RECKLESS AT HEART

A PINE HARBOUR NOVEL

ZOE YORK

THE KINCAIDS OF PINE HARBOUR

For the girl who went to Whistler

CHAPTER ONE

"DAD, I'M PREGNANT."

Owen Kincaid felt the three words more than he heard them. The immediate and heavy truth that this could—would—change everything. His daughter Becca gave him a beseeching look from across the living room. He knew in the back of his mind that he was supposed to say something supportive, something understanding. Hell, he understood all right.

He'd been there, done that, got the too-young parent t-shirt himself, hadn't he?

Eighteen years ago, in fact.

The roar in his ears made it hard to think. He couldn't figure out how to respond in any way that wasn't scary—or scared, if Owen was being honest. He'd been sprawled out on the couch, waking up after a midday nap before an evening shift tonight, when Becca came home ten minutes earlier. His cue to make some food and be a good dad. She'd disappeared into her room, then reappeared, finding him in the kitchen. "Can we talk?" she'd asked, her voice tight.

Then she'd turned on her heel, making him follow her into the living room of his small, three-bedroom bungalow. He'd been prepared for a confession about her car. A fender bender. Or ready to go to battle if she'd been let go from her job at the golf course, where she worked part time on the banquet staff. He could have commiserated if something had happened at school.

But this?

She was pregnant?

God. Fucking. Damn. She was eighteen years old. A baby herself. *His* baby.

She stood up from her seat across from him—carefully, warily—and moved closer. His fist clenched hard at his thigh, and she covered his white knuckles with her own fingers. She was shaking.

No.

"Dad, it's going to be okay."

That was his line. That's what he was supposed to say. But he couldn't, so he opened his arms instead, and she fell against him.

He'd known she was growing up. He couldn't keep her a kid forever. He thought he had done his best, but he'd failed. "Are you okay?" He finally said, his voice full of gravel and regret and undisguised anger, too. There was no hiding that, so he didn't try.

And she picked up on it, too, because she didn't answer his question.

"Don't be mad," she whispered.

"Not at you, baby." He closed his eyes and clenched his jaw, inhaling roughly before rubbing her back. "Did you... do you know...Does the fa—" Nope. That was a word that wasn't crawling out of his throat right now. Father. Some little punk-ass kid knocked up his daughter.

You were *that punk-ass kid nineteen years ago.*

But history wasn't supposed to repeat itself like this. He'd done his best, *they* had done their best, to give Becca everything despite how young they were when she arrived. Her mother may not have been his soul mate, but they were decent co-parents. They'd just celebrated Becca's birthday four months ago.

Him, his ex-wife, her husband, and Becca's shithead on-again, off-again junior hockey player boyfriend who dumped her a week later.

And the anger roared back to life. "Becca, tell me it wasn't Hayden."

"Daddy, don't be mad at us."

Us. There would be no us with Hayden. The kid had his eyes firmly locked on the NHL, and nothing—no one— would get in his way. Not a girlfriend. He'd made that clear to Becca every time they broke up. So there was no chance he'd prioritize a child. Owen could kill him. With his bare hands, and he'd enjoy every second of the murder.

"I'm sorry," he said gruffly. "I'm not mad."

"You are." She'd always been able to see right through him like that.

He shuddered and kissed the top of her head. "I was thinking you'd banged up the car, that's all."

"No." Another small sound.

He forced himself through a calming breath. "Well, that's good. Have you told your mom yet?"

"She's not home. I stopped there first on my way back from the store."

He froze. "Did you just find out?"

She nodded, a tiny little jerk of her head, and his heart cracked open. She'd taken a test and he was the first person she told. Because her mom wasn't home, and if she had been, Becca would have done it there. But still, he'd been the first one…and he'd reacted like it was the end of the world.

It wasn't.

The end of his Great Bachelor Plans, maybe. But not the end of the world. And it was the earliest of days. She had time to think and make decisions, and he couldn't get ahead of himself guessing what would happen.

"Ah, shit. I'm sorry. It *is* okay. It's going to be okay." He squeezed her again, wanting to make it all better, but this was monumental. And she needed Rachel. "One thing at a time. Do you want to call your mom now? She can come here if you want some privacy with her."

Rachel had three younger children and a loud husband, Hudson, who was a decent guy, but he treated Becca like a kid still. That wasn't going to help in the next while.

"I don't know. I don't want to tell her on the phone." Becca's voice was tiny now.

"Do you want me to call her? I can ask her to come over."

"Maybe."

Owen didn't know where his phone was. He'd find it in a minute. Had he left it in the kitchen? He'd been fiddling with that damn bachelor life wish list. Shit that didn't matter nearly as much as his daughter.

Becca was quiet for a long stretch. Then she gave him a tight squeeze before moving back. "Thanks."

"I love you." It came out raw, but at least that was honest.

"This doesn't have to change anything. I can still move out next summer." But her voice was small and unsure.

She knew he'd been counting down the months until she graduated.

And now he was the world's biggest asshole. Fuck. "Don't worry about that."

"Dad—"

"One thing at a time, kiddo."

Her face crumpled. No, she wasn't a kid anymore, was she?

"Look." He waited. "Look at me."

She paused, then lifted her head, her eyes watery but fierce. "What?"

"Whatever you need, I'll be right by your side."

"I don't know what I'm going to do."

"That's okay. You've got some time to think about it." He swallowed hard. He had an overnight shift to get ready for. "I have to go to work. Are you going to be okay?"

"Yeah."

"If you want your mom to come over…"

She nodded. "Maybe."

But by the time he was in his EMT uniform and getting ready to head to the Pine Harbour Emergency Services Building, Becca hadn't called Rachel, and to Owen's surprise, she'd decided she didn't want him to do that just yet, either. "I need more time. I don't want to tell anyone else."

He dragged in a rough, ragged breath. "Okay. This is our secret for now. Deal?"

She nodded solemnly. "Deal."

Owen hoped that promise wouldn't come back to kick him in the ass later. But Becca was a grownup now, at least officially.

Her teen years had sped by in a wild kaleidoscope of parties and growth spurts and the occasional scholastic achievement, but mostly it had been a period they had barely survived. He'd been looking forward to some breathing room next. To her moving out and finding her passion in life. And in the quiet that would follow, he'd had big plans for himself. Hobbies. Dating, and not just the furtive hook-ups of his past. A real social life that wasn't dictated by making sure his teenager was safely tucked into bed by her curfew.

That wasn't going to be a worry tonight, though. Becca was already wearing her flannel pyjamas and had scrubbed her makeup off.

Still… "I'm around the corner if you need me. I can be here on my pager if need be."

She shook her head. "I'm going to watch something and go to bed early."

"Call me if you can't sleep."

"I'm not going to call."

Owen ignored that. "Call me if you need *anything*."

"I need some alone time." She said it like a confession, and he realized he was crowding her. He'd want the exact same thing in her shoes—had, in fact, locked himself in his bedroom nineteen years earlier so he could stare at the ceiling.

"Got it. I'm going."

As she disappeared into her room, and he turned on his heel to head to work, a complicated wave of concern and regret flooded his mind. What could they have done differently?

Had he failed her somehow? Had they romanticized what it had been like to be teen parents? Becca was loved, God damn it, but that didn't mean having her so young hadn't been brutally hard.

Maybe the pregnancy wouldn't last. He had a flash of

guilt for wishing for a miscarriage, to take the choice out of her hands. More than a flash. That dark thought carried him all the way to work, where he parked out back and let himself in the side entrance.

In an ideal world, he'd make it to his office without running into anyone, and be able to bury himself in work.

It was not an ideal world.

The sound of voices drifted toward him from the kitchen. There were two cooking and eating spaces in the building, a full-fledged kitchen on the ground floor that was mostly used for the weekly training night for the volunteer firefighters, and a break room upstairs with a kitchen and microwave. That was where his paramedics grabbed a bite in between calls. Nobody had time to clean up from a full meal, and God forbid anyone left something behind for Owen to find.

He didn't strictly speaking have a *don't use the downstairs kitchen* rule, but it was understood that the space was only for cooking larger meals for the whole group. Or so he thought.

Laughter broke out. "Catch it!"

Catch what?

"We can't do this during the day. The EMT supervisor's a real—"

Owen stepped into the doorway and cleared his throat as he took in the scene. Two firefighters, not volunteers, but guys attached to his station from the main firehouse in Wiarton, were standing on either side of the microwave. One was holding a bag of popcorn. Owen knew his face was thunderous, because yeah, he had a tendency to be a real *something* when people were messing up his space. "I work evening shifts from time to time as well, you know."

The kid holding a bag of freshly microwaved popcorn

clearly did not know that, because he dropped it, sending greasy kernels skittering all over the floor.

"There's a microwave upstairs," Owen growled.

"Someone else was using it."

"Patience is a virtue."

The kid's face blanched. "We'll clean this up."

Owen glanced at the floor. "Soap and water to get the oil off the floor."

"Yes, sir."

Nights like this made him second-guess his decision to take the supervisor job when they built this new station. For most of his career he'd been happy to be a paramedic. The shift work had been tricky to work custody around when Becca was little, but when he was off, he was off, and in the summers he'd been able to be home with her for almost half the week. But as college loomed closer and closer for Becca, the promise of more pay—and a more regular schedule—had won out.

Somewhere along the way, he'd lost his sense of humour about things like tossing popcorn.

Owen felt old.

And as he sank into his chair behind his desk, he longed for the days when his daughter's biggest worry was whether she would get both Barbies she wanted from Santa.

At eleven o'clock, she texted to say good night. He was in the ambulance bay updating the whiteboard on the wall and he stopped as soon as his phone vibrated.

Becca: I'm going to sleep now. Front door is locked.

He grinned.

Owen: And what about the back door?
Becca: Left that hanging wide open for the
monsters to get in.
Owen: Love you.
Becca: Love you too.

The rest of the night passed without incident. He listened to some dispatch calls to make notes for performance review meetings, got ahead on some of his other monthly tasks, and finished his shift by taking inventory on the gear in his own truck.

When he got home, Becca's bedroom door was still firmly shut.

But she wasn't asleep.

His phone lit up with a text message as he was thinking about knocking to wake her for school. It was a group message, sent to both him and her mother. Apparently, Becca had decided it was time to tell Rachel.

Becca: Can we have a team meeting after school today? At Dad's place?

Team meetings are what they'd taken to calling co-parenting discussions when Becca hit the teen years and demanded they include her in any talks that related to her —which was every talk between him and Rachel.

On the screen, dots appeared. Then disappeared, and finally reappear.

Rachel: What time? I need to pick up the little ones at three-thirty.
Becca: Dad's on nights, so he needs to sleep but

he's usually up by the time I get back. Remember I don't have a class last period. How about two?

It was such a grown-up reply. Thoughtful, which she wasn't always, because teenage hormones were something wild, but when she was…man, she was a good kid.

Not. A. Kid.

But he thought of everyone younger than him as a kid, especially his own daughter, and God damn it, he was too tired to fix that right now. He sighed and shook his head, then tapped out a quick reply that it worked for him.

Fifteen minutes later, she found him in the kitchen. She was dressed already, in skin-tight jeans and an oversized sweater, with a full face of makeup on.

"I made oatmeal," he said gruffly.

She smiled faintly. "I probably can't tell you that I need to go, can I?"

"You've got five minutes. Eat a real breakfast for me, okay?"

She grabbed a bowl and the glass jar of brown sugar. "Oatmeal, huh?"

"It's good for you."

"You haven't made oatmeal in years."

"And I'm regretting that right now, so…eat up." As if more oatmeal would have prevented this turn of events.

She shoved the bowl into his hands. "Only if you eat some, too."

He didn't feel like eating, but she'd cornered him with logic. "Fine."

This had been their dynamic for so long. He did his best, even when it wasn't enough, but at least it was something. And she showed him how to be a better person, too.

Oatmeal for dinner. Then some sleep. Then… He

wasn't looking forward to what was coming later that afternoon. Depending on how it went, he might need a drink. Or a game of darts. He could pin his list of bachelor life dreams on the board and aim for each of them one by one.

CHAPTER TWO

KERRY HUMPHREY HAD BEEN LOOKING FORWARD to this afternoon for a solid week. She was on her way to Pine Harbour to see a new clinic space. She slowed down as her GPS warned her that the turn off the highway was coming up on the left. In the two years she'd been working in Bruce County as a midwife, she'd driven up and down the north-south highway along the Bruce Peninsula many times. She'd even turned right at the gas station ahead and gone into Lion's Head a few times. But somehow she'd never needed to go to Pine Harbour.

But if all went well in the next hour, it would be her new place of employment.

Technically, the Pine Harbour clinic would be a satellite office of their practice in Walkerton, an hour south. That was where one of the two hospitals they delivered at was located, and years ago it had made sense as a base of operations.

In the winter, though, the distance made those drives unnecessarily precarious for clients. So when her midwifery partner Jenna Foster, who lived in Pine

Harbour, saw what she described as "the perfect space" come available for rent, Kerry had thrown her support in for the idea.

Now it was a matter of seeing just how perfect it might be.

The first thing she saw as she drove into Pine Harbour was a diner nestled on the edge of the forest, a sprawling roadside restaurant surrounded by a giant gravel parking lot full of pickup trucks.

Mac's Diner read the faded sign.

The next block had a row of century-old homes, all in various stages of needing some upkeep. After the next stop sign—which was right next to a street sign that clearly indicated she was on Main Street, should there have been any doubt—the commercial centre of the town started. And also ended, because it was only two blocks long.

But they were two busy blocks, and she couldn't find a parking spot at first. She kept going, to the end of the street where a hill ran down to what was obviously the namesake of the town—a glistening harbour. At the moment it was mighty chilly looking, with crashing white-capped waves and chunks of ice along the shore, but she could imagine it was quite beautiful in the summer.

Doubling back, she finally found a parking spot in front of the library. Across the street, Jenna waited on the sidewalk, bundled up in a parka that was bulky enough on the front that Kerry knew she had a sleeping baby on her chest under the coat. Jenna had recently returned to their midwifery practice after her own maternity leave. She was talking animatedly with two people, a woman holding a clipboard who she introduced as the town's only realtor, Catie Berton, and an older man.

"I'm the landlord," he said with a kind smile. "But Catie's agreed to manage some of my rental agreements as I ease into retirement."

At first glance, the storefront was unimpressive. Dark, dated, and very empty, probably for a long time. But Catie had a good pitch, and it started even before she unlocked the door and turned on the lights.

She handed over the card of a local contractor who had done other work for the landlord, and promised that everything could be changed. "Whatever you see when you squint, whatever you imagine as we walk through, Jake can make that possible."

"We have pretty vivid imaginations," Jenna said. "But we know Jake is up to it."

Kerry's vivid imagination was usually limited to filthy fantasies. But she was open, and once they were inside, Jenna's enthusiasm was infectious. And Jake was Jenna's brother-in-law. If she had faith he could transform the space, Kerry believed her.

"This is my favourite part—Oh, no, imagine *this*—and over there!" Jenna led Kerry through, talking in half sentences about exam rooms, where a washroom could go with enough room for a scale and the sterile pee collection.

It turned out the squinting thing really did work.

"It's perfect." Kerry did a slow turn. "What are the parking options? I had to drive down the block to find a spot."

"There are four dedicated spots out back, let me show you." The landlord pointed the way. Kerry followed him, leaving Jenna—who now had a fussy awake baby to feed—with Catie.

The landlord opened the back door, and they stepped outside. The unexpectedly large parking lot behind the buildings had seen better days, but would meet their needs for sure. "One of these spots is for the apartment upstairs, but that tenant just gave me her notice, so it'll be a while before I rent it out again."

"There's an apartment upstairs?" The wheels in Kerry's head started turning. That would be insanely convenient. "How much is the rent for that?"

The amount he listed off was half the cost of her apartment in Walkerton.

"You're kidding."

"It's a small space," the landlord said. "Do you want to see it?"

Yes, yes she did. "Can you wait a few minutes? Let me go back and finish up talking about the clinic space with Jenna, because I think she wants to head out."

"Take your time. I'll go up and make sure now is an okay time to view it."

Back inside, she found Jenna saying goodbye to Catie. "I have to head out," her partner said. "I got paged. Dina Suarez is having contractions and on the way to the hospital. So I'm going to finish nursing James, then drop him at home with Sean."

"I'll follow you out to your car," Kerry said.

Jenna waited until they were alone on Main Street. "What's going on?"

Kerry took a deep breath. "What do you think about me moving to Pine Harbour?"

"Just like that?"

"Maybe?" Kerry laughed. "I don't know. Maybe. Yes. In for a penny, in for a pound, am I right?" She bit her lower lip. "It makes sense. We could operate this clinic autonomously. There's enough work, and it would open up an office space in Walkerton for another new midwife to join there. That's good all around, and would help us out for covering vacation time, providing back up…"

Jenna nodded as she trailed off. "Yeah, no, I get it. It's a great plan, and I can see the excitement all over your face. I want to make sure this is a good decision for you."

"I'm driving up and down the peninsula anyway, I might as well shift myself here and save some money while I'm at it."

"Are you doing it because it'll be easier for work? Or do you actually want to live in my little town of six hundred people, where the only coffee shop only serves actual coffee? No lattes, no cold brew, no shots of espresso."

"With the money I'm saving, I'll buy a fancy instant espresso machine for the clinic."

"It's not just coffee. Pine Harbour is an entirely different pace of life," Jenna warned.

"Maybe I'm ready for that." She'd been doing a lot of thinking about what she wanted in life. This could be a sign.

"Long way to go for dancing on Friday nights."

"Maybe I'll trade that for…" She trailed off, her breath puffing in the cold air between them. Jenna had to get going, too. "Help me out here. What are the best parts of Pine Harbour?"

"The people," Jenna said quickly. Then she laughed. "But if you're looking for fun, we have that too. Bonfire parties are popular in the summer."

"That's a good start."

"And there's a pub over in Lion's Head."

"Even better."

"They're pretty serious about their outdoor life here. The trails are great."

Kerry liked the sound of that. "I run sometimes. More if I'm being chased."

Jenna snapped her fingers. "There's a women's rec league. Soccer in the summer, ball hockey in the winter. Lots of chasing—or so I've heard. Sean has done some clinics with them."

Jenna's husband had once been an elite extreme distance runner—before being injured in the line of duty. Now he was a world-renowned coach, and people flew in to train with him. Kerry thought it was pretty amazing he also made time for the regular athletes in his home town, although the thought of being put through running drills by him was daunting.

One thing at a time. A pub sounded great. "Don't worry. I'm pretty good at making friends. In fact, I'm going to take myself out for a celebratory drink after we sign the lease papers. What's the name of that pub?"

Jenna grinned. "The Green Hedgehog. One day when I don't have a patient to meet at the hospital or a baby to nurse back to sleep, I'll take you there."

Kerry gave her partner a quick hug. "Sounds like a plan. I'll go finish up with Catie. Keep me updated on Dina's progress!"

Back inside, Kerry told Catie about her conversation with the landlord. The real estate agent locked up the front of the store, and together they climbed the stairs to the second floor. Kerry braced herself to not like the apartment, because when the landlord said it was small, that probably meant the apartment would be dark, crowded, and only worth the small amount of rent being asked.

That was the furthest thing from reality, though. Yes, it was tiny. One small bedroom, a living room with a kitchenette nook in the corner, and a bathroom that could only be described as minimalist and spare. But at the far end of the living room, two huge windows overlooked Main Street, flooding the space with natural light, even in the late winter afternoon gloom, and on the back wall there were wide windows set high in the exposed brick. Also on that wall was a giant cast iron clock.

"Oh, wow," she whispered.

"The clock doesn't work," the landlord said. "But it can't be removed."

Kerry didn't care if it didn't work. It would be right twice a day, and delightfully wrong the rest of the time. It fed all of her secret Pinterest aesthetics at a fraction of her housing budget. She was so in. "Where do I sign?"

After following Catie back to her office—which was also her hair salon, apparently, because being Pine Harbour's only real estate agent was more of a part-time gig—Kerry signed the paperwork for both leases.

Then she drove across the peninsula to buy herself a drink at the nearest pub.

The Green Hedgehog was a rambling building. Once a turn of the last century house, it had a significant addition that stretched over an entire block.

Inside, the foyer was decorated for the holidays.

A waitress passed by as Kerry paused at the *wait to be seated* sign. "Take a seat anywhere, hun," she called out.

There was an empty seat at the end of the bar that had her name on it, right next to a coat hook on a pillar. She took her coat off and hung it up, then hopped up on to the seat and leaned forward, resting her elbows on the bar top.

The bartender on tonight was a young white woman, pale and gothic, with a choppy hair cut, buzzed underneath. "Hey," she said, sliding a coaster in front of Kerry. "What can I get you?"

"Do you have anything special for Christmas?"

The bartender pointed to a standup sign further down the bar. "Mulled wine?"

"Sold, I'll take a mug of that."

When she set it front of Kerry a minute later, the bartender stuck around to be chatty. "Haven't seen you in here before. Are you visiting for the holidays?"

Kerry shook her head. "I'm moving here next month. Just signed a lease on an apartment."

"Here in town?"

"Across the highway, over in Pine Harbour. But I heard this was the closest place to get a drink, so…here I am."

"Welcome. I'm Lore. As in, my parents named me Lauren."

"Kerry." She lifted her mug. "Cheers."

"Who sent you our way?"

"Do you know Jenna Foster?"

Lore shook her head.

Kerry shrugged. "Well, that's who."

Lore laughed. "She's got good taste. What else did she recommend?"

"Bonfires, and the women's soccer league," Kerry said dryly.

"Hey! I'm on the soccer team." Lore jumped in the air. "Hey! Bailey!"

Kerry hadn't seen that coming. Laughing, she pivoted on her stool just in time to see a south Asian woman bounce up and slide onto the stool next to her.

"Did I hear someone mention the soccer league?" She stuck her hand out. "I'm Bailey Patel. Nice to meet you. Do you play?"

"I…" Kerry shrugged. "I run. Slowly. And my co-worker suggested soccer as an alternative to…" She trailed off, not wanting to insult the locals. "Other things."

Bailey and Lore didn't seem offended, though. "Fun things? We get it. But your co-worker is right. Pretty much the soccer team is where it's at for those of us in our twenties, caught between the two generations of people who have bonfire parties."

"Uh…" Kerry took a long swallow of her mulled wine. "I might be in the next bracket up, age-wise."

"We won't tell anyone," Bailey whispered. "Not if you're willing to play defence."

Kerry had her first Pine Harbour social calendar booking. The women filled her in on the soccer team's website, which listed the season dates. "But we also practice in an ad hoc way before the season begins. Next year we might even rent space over the winter."

Kerry had just finished taking down their contact information when there was a decent-sized thud as the front door of the bar swung open and bounced against the doorstop. In walked a tall monster of a man, wearing a dark parka, a snow-covered toque, and a grim scowl.

He lifted a hand at Lore. She wordlessly acknowledged him right back as he kept going past the bar and through an archway into a back room. Kerry didn't stare—she had better self-control than that—but she couldn't stop herself from surreptitiously tracking him until he disappeared. She had a thing for big guys, always had. There was something magnetic about the way this one stalked right past her, his strides powerful, his presence commanding. The bartender immediately grabbed a glass from beneath the counter and poured a perfect pint of stout. She looked around, maybe for the waitress, before ducking out from behind the bar and disappearing after the man herself.

Beside Kerry, Bailey sighed. Whatever caused Lore to hustle after the man was none of Kerry's business, and she was quite good at minding her p's and q's. Bailey, on the other hand, clearly wanted to talk. "That's Owen Kincaid," she whispered. "Lore was in the army reserve for a couple of years, and he was her platoon sergeant."

The military was a big part of life around here. Kerry had clients from the training base around the bay. "Nice that she read his mind."

"Mmm." Bailey nodded toward the back room. "They have some pool tables back there. Do you want to play a game?"

On the one hand, Kerry liked the two younger women and was looking forward to getting into a sports league. But she wasn't interested in stalking a man she didn't know around a bar she'd never been to before, no matter how big and burly and shiver-inducing he might be. She wiggled her mug of wine. "I have to drive home, so this is it for me. Can I have a rain-check for another time?"

"Sure." Bailey was craning her neck now. "I might… just…you know…"

No skin off Kerry's nose. "Go. I'll wait here for Lore and then settle up."

As soon as she said that, the bartender returned. She caught sight of Bailey and pointed to the bar stool. "Stay!"

"What?"

"You were going to perv on Owen, and you know he's off-limits. Becca would kill you."

Bailey laughed. "If I'm going to crush on any of the Kincaid brothers, it won't be the grumpy old man, don't worry."

The guy who stalked by was hardly old. He couldn't be much older than Kerry, but not her circus, not her monkeys. This conversation was probably her cue to not overstay her welcome. She pulled a few bills out of her wallet and set them on the bar. "I'm going to head out now," she said. "But I'll be back in a few weeks. And I'm going to sign up for the soccer league as soon as I get home."

Bailey punched her fist in the air. "Yessss!"

Lore laughed. "Welcome to the peninsula, Kerry. It's never boring here."

CHAPTER THREE

THE DAYS LEADING up to Christmas were somber and quiet. And then Becca decided, on Boxing Day, that she was going to keep the pregnancy.

Which meant that on the stretch of down time between Christmas and New Year's Day, Owen's house became ground zero for Processing Feelings About the Pregnancy. He'd prefer to live in denial, but it didn't matter. Constant processing was what the women in his life needed.

"Mom is so mad at me," Becca said one morning after a rapid-fire text exchange with Rachel.

"She's not mad."

"*I just want you to remember you have options,*" she read off the screen.

Owen rolled his eyes, which made his daughter huff. "What? That's not anger I'm hearing in those words, it's concern. She's worried you don't know what it will really be like—and before you say anything, let me remind you—"

"That you two know what it's like," Becca said, cutting

him off. "I. Know. I was your mistake, right?" She jumped up. "I don't know why you need to take her side."

Because nineteen years ago, he'd made Rachel a promise that no matter what, that was exactly what he would do. *We're in this together, through thick and thin.*

"This" had turned out to only be parenting, although they'd given marriage a try. But that required love, and what did two eighteen-year-olds know about that? Not enough. When they broke up, he made her the same promise again. *We're still in this together, no matter what. You're her mom, and I'm her dad, and nothing will ever change that.*

He'd kept that promise. It had been damn hard at times, and there were moments—scary in hindsight—where he could have lost Becca. Could have made the wrong decision and wound up all alone with nothing but regrets.

Sometimes parenting required more patience than humanly possible. He stood and got in front of Becca, setting his hands on her shoulders, making her look at him. "You are not—were not, would never be—a mistake. Got it?"

"Got it," she mumbled.

"I'll talk to your mom. But I want you to remember that because we're your parents, we are allowed to worry about you."

"Tell her—"

Lord save him from a bossy eighteen-year-old. He turned Becca around and pointed her in the direction of her room. "I don't need you stage managing this conversation. Leave what I'm going to say to me."

After texting Rachel, who leapt on his invitation to come over later and have a team meeting, he paced around the house for a bit, looking for something to do, but everything annoyed him. Finally, he knocked on Becca's door and told her he was going to the station to get a quick workout in before her mom was coming over. He needed to burn off the nervous energy zinging through him. It was making his bark worse than usual.

Pine Harbour was too small to have a proper gym, so lifting heavy stuff had to happen at work or with one of his army buddies. A few people had proper home gym setups, with weight racks and benches. Not Owen, though. He lived in a three-bedroom bungalow with no basement. Between his eighteen-year-old daughter, who needed her own room, and the fact that three of his four younger brothers were nomadic and often needed a place to crash when in town—necessitating a guest bedroom—building a home gym for himself had been on his "when Bec moved out" to-do list.

As he'd put up the Christmas tree, just a few weeks earlier, he'd had the naive thought that it was the last year for over-the-top piles of presents. And he'd miss it, in a way, because it was the end of an era, but he'd also fantasized about next Christmas doing something radical like buying her a trip to Mexico with her college friends so he could spend the holidays converting the spare room. He even had a treadmill picked out. The only redecoration of the spare room that would be happening now would be converting it to a nursery instead.

Owen's Dad Years weren't over after all.

While he was at the station, he checked his email, then stomped up the back stairwell to the private gym space reserved for firefighters and paramedics. He had it all to himself, which he liked, so he cranked Guns n' Roses—a musical choice the younger first responders rarely tolerated.

When he got back to the house, his muscles well-used and his brain a bit clearer, his ex-wife was waiting for him in the driveway.

He gave her a sweaty one-arm hug and she launched right into an emotional outburst. He cut her off. "Rach, we gotta stop. She knows what she wants. We don't have to understand it, but we do have to accept it."

"Do we?" She huffed out a frustrated breath. "I know. I *know*." But she didn't, because the silent beat that stretched out next practically vibrated with tension. Then she turned on him. "Now is not the time to be pointing fingers."

Calm blue ocean, Kincaid. "It's really not."

"But—"

"You just said—"

"She's eighteen years old and pregnant, Owen. Eighteen. Where did we go wrong?"

At least she said *we*, and not *you*. "I dunno." He swallowed hard. "I've been thinking of pretty much nothing else since she told us."

"She says Hayden still hasn't responded to her text messages."

"What do you want me to do, go over there and drag him out of his house by his hair?"

Rachel gave him a beseeching look. "Yes?"

Owen laughed, but it felt hollow. "Yeah, me too. But I can't."

"Stop being a reasonable grown-up."

The thing was, Owen didn't feel reasonable on the inside. He was scared and out of his depth, and this whole situation was bringing up all kinds of uncomfortable feelings from their distant past.

He wanted Hayden to do the right thing, but he knew how stupid eighteen-year-old boys could be—and how they didn't have the emotional maturity to understand what the right thing truly was.

And did he want Hayden to follow in his own steps, when in the end, Owen hadn't been a good enough husband to Rachel? Hadn't loved her enough? Sure, he'd married her, but he hadn't turned into the partner she needed. Owen *was* the punk-ass kid. He left town as soon as they broke up and partied a little too hard while at firefighter school.

Not hard enough to bury the guilt, though. Not when the partying just made a fresh layer of guilt to pour on top of the layered Dad Guilt.

That feeling had never gone away, not even after Rachel married Hudson, who had given her three more kids and a big house on the edge of town.

He pointed out the house. "Let's go inside."

Rachel's jaw jutted to the side, then righted itself. There was no more anger there. All of that had been fought over —many times—almost two decades earlier.

They'd both moved on.

"Maybe it won't be as hard for her as it was for us," he said as he let her inside. There was no sign of Becca, but her car was in the drive. He lifted his voice. "Bec! I'm home, and your mom is here." He turned to Rachel. "Coffee?"

"Always."

He got that going, then texted his daughter that she needed to make an appearance in the kitchen. Rachel laughed at him as he muttered about technology.

He scrubbed a hand over his face as something else occurred to him. "Listen, I gotta warn you about the latest thing she's been talking about. She's been doing her research, and she knows how many hours she needs to get maternity leave benefits. If she can't find a second job here, or get more hours at the country club, she's talking about heading to the city."

"A job? In the city?" All the relief fled from his ex's face. "No, Owen. That's shortsighted."

"I agree."

"Then we need to keep her focused on staying in school. Got it?"

"Got what?" Becca asked from the doorway.

Her mother paused, then launched into a classic too-much-information dump. "I think it's great that you want to get a job, honey, I really do. But the city is expensive, and will be even more so when you're only getting the EI payments for maternity leave. It's hard to live on that, and—"

Owen stepped in between them and held up his hands, cutting her off. "One thing at a time. Bec, we see how you're trying to manage this, okay? But we love you and we want to support you, too."

"It doesn't feel very supportive right now," his daughter said softly, her eyes big and wet as she glared at her mom. "I'm not asking for anything. Do you hear me asking for anything?"

"You don't have any money," Rachel exclaimed. "How are you going to move to the city?"

"I'll sort that out."

Owen didn't want her going anywhere. He changed the subject. "One thing at a time. First, you need to go see the doctor."

Becca made a face. "I don't want to go see Dr. Malcolm. I looked up the midwifery practice Jenna Foster works in. I like the sound of their whole deal. Do you know the difference between informed consent and informed choice?"

Owen blinked at his daughter. "Yes. Hi, I'm your dad. I'm a trained paramedic with two decades of experience. I've even attended births, you know that? We get called out to home births with those midwives you've just discovered on the internet."

Not to mention he knew Jenna, both from working with her, and working with her brother-in-law, and the fact their town only had six hundred people in it.

Calm blue ocean.

Becca made a face at him. "No need to be snippy."

This time it was Rachel that got between them. "Okay, so we have an action plan?"

Owen dragged in a breath. "Sounds like it."

———

BECCA'S first appointment fell on a day off for Owen, so he volunteered to drive her the hour south to Walkerton, where the clinic was, and be moral support. Her ex-boyfriend Hayden still hadn't responded to her messages. Owen wanted to kick his ass, but that wasn't productive.

Right now, no matter how he felt on the inside, he needed to keep his yap shut and let Becca deal with the whole situation as she wanted.

It was easier said than done.

At least the appointment was well outside of Pine Harbour, off the peninsula. And Jenna Foster had promised Becca's privacy would be protected at every turn.

At the clinic, the receptionist gave Becca an intake form, then told them to take a seat. "The midwife will be out shortly." She pointed at a short hallway. "She'll come and get you when it's time."

Owen didn't miss that Becca's hands shook as she filled out the paperwork. He wrapped his arm around her and squeezed. The seconds ticked by, loud as if there was actually a grandfather clock right next to him, instead of just his own nerves.

When the door at the end of the hallway swung open, instead of Jenna Foster, a dark-haired woman with olive skin stepped out. She was wearing bright, glossy red lipstick, and was short enough that she had to go up on her toes to reach the charts filed away on top of the filing cabinet behind the receptionist. As she looked at the first one she grabbed, then shook her head, put it back, and grabbed another, her short, brown waves bounced.

Owen was transfixed.

Her body flexed, taut like a dancer's, as she slowly lowered her heels to the floor. The midwife's office was not the place to notice tight, round curves or the flex of her calf beneath the cut-off hem of a pair of jeans.

Not the place at all, Owen. Eyes anywhere else, man.

But it was hard to look elsewhere, because this tiny woman sucked all the air out of the room. And she hadn't even looked up. She was still reading the chart in her hand, like she was pouring all of her attention into the pages.

When she turned around, she immediately looked at his daughter, her face brightening up. "Becca Kincaid?"

He should have seen that coming. Of course she was Becca's midwife. That was exactly the right next punch for the universe to deliver in the *Take That, Owen Kincaid* march of events. He locked down any awareness of this person as a woman. She was his daughter's caregiver, apparently. Or one of them. He squeezed Becca's hand. "That's you, honey."

She didn't move.

"Bec?"

She shook her head, and he could see tears swelling along her eyelids.

Aw, shit. He wrapped his arm around her and squeezed. "Come on. I'll go in with you."

The brunette came closer. Close enough to speak in a low voice and still be heard, but not so close as to freak out his daughter. She crouched low and gave them a friendly smile. "I'm Kerry Humphrey."

"Becca thought we'd be seeing Jenna," he said by way of explanation. He had a lump in his own throat. His daughter wasn't the only one thrown by this unexpected change of plans.

"Ah. Sorry about the miscommunication. Jenna's at a birth right now. But we can do the intake together, and she'll be here for the next appointment. Why don't we go into the exam room and I can explain our model of care. We work as a group, so you might see any of us for your appointments."

"Sure." Owen moved to stand up.

Kerry pivoted her gaze in his direction, her gaze sliding quickly from friendly to coolly professional. "Can I see Becca alone first? You're welcome to join us in a few minutes."

No. She's my baby and she's scared. But that wasn't how medical appointments worked, and he knew it. That lump in his throat got harder and he puffed out his cheeks, trying—and failing—to match her professional tone. "Of course."

Becca gave them both a nervous look.

"Go on," Owen said, trying to be gentle for her. *Fuck.* Rachel should have brought her, he was making a mess of this, like a bull in a china shop. "I'll be right here."

———

KERRY HAD SPOTTED the terrified young woman as soon as she'd stepped into the waiting room. She'd noticed the way the man had his arm possessively around her, too. She didn't recognize him at first, not without the parka and the toque, but as soon as she looked at the file, she recognized the last name, and the address. *Pine Harbour.*

He was older than her, by a fair margin. A big, tough-looking guy, with a bit of silver at the temples. Almost twice Becca's age, Kerry would bet. Lore's words rang in her head. *You know he's off-limits. Becca would kill you.*

Well. Holy shit. This was trial by fire for her new community, but Kerry knew what to do. Talking to clients one-on-one was standard procedure any time. Moments like this were exactly why they had that practice in place.

She closed her office door as Becca sat down, then took her own seat. "Welcome to our practice." Smiling, she waited for Becca to nod, then continued. Each beat of her introduction was followed by a pause, making sure the young woman was easing toward being comfortable. Trust was so important here. "Let's go over the information you put on the intake form. I'm going to ask some questions that will help us support you with this pregnancy. Feel free to ask your own questions as we go, and know that every-thing we talk about is strictly confidential."

"Okay."

"How is your pregnancy going?"

Becca shrugged. "I dunno. It's early. I feel fine."

"That's great." Kerry paused. "How do you feel about being pregnant?"

The young woman's eyes snapped up, meeting Kerry's gaze. "Because I'm young?"

"Sure, yeah. Your age might be a factor there. But I ask every woman who comes through that door the same question, I promise. A pregnancy can be an unexpected thing to adjust to at any age—and, at any age, it could be a good time or a bad time for the news."

"Oh." Becca shifted in her seat. "My parents aren't thrilled, to be honest. But I'm..." She put her hand on her midsection. "I'm happy. I know it's going to be hard, but my parents were young when they had me, and I think it's going to work out."

Kerry jotted a quick note, *optimistic*, next to that set of questions, and moved on. "What is your current relationship status?"

Becca made a face. "It's complicated."

"Do you live with your partner?"

"No. I live with my dad."

Kerry made another note about the possibly unsupportive parents at home. If they had concerns about Becca's complicated relationship with the older boyfriend, that would be important to track as the pregnancy progressed. "Okay. Now I'm going to ask you a couple of other routine questions that I ask everyone—and this is why it's important that we first talk alone, okay? These are health and safety questions. Everything we discuss in here is just between us."

"Sure."

"Have you ever smoked or used tobacco or nicotine products?"

Becca hesitated.

Kerry waited.

"No, not really." The teen made a face. "I tried a few times."

"Did you use any tobacco or nicotine products in the three months before you became pregnant?"

"No, it was last summer."

"Does anyone smoke in your house or vehicle?"

"No."

She repeated the same set of questions about alcohol and recreational drugs, then moved on to the intimate partner violence screen. "Since you've been pregnant, have you been slapped, kicked or otherwise physically hurt by someone?"

"No." Becca's eyes widened.

Kerry noted that, then asked the next question. "Have you ever been emotionally or physically abused by someone important to you?"

"No."

All of her negative answers seemed genuine and without stress, but the age gap between her and the boyfriend and the tense dynamic between them in the waiting room still gave Kerry some concern. Another note, then she paused and pointed at the door, toward the man on the other side. "The person with you today, do you want them to come in for any part of the appointment?"

"Oh yeah, my dad's great."

Kerry's pen slid against the paper. *Her father.* Oh. She backed up her mental process, all the way to when she first stepped into the waiting room and saw the big guy sitting on the couch, who had to be older than her, with his arm around the slight, scared-looking teenager.

The name, the accidental connection to gossip at the Green Hedgehog. What a rookie mistake. And then she zoomed, fast forward, to what Becca had just said. *My parents aren't thrilled. My parents were young when they had me.*

"You mentioned he wasn't thrilled? I just want to make sure you're comfortable and supported here."

"Oh." Becca grimaced. "Yeah. Well, I am. My parents both mean well. You'll meet my mom at the next appointment. They think I'm reliving their mistakes, but like, I'm their mistake? And I'm pretty cool. Obviously. So they'll deal. It's fine. He can come in. His bark is worse than his bite."

"All right. Let's zip through the rest of these questions and figure out your probable due date. Then we'll get him to come in and we can discuss appointment schedules and what comes next."

By the time Kerry opened the door and invited Becca's father to join them, the teen had relaxed and opened up a bit about her ex-boyfriend, who hadn't responded to her texts about the pregnancy yet, and her worries about having enough hours to get EI for her maternity leave.

Becca's demeanour didn't shift at all when her dad sat down next to her, either. They leaned in to each other, exchanging a warm, silent communication.

Kerry's concern eased all the way.

But the warmth this man had for his daughter did not extend to her midwife. When he pivoted his attention to her, his gaze was hard and cold. "Are you done grilling her?"

Kerry felt her eyebrows spike toward her hairline, and it took all of her self-restraint to catch them and ease her expression into something more like gentle taken-aback-ness rather than the sharp what-the-fork reaction she was really having.

Nodding slowly, she held his gaze. Dark grey eyes glared back. "There was no grilling. I explained to Becca that it's routine practice to cover off some of the basics alone, and then bring in the support person for the appointment. It's great that you could be here. I understand Becca lives with you?"

"Yes."

"And is your name Kincaid as well?" She was already pretty sure it was, but the gossip had led her astray already once today.

"Yeah. Owen Kincaid." As Becca had warned, he practically barked it out.

"Nice to meet you." It was the polite thing to say, but she wasn't sure it was true. *What's your forking problem* wasn't appropriate to ask, but she really wanted to know.

It would come out in time. It always did. He wouldn't be the first person to be bristly with her, and he wouldn't be the last. She pushed it out of her mind and carried on with the rest of the appointment.

Becca was almost ten weeks pregnant, going by the date of her last period, but her cycles weren't regular, so Kerry gave them paperwork for a dating ultrasound.

"I'll call you with the results of the scan, and based on that, we'll set up appointments. Monthly for a while, then they'll get closer together."

"Do you ever do weekend or evening appointments?" This was Mr. Kincaid asking, his voice catching on the words like they were barbed. "Becca has school until June."

"Dad, it's fine."

"Our clinic days run until five, but depending on what time school lets out, I could stay a bit later. And it depends what office you want to see us in as well. You live in Pine

Harbour, right?" Kerry pasted on her best you're-in-luck smile and leaned forward. "That should make it easier, then, especially as the appointments get closer together. We're opening a satellite office in Pine Harbour next month."

"Oh!" Becca said.

Her father scowled. "Oh."

She glanced back and forth between them, trying to translate the monosyllabic responses. "You can still come here for appointments, if that's your preference."

Becca didn't reply and her father waited. At least he seemed to follow her cues. Finally, she shrugged. "I don't know. It's a long drive."

Kerry took a deep breath. "Either way, the appointments are confidential. Think about it and let me know. You'll get an email with the next appointment details in a few days, and you can pick the location later."

Owen was the first to stand. He already took up a lot of oxygen in a room while sitting and scowling. When he pushed to his feet, he towered over her. She'd have to jump onto her chair to look him in the eye, and if she tried that, she'd probably go sailing onto the exam table. Instead, she did her solid best to ignore him and focus on Becca as the Kincaids left.

It took less than ninety seconds for the clinic receptionist, Sarah, to appear in Kerry's doorway. "How'd that go? You were in here with her alone for a while."

"She was great," Kerry said simply.

"I don't mean the girl. How did it go with Mr. Alpha?"

She gave Sarah a pointed look. "No gossiping about the clients. Or their fathers."

"Ooooh." The receptionist sagged against the door frame, then leaned her head back, laughed, and fell forward into Kerry's office, sinking into the chair Mr. Alpha himself had vacated just a few minutes before. As much as Kerry didn't like to admit it, the nickname fit. He had a certain leader of the pack, don't mess with my daughter vibe usually reserved for fictional characters.

Sarah blew a raspberry. "Her father. That explains a lot. I had some questions about their whole dynamic."

"You and me both," Kerry admitted.

"He's pretty hot for an old guy."

She made a noncommittal face. "I don't have a read on him yet. He didn't say much. But Becca's great."

"No commentary on the hot dad?"

"Nope."

"That's no fun."

Kerry winked. "I save all my fun for after hours. Are we still on for dancing on Friday night?"

She didn't have many more weekends of dancing left before she moved north. "You know it."

When Sarah left, Kerry finished her notes, then checked the computer system to remind herself of her afternoon schedule. Lunch first, then two more appointments. That would give her enough time to call around and get some quotes for movers.

She had moved seven times in the last fourteen years. Until now, she hadn't had the funds to afford professionals. She had a short list of moving companies she'd cribbed from review sites. The first place went straight to an answering machine. She left a message with her quote request, then moved on to the next. A person answered there, but only took the same information and told her someone would call back in a few days.

That wasn't promising.

Maybe the third try would be the charm. This one

she'd put a star next to anyway, because she liked the sounds of it. A local company run by army veterans.

She punched in the number. Someone picked up on the second ring. "Warriors Moving, Adam speaking."

"Hi, I'm looking for a quote. I have a small one-bedroom apartment. A bed, a couch, a television, two bookshelves, and some boxes. Moving from Walkerton to Pine Harbour at the start of next month."

"Sure thing, let me just grab our rate card. You can see this on our website, too." He kept talking in her ear, and she pulled that page up on her computer. When he gave her the quote, it was exactly what she saw, and probably more than competitive against the other services she'd called.

Plus there was something about his voice that she liked. "Sounds good. Can I book that now?"

CHAPTER FOUR

BY THE TIME Adam from Warriors Moving showed up at Kerry's apartment on the last Saturday in January, she felt like she knew him. He'd called once to go over the details, then again to let her know who her movers were and what time exactly they'd be arriving. On that second call, he asked if she'd prefer to receive text message updates, which she agreed to, and on the day of the move, he texted to say there had been a last-minute change and he'd be on the crew himself.

When he knocked on the door, he cheerfully introduced himself, and then pointed to his friend. "And this is Stevie. He's the strong, silent type. Are you ready for us?"

Behind him was another man, maybe around the same age. Younger than her, in their twenties. She thought back to their flyer. Veterans shouldn't be that young was her first instinct and then foolishness quickly followed, because of course vets were young. Most people didn't stay in the military that long. She knew that from her work with young parents around the nearby training base—half of them were looking at getting out soon.

"Come on in. I'll get out of your way," she said, scooting to the side.

Adam winked at her. "You're not in anyone's way."

She headed out onto the landing anyway to check her messages. The *are you ready for us* double entendre had been easy enough to read straight, but the wink confirmed that Adam was flirty. She both liked it and it made her feel the full weight of her thirty-three years, and that tug inside that told her flirting with guys in their twenties didn't lead to babies.

Meddlesome ovaries, trying to restrict her dating life to suitable candidates only. She wouldn't fall for that.

Her couch came out first, with a lot of grunts from Stevie and cheerful warnings from Adam as they made their way down the stairs. Then her boxes paraded past, one by one. The last thing to be loaded into her truck was her bed, in pieces.

Which meant that when they got to Pine Harbour, her bed was the first thing to be assembled in her new apartment.

"Clever," she said as Adam and Stevie set the mattress down on the bed frame.

"Last thing in, first thing out." Adam tapped his head. "Not just a hat rack."

She laughed.

When they brought in the bedroom boxes, she dug through them and found her sheets, pillows, duvet and quilt. Even if the rest of the apartment was a disaster of cardboard and disorder for the next few days, she'd be able to sleep in comfort.

But by the time she made it into the living room, the thought of doing any more work or going grocery shopping was not at all appealing. So when the guys were done, she followed them downstairs. "Are you local?"

Adam nodded. "Born and bred."

"Can you recommend a place around here to get dinner?"

"Mac's Diner on the edge of town is where everyone goes. Or you can head to the Green Hedgehog in Lion's Head if you want more of a pub. That's the best place in the middle of the peninsula to grab a beer and make friends."

Kerry was quite sure Adam Kincaid had zero problems making friends. "Good to know. I'll start with the diner."

That got her another wink. "We're heading there, too."

She would make sure to buy their dinner before she left with her takeout. "Great. See you there, then? I'm just going to lock up and take a minute to myself."

"Sure thing." He grabbed the clipboard his silent buddy had gone to the truck to grab. "Can I get a signature for our boss?"

———

OWEN SPENT the day at a leadership conference for his army reserve unit. All he had wanted all day was a hamburger. A big, thick homemade patty topped with mushrooms and Swiss cheese, on a definitely-bad-for-him Brioche bun.

He hadn't anticipated Becca bursting into tears as soon as he pulled the ground beef out of the fridge.

"What?"

"Are you going to *cook* that?"

He blinked at her. "That's usually what happens, yeah."

"Dad, it smells so gross. God. Please, no." She gagged and ran from the room.

All right. So they were hitting that stage of pregnancy. He sighed, shoved the beef into a resealable bag, and tossed it into the freezer. His homemade burger plan would have to wait a month or maybe six. He gazed longingly at the mushrooms he'd picked up, decided it wasn't worth risking those either, and stomped after his daughter.

"I'm going to Mac's for takeout, do you want anything?"

From the other side of her closed bedroom door he heard a groan.

Knocking, he raised his voice a bit. "Bec? Can I come in?"

She opened it and gave him the saddest face he'd ever seen. "Can you get me some French fries?"

He frowned. "Yeah."

"I can't keep anything else down, Dad."

"It's fine. But you should call your midwife."

"She has a name, you know. You keep calling her the midwife. I told you, I talked to Kerry last week about this, and she said it was normal."

"Does she know you want French fries for dinner?"

"She told me to eat crackers. Fries are the same as crackers."

"They are not."

"Are they not, though?" She gave him a skeptical look.

He waited, but she wasn't going to budge.

"I'm fine as long as you don't cook any meat," she said with a pout.

God help him. "All right. I'll be back. Should I eat my burger at the diner or can I bring it home?"

She rolled her eyes. "You can bring it home. You just can't *cook it* at home."

"Good to know."

By the time he pulled into the gravel parking lot, there was a text message from Becca, too.

> **Becca: And a milkshake! Vanilla. Kerry said I can drink milk, so don't even start.**
> **Becca: I love you.**
> **Owen: You're pushing it, kiddo.**
> **Becca: la la la la love you.**

The place was busy, so instead of standing by the counter, he turned and scanned the room. On any given day, there was a solid chance of an army buddy or a fellow first responder sitting in a booth.

Today was no different. Sprawled in a corner spot was his youngest brother, Adam, and a fellow ex-soldier, Stevie. Owen waved at them, then put in his takeout order with the waitress—including the milkshake for Becca and a slice of pecan pie for himself, because why the hell not—and pointed across the room. "I'll be over there, holler when it's ready."

Adam and Stevie both had drinks, but no food yet. They all shook hands, and Adam gestured to the seat next to Stevie. "You want to join us?"

"I'm good. I've been sitting all day. Ryan Howard and I were at a leadership conference for the brigade. And I'm taking dinner home, anyway."

"Sitting all day sounds good right about now," Adam said. "We just finished a move."

"Just the two of you?"

"Yeah. Small job. Nice lady. Real pretty. She's getting

takeout, too, actually. Let me introduce you."

Owen opened his mouth to protest, but Adam was already waving his hand in the air. Under his breath, Owen muttered, "What are you doing?"

Adam grinned at him. "Reminding you that there's more to life than work and fatherhood."

Easier said when one didn't have a mortgage or a kid to support.

His brother couldn't read his mind, though. "Kerry, this is Owen, my big brother."

Owen's heart sank as he turned around. There was no way to avoid the awkwardness of the next moment, he realized that, and yet he still wanted the ground to open up and swallow him whole.

Standing in front of him in a tight, white parka, snug black leggings, and oversized winter boots was his daughter's midwife.

Her gaze landed on his face and she froze. He froze, too. Nobody else knew about Becca's pregnancy yet. Then she smiled, as if they'd never met. "Nice to meet you, Owen. I'm Kerry."

"Kerry works with Jenna Foster."

"The new clinic," Owen said, leading them as quickly as possible through this charade.

"That's the one." She turned and looked at the counter. "My dinner's going to be ready any minute now, so…"

It wouldn't be, though. Not if she'd just come in and placed her order after him.

But he watched her walk back to the counter, then turned sharply back to his brother, who was shaking his head. "What?"

"Man, you are hopeless. She's exactly your type."

"I don't have a type."

"Becca's leaving the house soon, it's time to get back—"

Owen glanced over his shoulder. The white parka and dark curls were hovering near the cash register. No easy out from this conversation.

"I've got her number if you want it," Adam said, laughter bouncing through his words.

Owen growled and waved him off.

The thing was, his brother wasn't wrong. In another time and place, Kerry would be the exact type of woman he'd want to spend time with. Get to know, get to taste, get to savour. But Becca *wasn't* leaving the house any time soon. And even if he had the bandwidth right now for some fun, her midwife was off-limits in that regard.

But he didn't have the bandwidth. He'd never been great about juggling a private life and parenting. Add in pregnancy hormones to the mix and he was on thin ice.

Six more months. *Then the newborn period.* It wasn't going to end any time soon.

When he glanced over his shoulder the next time, Kerry wasn't anywhere to be seen, so he figured maybe it was safe for him to escape back in the direction of the cash register. "I should go check on my order."

He said it in the direction of his brother, but he didn't wait for a reply before stalking off. As he waited by the cash, his phone vibrated. Expecting another request from Becca, the back of his neck heated up with stifled frustration as he pulled the phone from his pocket. But it wasn't his daughter.

It was his ex-wife.

Rachel: Do you want to come over for dinner tomorrow night? Hudson got a new smoker.

Owen: Becca's developed an aversion to meat.
Rachel: Aw, crap.
Owen: I'm at Mac's, picking up dinner because she
didn't want me to cook burgers in the house.
Rachel: I'm sorry. I'm laughing, but I'm also sorry.
Owen: It's fine. This too shall pass.
Rachel: The smoker is optional. I could make a
lasagna?

He made a face. He appreciated the way Rach and Hudson included him in things like their family dinners, but right now, he wanted to hibernate. But he had a daughter, and she had three half-siblings. Turning, he glanced back across the diner at Adam, now engrossed in a story he was telling Stevie. As much as his brothers had been royal pains in the ass over the years, they had also been his raison d'être. Family was everything, for better or worse.

Owen: Sounds good. Did you ask Becca?
Rachel: Not yet. I'll text her. I wanted to check with
you first.
Owen: K.

Text bubbles appeared, then disappeared. He could imagine Rachel's words flying across the screen, then being deleted. They'd been total crap as spouses, but especially as Becca had slid into her teen years, they'd become good friends. Friends who knew each other well enough to guess what the other was trying—and failing—to say.

Owen: I appreciate the invite. I like our family
dinners, you know?

Rachel: Me too.

He shoved his phone away, then glanced up at the waitress. "Order for Kincaid?"

"Two more minutes," she said crisply. "Just waiting on fresh fries for you."

Two minutes. Just enough time to remind his other family member here that he was appreciated. Owen strode back to Adam's booth.

"What's up?" his youngest sibling said, glancing up from his food.

"Do you have the day off tomorrow?"

"Yeah, sure do."

Owen nodded. "Good. Let's get together with Will and work on the car."

"Not too early. I'm going out tonight." Adam fist-bumped with Stevie across the table.

Owen gave him a half-smile. "Not too early."

Just like that, he had a fully packed social calendar for the rest of the weekend. Family stuff, sure, but that was what he could handle right now. It might not be the social life he'd dreamed of for this year, but beggars couldn't be choosers.

Back at the cash, he paid for his food, carefully wrapped up for him to take home to his daughter. He tipped the waitress, waved goodbye to his brother, then stepped outside.

The first thing he caught sight of was a white parka bounding back across the parking lot. He told himself to take a sharp right turn. And he did—but not until after something in his chest lurched hard. Something a lot like *what if* and *if things were different.*

He looped around the perimeter of the parking lot to

get to his truck, a list of all the filthy things he might want to do with his daughter's midwife if they'd met any other way, at any other time, spiralling through his mind.

CHAPTER FIVE

ON KERRY'S first morning as a Pine Harbour resident, she woke up to sunshine streaming through the oversized windows. She went downstairs to the clinic, where Jake Foster had transformed the space into Jenna's vision—on time and under budget. Kerry's sole contribution to the decor was the fancy espresso machine, and she was grateful for it this morning. The night before at Mac's, she'd discovered that Jenna hadn't been kidding about Pine Harbour being a latte-free zone.

She'd made an outsider rookie mistake by falling for the cute poster above the booth closest to the door asking, *How Do You Like Your Coffee?* It proclaimed four options. One for black, two and three for gradients of cream, and four for a delicious frothy mug topped with cinnamon.

"Not on the menu," she'd been told with a hearty laugh.

She could roll with that. Making frothy coffee at home would save her money in the long run, anyway. And nothing would get her down this weekend. It was the start of an exciting new adventure. First she would play barista, then she had big plans to explore her new town.

She filled her travel mug with perfectly brewed espresso and velvety steamed milk before bundling up for the cold weather and heading out on foot.

Pine Harbour was mostly neat blocks of residential neighbourhoods, a mix of post-war cottages, more modern bungalows, and on most corners, an oversized Victorian house like the ones Kerry always dreamed of living in one day when she was a little girl in an apartment in the city.

Every lot was large, the houses set back from the street, with space in between for driveways that often had more than one vehicle in it. A truck, a car, and on the second block, she saw two snowmobiles, too.

When she reached the outskirts of town, she looped back to the main drag and turned toward the lake. A hill separated the bulk of the town from the harbour. Main Street ended in a T-junction at the road that ringed the harbour. There was a sign advertising a marina, shuttered for the winter. Closer to her, across from the marina on the town side of the intersection, sat an abandoned gas station, nestled back into the pine trees climbing down the hill. To her right, across the road from the gas station was an empty lot covered in weeds. It lacked the sweet picturesque nature of the rest of the town, but the view of the harbor was stunning—and Kerry had it all to herself at this particular moment.

Wind whipped across the lake, churning the dark grey water into terrifying white caps, which bounced into the substantial ice and snow crests on the shore.

Kerry fell in love immediately. She crossed the road and turned right, following the sidewalk all the way around the harbour until the road curved away from the water again. There she found an entrance to a hiking path which was closed for the season.

Apparently the hiking trails went all the way from town to the provincial park. She took a picture with her phone so she wouldn't forget to look it up online, and then turned back toward the water. Pine Harbour was full of unexpected treats and delightful secrets.

As she got closer to the T-junction, and the hill at the bottom of Main Street, she realized the empty lot was no longer empty—there was a car parked on a diagonal in the middle of it, the driver's door hanging wide open and the front hood propped up. A big ol' beater of a car, something straight out of a seventies buddy cop TV show. On the other side of it was a pickup truck, and it looked like three guys were trying to boost the car off the truck's battery.

"How's that? Still nothing?" called out one of the men working on it.

"Nothing. Might need to get it towed back to your place. I told you not to take it for a drive."

"It was running just fine," the first guy said.

The third guy popped out from beneath the hood, and Kerry recognized her mover, Adam. And because there was nobody else around, her movement caught his eye. He waved, then gestured to the others. With a sinking feeling, she realized the tallest one, with his back to her, must be Becca's father.

The one Adam had tried to introduce her to last night, because her new town was just that small. Picturesque, perfect in many ways, but there was Owen Kincaid— glowering at her two days in a row.

———

OWEN PIVOTED around when Adam gestured across the road, but immediately turned back on his heel.

"What are you doing?" he muttered to his brother.

"Being friendly."

He made a face, then glanced over his shoulder. Becca's midwife—*Kerry, she has a name*—had stopped. She was coming over. Great.

"Leave her alone," he muttered at his brother, then picked up the pliers. "Let's get this shit-box working again."

Adam ignored him and slid out of the way, so when Kerry stopped in front of them, Owen was closest to her.

His brother wasn't subtle about it, either.

She gave him a polite smile. "Hi."

All the perfectly normal greetings Owen could usually produce died in his throat. "Yeah," he barked out.

Kerry's eyebrows jolted upwards.

He sighed and turned back to the car.

"Car trouble?" Kerry tried again, this time to Adam.

"More like a trouble car," he said easily, then gestured to their other brother. "This is Will. It's his disaster on wheels."

Owen ignored the rest of the introductions. He tried to ignore the conversation about the car, too, although it was hard not to notice the way she leaned in, the way she used her smile to get more information as she asked a few more questions.

It was hard to ignore *her*, bundled up in her bright white parka like she'd just walked off the pages of the Canada Goose catalogue. Owen didn't breathe properly until she said goodbye and headed up the hill towards town.

When his brothers returned their attention to the car, Adam was frowning. "What's going on with you?"

"Nothing." Owen squinted at the connection to the battery. He could feel Adam's suspicious gaze lingering as he tightened the wires. "Try that again."

It didn't work.

Will swore under his breath.

Adam crossed his arms over his chest. "This thing is a piece of junk."

Will frowned. "It's a piece of history."

"It's history, that's for sure. At least until we talk to Josh." His second youngest brother was a mechanic who worked on the racing circuit in the States. Josh could fix anything, but they had reached their limit. Owen straightened up and flexed his freezing fingers. "Time to call for a tow."

They didn't bother to wait for the truck from the garage to show up. It would be a few hours, because it was low priority. So his brothers piled into his truck and they went back to his place, where they had been working on Will's car when he'd gotten ambitious and decided to take it "around the block". Owen had the bigger garage, so the piece of junk—or piece of history, depending on how you looked at it—lived at his place.

He didn't know what had gotten into Will today, but he'd taken it further afield than just around the block, and as he'd gone down the hill toward the harbour, the shitbox had died on him. He'd coasted into the empty lot and called for help.

Back at Owen's place, his brothers followed him into the house. Becca's door was shut, so he told his brothers she was napping and led them into the kitchen, the furthest point away from her space.

"Is everything okay?" Of course Will picked up on the fact that Becca napping wasn't normal. Owen shouldn't have said anything.

"Yeah. She had a late night last night. She's pulling more hours at the country club, that's all."

"You gotta be careful she's not burning herself out with work." That was the school principal speaking. The professional who had a different perspective on kids than Owen did as a dad. "Is she stressing about next year? She hasn't picked a college yet, has she?"

Owen wasn't getting into that. He pulled open the fridge. "Beer? Coffee?"

Adam went for the former. Will asked for the latter.

Owen had both—but not at the same time. He downed his beer quickly. It didn't do much for his cold hands, but it felt good going down, and distracted him from the slight tremor deep inside. Big feelings, he'd have called them when Becca was little and still learning to control her emotions. *It's okay to have big feelings. It's not okay to hit when we're mad.*

He didn't want to hit anything.

He didn't know what he wanted. *Lies.* He wanted a white parka wrapped around a dark-haired beauty. He wanted freedom. He was trying so damn hard not to give in to the resentment of having to put off the next stage of his life, again.

Over the years, all of his brothers had been good confidants. When he broke up with Rachel, Seth—now a float plane pilot up north—and Will had listened to his shit with maturity way beyond their teen years, and promised him he would still be a good dad if he needed to leave.

He'd tried to live up to that belief, and turned back to them over and over again. As he re-negotiated custody when he came back, as Becca slid into her teen years like she was being chased by wild dogs.

But he couldn't talk to them about the pregnancy. Not yet. So he downed a beer, then he poured himself a cup of coffee. Mr. Responsibility.

His brothers had gone back to arguing about the car.

"Speaking of old and wonderful things—"

"That's a perversion of what I just said and you know it," Adam said blandly.

Will kept going anyway. "I'm starting something really cool at the school."

"You just said cool at the school. Ergo, it won't be, because it has a Dad Joke-level of rhyming built right into the premise. Can't support."

Will rolled his eyes at their youngest brother. "Fine, I won't tell you about it, but you'll be sad you couldn't get in on the ground floor and be a founding member of the Vintage Media Lab."

Owen had been watching their conversation silently, but now he leaned in. "The what now?"

Adam was hooked, too. "Excuse me, I always want to be the founding member of everything."

Will grinned broadly. "Then it's time to dig out any old electronic equipment you have, because I want it all. I'll make a 'Donated by Principal Kincaid's Whiny Little Brother' plaque and everything."

Adam ignored that. "Do you want VHS tapes?"

That made Will pause, suspiciously. "Depends what's on them."

"Fuck off. PG shit only. I know this is for kids."

"Yeah. Our librarian will take a look at them. But if you've taped over them with anything…"

"All of my sex tapes are digital only, never fear."

"We didn't need to know that," Owen said. "Moving on. What else do you want? I've got a stack of CDs I can go through."

"Excellent. Did anyone keep Dad's old eight-tracks?"

Owen squinted, trying to remember. That year had been a chaotic blur. "Maybe Seth has them."

Adam's eyes lit up. "He could bring them down, and then take us back up north with him. We could do a brothers' trip into the wilderness."

"Into the frozen tundra?"

"It's hardly the tundra. And I've always wanted to go on one of those ice fishing expeditions he runs."

"You haven't done one of those because you work part time for a moving company and you don't have the disposable income for a float plane to come and fetch you for weekends away."

"Family discount."

"That's not the Kincaid way," Owen barked.

Will shot him a warning look. Part *what crawled up your ass?* And part *give the kid a break.*

Adam shrugged. "I know. I don't actually want Seth to pay for anything."

Owen started ticking off the points on his fingers. "He pays for the fuel. His time is money. He—"

"He's also our brother, and did you ever consider that he might want to spend time with Adam?" Will said. "Seth's a grown-up, too, and he can say yes or no. Besides, pretty soon, we're only going to have each other."

Another reference to Becca moving away for school. Adam had said the same thing last night. Little did they know. But they didn't, they couldn't, and Owen knew that, but he barked anyway. "Jesus, that's maudlin. You planning ahead to when we all need to move back in together to make ends meet on our fixed income retirement?"

Will shrugged. "Would that be so bad?"

Owen rolled his head around, cracking his neck. "I'm planning a good long run of living on my own before we need to come to that point. Talk to me in forty years about being old."

"Maybe if we talk now, about other shit, you won't spend the next forty years alone and miserable."

"Who said I'm miserable?"

Will was saved from answering that by the arrival of his niece. Becca wandered into the kitchen. "What are you guys yelling about?"

"Uncle Will's car broke down."

"The clunker?" She said it with all the genuine love a niece could have for an uncle, but it still made Adam howl, which made her giggle.

And that made Will smile, even though his precious hunk of junk was being insulted. Becca poured herself a glass of water, then leaned against the counter and settled in to roast the older generation. "Look at you all in your matching boots and big, burly plaid shirts. How are you all single?"

"That was the other topic of conversation. How we're all going to live together when we're old," said Will.

"I can totally see that. You'd be the baddest old guys on the block. My daddy and his ferocious brothers," Becca teased.

Adam hooked his arm around her neck and she squeaked as he gave her a noogie. "Who are you calling ferocious?"

"Definitely not you," she grunted as she kicked him in the shin. "Picking on a—" Owen could hear her pause, like she was maybe going to say *pregnant woman*. But she didn't, and his pulse slowed down. "Picking on a little girl. Only bullies do that."

"You started it." Adam threw his hands in the air. "But I'll call uncle."

It was a game they'd played since she was little and Adam had been the doting teen halfway between her and her dad in age. He'd pick a mock fight, she'd "win", and he'd have to beg for mercy. She used to think it was the funniest thing in the world to make her uncle cry *uncle*.

It still made Owen laugh.

He didn't miss the look Will shot him across the room, as if saying, *see? She's fine.* But his brother didn't know the rest of it.

"What's wrong with plaid shirts and boots?" Will asked.

She gave him an innocent shrug. "Nothing."

"She was just starting shit," Owen rumbled.

Becca glanced sideways at Will. "Why do you ask? Is there anyone you're trying to impress with your sartorial choices?"

His brother stared straight ahead. "No."

"There is." She bounced up and down. "Uncle Will has a crush on someone!"

The hair on the back of Owen's neck stood up, like the word *crush* might shine a spotlight on him. Not that he had a crush on anyone. *She has a name.* He had grown-up, complicated fantasies, and that was completely different.

"Leave him alone," he said gruffly. "Go back to picking on Adam."

She twirled toward her other uncle, but then pulled her phone from her back pocket.

"Saved by the silent text message," Adam teased.

"Who's that? Hayden? Haven't heard much about your hockey player lately."

Owen thought about throwing his full mug of coffee right across the room, anything to save Becca from having to answer that question, but his daughter just shrugged and smiled, seemingly unperturbed by the reference to the shithead who wasn't returning her messages. Unless there was an update Owen was unaware of. Concern roared to life inside him, shoving away his selfish thoughts about his own non-problems.

That night he asked Rachel about it when they had a moment alone before dinner.

"He's in the middle of the hockey season," she said. "I'm not excusing him for that, but Becca might be. I'll talk to her about him."

"Tell her—" Owen cut himself off, then groaned. He was about to do to Rachel what Becca did to him, try to stage manage a conversation. "All right. Thanks."

Rachel gave him a serious look. "You need to prepare yourself for her giving him a lot of slack here. She's his biggest fan."

He was painfully aware of that fact. "Yeah."

CHAPTER SIX

THE LAST WEEKS of winter sped by in a blur of meeting new neighbours, learning more about Pine Harbour, and spreading the word about their new clinic to get more clients.

All in all, Kerry was loving her new town. But every so often, she'd bump into Owen Kincaid, who she'd renamed from Mr. Alpha, which was way too generic, to Mr. Broody. The intense brooding presence he'd projected during Becca's first appointment continued. He was cold and awkward each time she ran into him, and Becca's mother Rachel came to her next two appointments. For the first one they drove to Walkerton but then Becca surprised her and announced she was fine with the Pine Harbour clinic. Kerry was happy to see her young client get more comfortable with being pregnant in her own community. That would ease the transition to being a new mom.

At each appointment, they didn't just talk about the physiological changes of pregnancy, but the emotional impact as well. Becca had supportive parents, but her ex-boyfriend wasn't in the picture.

"He's a hockey player and it's the end of their season," Becca said. "Maybe once he's through playoffs…But if he doesn't want to be involved, that's his choice."

"There are resources for single parents. We can talk more about that as you get closer to delivery." It was a topic close to Kerry's heart, and not just out of professional interest.

Every month, as she hit the middle of her menstrual cycle, she found herself googling sperm donation and egg freezing. She wasn't ready to make the leap yet, but her biological clock ticked a little louder each month. It didn't help that she was surrounded by babies and pregnant bellies all day, every day. Would she want to do that on her own? Her answer depended significantly on how annoying she found the partners who came in with her clients on a given day.

No partner was certainly better than a toxic one.

But then she would go out for a trail run, or to the Hedgehog, and she would think…this would be over. Done with. Maybe once in a blue moon she might stalk in for a grumpy beer, like Becca's father had that first night she'd seen him—but he hadn't been back. Being a single parent would mean no more extracurricular fun.

And Kerry liked her extracurricular fun. It had been a surprise to her when her biological clock had started ticking, ever so quietly, a year ago. All the way through school and as she started her career, she had thought that maybe babies were only professionally interesting to her—and then something started to change.

She still didn't understand it, but she was going with the flow for now. Dreaming and researching, considering all of her options.

"You're lost in your thoughts," Jenna said over lunch one day. "Is everything okay?"

Kerry nodded. "I'm fine."

"Do you want to talk about our cases?"

Once a week, they caught each other up on their patient files. It helped for when they covered each other off, for appointments. "Yes, absolutely." She stood up and shook off her thoughts of babies and the future. Right now, in the present, they had work to do. "Who do you want to start with?"

"Dina Suarez is fully discharged now, we had our last appointment yesterday." Jenna pulled out her phone, where she kept a running summary of her case notes. "I have two intakes this week. One is second trimester already, a transfer in from Dr. Malcolm because we have space on our calendar."

"Excellent."

"And the other is a nineteen-year-old from Tobermory. She doesn't have a car, so I was thinking of offering more home appointments. I know that's not standard care, but..."

Kerry nodded. "Yeah, no, I get it. If we can do that now, while we aren't swamped, I don't see why not." She chewed on her lower lip. "That's two teen pregnancies in our care at once. See if she might be interested in a peer session with Becca Kincaid."

Jenna made a note of that, then moved down the list.

Kerry's thoughts drifted again as they finished up their meeting. Teen pregnancy was a statistical reality. How many other young moms were there on the peninsula that they didn't see in their care? She should touch base with public health. "What do you think about offering our space for a teen mom peer group? Not just for our clients, but a drop in for anyone?"

As soon as she said it, she knew what Jenna would say. The only space big enough was the kitchenette break room they were in, and it had a max capacity of ten people.

But her colleague surprised her. "If we can't host it here, we can find the space. That's a great idea."

AS THE WEATHER started to warm up, and soccer season loomed in her near future, Kerry made a resolution to make dinner for herself a bit more often and rely less on the easy and delicious takeout menu from Mac's.

One night she drove over to Lion's Head to get groceries in order to stick with that personal pledge, and standing in front of the celery she wanted for her tuna salad was Mr. Broody himself, his back to her. She didn't care for the way she knew instantly who those broad shoulders belonged to. The unseasonably warm early March weather meant she had left her coat at home and only wore a sweater, but Owen had taken the wardrobe shift to another level. Instead of the long-sleeve layers she'd seen him in before, today he was wearing a black t-shirt that stretched snug across his back and rode high on his biceps. She was surprised to see he had a delicate tattoo that curved almost all the way around his upper arm. A filagree moon, jewels hanging from it. Since he was standing where she needed to be, and wasn't moving, she couldn't help but look at it. It was right in front of her.

It wasn't the kind of tattoo she'd have guessed he'd have. Or any tattoo, for that matter. The uptight para-medic was a grouch who she'd have pegged for a rule-follower. And if told that the man had a tattoo, she'd have guessed something simple, maybe a mistake from his youth.

The pretty moon with even prettier droplets hanging off it didn't match her idea of him at all.

Those droplets shifted in front of her, Owen's arm flexing, the muscles rolling beneath the tattoo as he reached out and grabbed two bunches of celery at once. Kerry stood her ground as he pivoted towards her.

It wasn't really fair, the way she had advance warning that their gazes would collide and he didn't. She didn't care, of course. He'd proven to be completely unfriendly at every turn, so if her presence unsettled him, that was his problem, not hers. "Hi," she said brightly.

Storm clouds gathered fast and swift beneath his dark eyebrows. "Kerry."

"I need celery, too." She pointed past him.

He followed the line from her finger to the vegetables, then back again. With a grunt, he nodded, then turned on his heel and headed to the bakery at the back of the store.

"Nice to see you, too," she muttered.

It was exactly how every single passing encounter had gone. Eye contact, grunts, maybe a word or two, and then a quick retreat.

She didn't like it.

And more to the point, she didn't like that she didn't like it. What did it matter if he didn't have much to say to her? But it did matter, and that bothered her, too.

Owen Kincaid bothered her greatly.

The interaction lingered in her thoughts as she went home and made herself dinner.

Celery and shallots chopped. *Owen's thick arm, decorated with a pretty tattoo.*

Tuna and mayo added. *The way he said her name, like the barest of acknowledgements. Kerry, the person in front of him.*

Some dill, too, snipped up with kitchen shears. *The tall stretch of him as he stalked away.*

With a grunt of her own, she pushed away from the kitchen counter and grabbed a clean spoon from the drying rack. She was going to eat her tuna salad out of the mixing bowl and find something—anything—to watch on TV. Something, anything, to get her mind off Becca's father and the way he looked in a black t-shirt as he avoided any and all interactions with her.

Because Kerry recognized the discomfort deep inside her. Something about the paramedic chief had grabbed onto her imagination, and she was projecting on to him all of her typical desires. She had a type, after all, and if she squinted, Owen Kincaid could be molded into that man. Big, strong, capable.

She didn't usually have time for grouchy and grumpy, and definitely not *broody*, that was the worst, but for some reason that wasn't a turn off as much as it should be.

It should be a turn off because he's a client's father. It should be, but it wasn't.

Kerry froze in the middle of her tiny kitchen. The spoon fell out of her hand and clattered to the ground with an angry, sharp sound.

No.

She needed to go the Hedgehog for a drink and flirt with literally anyone else, because she was horrified to realize that deep down, she was absolutely fine with having a secret little crush on Becca's father.

And it wasn't just the way he looked in a t-shirt. It was, perversely, a little bit the way he grunted and growled, like he might kill someone who looked the wrong way at his daughter—even if that person was her midwife, because he was clearly not okay with Becca's pregnancy and the absent teenage father.

Kerry laughed out loud. He was projecting onto her, and she liked it because he was conventionally attractive? Oh, boy. She needed to get laid and fast.

CHAPTER SEVEN

THE NEW PINE HARBOUR EMERGENCY SERVICES building—which wasn't actually new anymore, having been built almost two years earlier, but which would be known as the New Building for at least another decade—wasn't technically a full firehouse. It was, primarily, an EMT station, with two fire trucks stationed there as well, for the volunteer firefighters who filled in the gaps in service on the peninsula.

But once a firefighter, always a firefighter. Owen had gone back to fire school after becoming a paramedic, to make himself more employable after his blink-and-you-missed-it marriage to Rachel burned out. That meant he was the right guy to supervise the whole building. Also the right guy to cook everyone dinner.

He did this once a week, at the volunteer training night. On the menu tonight was chicken thighs, dry rubbed with Korean barbecue spices, a celery and lettuce chopped salad, and oversized dinner rolls. As he prepped the salad, he replayed the conversation with Kerry in his head. *Conversation* was a generous word for the way he'd stared at her, said her name, then bolted.

God damn it.

"Need help?"

Owen's chef knife skidded against the cutting board as the question interrupted his thoughts. He glanced at the doorway and found Adam leaning casually against the frame. "What are you doing here?"

"It's training night."

Owen scowled. "You're not joining the team."

"That's not up to you." Adam gave him an easy grin. He wasn't wrong. It wasn't up to Owen, because the volunteer fire brigade was their own thing, separate from the EMTs. Owen supervised the building, but not the fire-fighters themselves.

But they'd talked about this. Repeatedly. Owen shook his head. "You should listen to me."

"I do. I listen to what you say, and I watch what you do. This is what I want to do with my life next. Trust me."

He did. Sort of. But Adam had only been nine when Becca was born, when Owen had been thrust into being a parent, a grown-up. And even though he was twenty-seven now, this was his third declaration of what he wanted to do with his life. So Owen trusted Adam to make his own decisions in the same way he trusted Becca, and frankly, he worried about their choices in the same way.

Especially if their choices could be deadly.

Adam looked pointedly at the vegetables on the counter. "So? Need help?"

Owen took a deep breath, then waved him in. "You can make the salad dressing. And we can talk about your plans to go back to school."

"The only school I want to do is fire school, and you know that."

But Owen wanted more than that for his youngest brother. Adam had joined the army right out of high school, did a couple of tours overseas, and when his contract came up, he got out unexpectedly. They'd all been relieved, but when he moved back to Pine Harbour, the only job he showed any interest in was working with Warriors Moving. Owen liked the guys who ran it, but it was a stop-gap thing. An opportunity for veterans, like Stevie, who weren't in the right headspace to look for a more permanent second career.

Adam wasn't like that.

Owen wasn't stupid. He knew there was always a risk of PTSD after deployment. He'd seen it in his own ranks, with Matt Foster, a paramedic who worked for him. But Adam checked out. He was happy enough, had a good social network, and his life stretched out in front of him full of potential.

And now the dummy wanted to be a firefighter.

No way was Owen getting into a fight with him over it, though. "Start making that dressing."

"If I cook, I stay for training."

He was staying anyway, Owen might as well get some kitchen help out of the deal. "Listen, when Will gets here, I need to tell you guys something."

"That's right, Will comes to fire training night. Will's allowed to do whatever he wants."

Will was a grown-up, Owen wanted to snap back, but so was Adam. But the difference between Adam and their middle brother was that Will was an elementary school principal by day. Sure, he volunteered on the fire team, but the chances of him actually running into a burning building and not coming out were low.

The chances of Will having a heart attack at forty-eight and leaving his family reeling were low, too.

God damn it. Owen forced that thought out of his mind and turned on the charm. Adam liked charm. He used it, but he was susceptible to it as well. "Look," Owen said. "I know I have different rules for Will and Seth than I do for you and Josh. And I know—I *know*—that it's not my place to have rules for grown men, period. But I do, because I'm your big brother, so humour me, all right?"

Adam chewed on his lower lip, then nodded. But he wasn't going to let it go that easily. "Speaking of Will..." Owen waited while his brother paused for dramatic effect. "I was thinking of getting Kerry's number for him, since you weren't interested?"

Inside his head, Owen rose to the bait. He rose swift and angrily, in ways he didn't want to analyze. But on the outside, he waited it out, stone-faced. Adam was a natural flirt, always had been, and that extended to match making. He would stop if he got the idea that Owen wasn't interested.

"She's really nice, you know. If you give her a chance."

"Are you hanging out with her now?" Owen's gaze narrowed despite his best efforts to appear unaffected.

His brother didn't back down. "She's come into the Green Hedgehog a few times."

"Ah."

"You should come out, too."

"Maybe." But they both knew he wouldn't. "Listen, about Kerry—"

"I know."

"It's not about me."

"Yeah. I *know*. Becca told me she's pregnant," Adam said. "That's a hell of a secret you've been keeping since Christmas."

"Wasn't mine to tell."

"Kerry won't be her midwife forever."

"Doesn't matter. She is right now."

"Is that why you're so freaking rude to her?"

Nah, that was all on Owen's darker side, which would never see the light of day. He grunted and let his brother take the noise as acknowledgement.

Will sauntered into the kitchen. "Are we talking about Owen's parenting choices?"

Direct hit and his middle brother didn't even know it. "Sure are."

"No," Adam corrected. "Did you get a text from Becca?"

She was telling people by text? Owen scrubbed a hand over his face. There were too many moving parts to the puzzle that was his family sometimes. She'd just told him and Rachel this morning that she was ready to start sharing the news.

"That's what—ah, shit." Will pulled up a chair. "You've been dealing with this all on your own?"

"I'm her father. And I'm not *alone*. Rachel's been good. Mostly. We're trying, okay?"

"Sure."

Owen looked around the kitchen, then out to the hall, where people were gathering. "This isn't the time or the place."

"Yeah." Will didn't move, though. "Adam, shut the door on your way out."

"Both of you, get going to training. I've got clean up to do, then I'll be in my office."

Will shrugged. "I can skip the first part of training. Or all of it."

Owen wasn't sure he was ready to talk. But the thing was, this had been coming for months. He was never going to be ready. "Yeah. All right."

Will waited until Adam was gone, then kicked another chair out from the table. "Have a seat."

Owen dumped himself onto the chair and leaned forward, resting his face in his hands.

"So we're going to be uncles," Will said slowly. "Becca sounds pretty excited."

"She is."

"And you?"

He lifted his head and rocked his jaw to the side. "It's not about me."

"It is right now. In here, just between us. You carry the weight of the world on your shoulders, Owen. You always have."

He never had a choice in the matter. "I do what any of us would do."

"None of us were the oldest. You've been carrying the load since Dad died."

"And now Adam wants to be a full time firefighter," Owen hissed, flinging his hand toward the training room on the other side of the wall. "Everything's..."

"What? Everything is what?"

Falling apart. Everything was falling apart, and Owen couldn't stop it. He was watching his daughter and his youngest brother make the same mistakes of their previous generations, and he couldn't do shit fuck all. "Everything is complicated," he muttered. "And they don't see the consequences of their choices."

"They being Becca and Adam?"

And Josh, who was chasing his dreams around a race track and not getting anywhere. And Seth, flying all over the north. Owen was so tired. He shrugged. "You're the only one who I don't worry about on a daily basis."

"I was thinking of getting a pet tiger," Will drawled.

Owen didn't laugh.

"Are you thinking about Mom and Dad?"

"I'm desperately trying not to," Owen said dryly. But the muscles around his mouth twitched, betraying his attempt at humour as a cover.

Will always had been better about talking about them than Owen was. "Yeah."

"You aren't Dad."

"Nah, I only had one kid, not five. And I was only a firefighter for a few years. I only work in a firehouse now, and I'm watching his youngest—who he never got to see grow up and join the army—want to follow in his footsteps."

"You think Adam is following in *Dad's* footsteps?" Will shook his head. "Not Dad. You."

Owen groaned. "That's even worse. I did what I had to do to stay close to Becca. Adam doesn't have—"

"He has you. And me, and Becca too. Sure, he's not a young father, but he's as tangled up in family as you are. We only have each other, bud. You taught us that."

He hadn't meant it like this. He had never wanted his brothers to take on dangerous jobs the way he had. "Why couldn't he be a house painter or something?"

"Way up high on ladders?"

"Fuck off."

Will smiled. "Adam's going to be okay. Becca is, too. And so are you."

Owen frowned. "I know I am."

"You've been extra grumpy lately. Maybe you should get out of the house."

"I'm here, aren't I?"

"Out of the firehouse, too." Will narrowed his eyes. "When was the last time you went to the Green Hedgehog?"

"Did you and Adam tag team me with this?"

"Hand to God, we did not. Why?"

"Nothing." He rolled his neck. "I'm fine. I promise, I'm not being too hard on Becca about this. I'm giving her the space she needs. I'm doing my best."

"She's going to be okay."

"That's what I told her as soon as she found out."

"Good."

Owen gave his brother an appraising look. "Can I ask you an honest question?"

"Sure."

"Would you be saying the same thing if she were a student of yours, and not your niece?"

Will didn't even hesitate. "Yes."

Owen wasn't sure why he'd asked that. Doubt swam in the same waters as fear, probably.

"We're all just trying to do the best with what we've got," his brother said. "And you know this—young adults are resilient, and they need to make their own decisions so they can learn from them."

"All right. Life lesson noted."

"If we're asking honest questions, can I ask you one?" Will looked like he was on guard, but fair was fair.

Owen nodded.

"Would you do anything differently? Becca's in your shoes now. Looking back..."

"No." Owen shook his head forcefully. "That's never

crossed my mind. I just didn't know how hard it was going to be."

It wasn't having Becca so young that he resented. It was then having two young brothers dumped in his lap when their parents died. Having another two teenagers who knew keenly he was *not* their parent. A house he couldn't afford, that had to be sold, and then years of renting before he could buy his little bungalow.

If his parents hadn't died, it just would have all been a little easier.

The previous generation of Kincaids worked themselves to early deaths. Owen didn't want any of his brothers to follow in their parents' footsteps. He'd been counting down the months to freedom, to his own chance to enjoy life to its fullest.

But looking at Will across the table, he couldn't bring himself to say any of that out loud. His pessimism was his own burden, not to be shared with his brother. So he stuck to repeating part of the truth. "Becca is the best part of my life. Hands down."

WHEN HE GOT HOME from work, there was a note on the fridge that Becca had run out to Mac's to get fries. Owen texted her to let her know he was back, then he pulled out the step stool that lived beside the fridge and opened the door to the storage crawlspace above the back porch.

The box of CDs he wanted was at the back and covered in a thick layer of dust.

Today had been a disaster from top to bottom, but maybe he could salvage it by putting together a box for Will's Vintage Media Lab.

Twenty minutes later, he had his laptop out, surrounded by memories. His plan had originally been to rip the music off the CDs to keep in .mp3 form before he donated them. But he was having a harder time parting with some of the plastic jewel cases than he thought he would.

It didn't make any sense—that box had been in the crawl space since he bought the house. Nostalgia worked in strange ways.

He heard Becca's car pull into the driveway, then turn off. The headlights flashed, then he heard her footsteps on the stairs. When the door opened, he waved from the couch. "I'm here."

"Oh my God, Dad. What are you doing?"

"Going through my old CDs for Will's Vintage Media Lab project."

Becca dropped her bag on the floor, then joined him on the couch. She had a cardboard box full of fries. "Hungry?"

"I'm good." He glanced at the fries, then at his daughter. It was a full box, and they looked fresh. He'd been home for at least a half an hour, and Mac's was a two-minute drive away. Fries weren't the only thing she'd gone out for, but Will's caution rang in his ears. She would need to make her own decisions, and learn from them. "How was your day?"

She shrugged. "School was fine."

That was it. He poked further. "And you told your uncles about the baby."

"I said I was ready to start telling people."

"I know." He took a deep breath. "I guess I wasn't completely prepared."

"Did they both descend on you at the same time?"

"One-two punch. Adam first, then Will slid in for a good ol' guidance counselling session."

Becca giggled. "He's good at that. I got it, too. He suggested some college programs that are all distance education."

"Oh yeah?"

"I dunno. Don't get your hopes up. One thing at a time."

Owen laughed. "Hopes properly stored at a very low level."

She leaned over and picked up the album on the top of the pile. "Lonestar. You used to play this when I was little."

"Stop making me feel old." But he didn't mean it. Every year with Becca had been full of memories just like that.

"You aren't old," she said softly. "You're pretty much the same age as the other moms on the pregnancy groups online."

He didn't miss the weird note in her voice. He set the CDs aside and looked at her, really close. "How you doing?"

"Oh." She shrugged. "You know. It's fine."

"Two words often used to describe things that are not, in fact, fine."

She blew a raspberry.

Owen frowned. "Do you need something?"

She shook her head. "No. *No.* And I don't want—" She stopped, raised her hands as if to reset the conversation. "It was just a down-in-my-feels moment. I'm all good. Let's talk about the CDs. Are you getting rid of all of them?"

"They aren't going that far. But actually, I think I'm

going to keep a few." He held up a Rascal Flatts album. "Like this one. Speaking of taking me back. I listened to it a lot when I was away at school, when you were a toddler. That was *my* deep-in-my-feels period. I missed you so much, and I just wanted to find the path that would bring me home to you."

Becca's eyes welled up. "Dad!"

"What?"

"That's really sweet." She wrinkled her nose, clearly trying not to cry.

He held out his arms, and she scooted sideways. As she leaned on him, she took the plastic CD case and turned it over in her hands. "You know, it's kind of like an archeological dig for your emo journey."

"Whoa, let's not go too far." He laughed, but she wasn't wrong.

They went through the rest of the CDs together, playing some of the songs as they went, tracing his emo journey, as she put it.

But he wasn't prepared for the last jewel case Becca picked up. It wasn't metal, and it wasn't country, the two types of music he usually listened to.

"What's this one?"

Owen took the Dire Straits album, his throat closing up with emotion. The answer came out strained to his own ear. "That was your grandpa's."

"Can we listen to it?"

"Yeah, of course." He blinked, his eyes suddenly hot and scratchy. He had to disentangle himself from his daughter, which was for the best. He didn't want her to see his eyes get wet, or the way it took him a second to pull himself together before he could put the CD in the computer.

His dad had probably been Owen's age now when he bought it. He hoped like hell that Becca would never be having the same conversation one day with her kid about the Lonestar CD. He wanted to be around to share the music himself.

"What are you thinking about?"

He glanced back at his daughter as the music started. "Lots of things. Probably the last time I heard this CD was when you were a baby."

"And now I'm having a baby."

Zing. Sometimes his daughter was too smart for her own good. He nodded reluctantly. "Yeah. There's some circle of life stuff going on in my head."

"I *knew* it was an emo journey!" And sometimes she was a teenager, through and through.

He chuckled, grateful for the laugh. "Yeah. Listen, Bec…"

"Mmm?"

"I know I've had quite the period of adjustment to the pregnancy. But I see how happy you are, and I just want you to know that I'm not angry."

"I know you're not." She tried to hold his gaze, but blinked and looked down after a second.

"Becca."

She rolled her head. "I know, Dad! I know you're not mad! But you're disappointed that I'm repeating the whole…" She waved her hand. "You know."

"It's more complicated than that. It's not disappointment, honey. It's fear. When you were a baby—the most perfect baby I had ever seen in my entire life—you were the only thing that felt right. I don't want you and *your* baby to be lost in a storm like that."

She slowed her movements and looked at him. "Oh."

"Your mom and I love you so much. With all of our hearts. But things were rough for us."

"This is about Hayden."

He took a deep breath. "Yeah."

"*Dad.*"

"What? You don't talk about him at all."

"Because you don't like him."

She had a point. He softened his face as much as possible. "Have you been talking?"

"Yeah. Some."

"You know, your mom and I know something about having a baby with someone who isn't…"

Becca tensed. "Isn't what?"

He stumbled. "Has your mom talked to you about this?"

"She tried. Just about as well as you are." She moved away from him, but didn't leap off the couch.

He held his breath.

"It's complicated."

He willed himself to not make a face at her earnest confession. He could imagine just how *complicated* it was for the hot stud hockey player to suddenly be faced with the consequences of being reckless.

Becca licked her lower lip, then sighed. "He doesn't want the coach to know." *Do not react, do not react, do not…* She threw her hands in the air. "Which is stupid, right?"

Owen let out the breath he'd been holding.

And his daughter laughed. *Thank God.* "Yeah, it's stupid," she said quietly. "But I don't want to cut him out of my life completely, because maybe once the baby is born he'll change his mind. And if he doesn't, so be it. I'm not going to lose sleep over him, if that's what you're worried about."

Owen reached out and cupped his daughter's face in his hands. "You are the best person, you know that? And I worry about everything, but only a little. Because I know you have a smart head on your shoulders. I do." To reinforce the point, he kissed her forehead before sitting back. "And whatever happens, you know I've got your back, right?"

"I don't need you to go and beat him up."

"I would."

"*Dad!*" She burst out laughing. "Have you considered that he might hurt you?"

"Not even for a second. I have old man strength."

"I thought we agreed you aren't old."

They had agreed on nothing of the sort. "Agree to disagree."

"Uh uh." Becca shook her head. "You're still a young man. Young enough to have babies of your own, all over again," she teased.

He howled. "Nah. Never gonna happen."

She giggled. "You never wanted more kids after perfection on the first try?"

"Exactly." He chuckled and leaned his head back against the sofa cushion. Once upon a time, he had thought he'd have a big family, just like his parents. But his path had gone in a very different direction, and that had been for the best—because then he did have a big family, suddenly, and it had been chaos. They'd all barely survived. No, he had no interest in starting that all over again.

And once Becca was past her maternity leave, she might move out on her own with the baby, and he could get his Great Bachelor Plans back underway.

CHAPTER EIGHT

IN EARLY APRIL, Owen had a conversation with Matt Foster, one of his paramedics, that didn't seem like a big deal at the time.

He received an email, read it, sighed, and went to find the right sucker to take it on. Matt didn't mind being volun-told to do things, especially if he could make some overtime pay in the process. He was a young husband, with a step-daughter and another baby on the way.

Owen found him doing inventory on one of their ambulances. "Hey, I've got a job for you. Public Health is pulling together a regional health providers working group on opioids and community impact of methamphetamines. They're looking for volunteers. Monthly meetings for the next six months, looking at the peninsula interagency..."

"Full disclosure, you lost me at working group. Briefly grabbed my attention again at meth in the community, but the six months thing is a deal-breaker." Matt slapped him on the shoulder. "Sorry, man. Sometimes you can talk me into this shit, but not for this summer. I'm going to be on a reduced workload, winding down my shifts so I can take a few months of parental leave, remember?"

Fuck. Where had Owen's head been at? Matt's wife Natasha was due right around the same time as Becca. "I knew that."

"Does it need to be a paramedic? Kerry Humphrey has shown an interest in the interagency stuff."

Owen scowled. It was the safest expression he could manage, and everyone read it as a grumpy anyway. That reputation didn't hurt him. "I'd rather keep it in house. We have unique concerns. It's fine, I'll go myself."

He went back to his desk, replied to the email, and moved on with his day, the moment forgotten until two weeks later when his door swung open and someone started yelling at him.

"Do you have a problem with me?"

He lifted his head and found Kerry glaring at him. That was a complicated question. Yeah, he kind of did, but it was the type of problem a man should keep to himself because it was really his issue, not hers. Lord help him if she ever found out. So he did the smart thing and kept his trap shut.

She threw her hands in the air.

"What?"

"What *what*?" She howled, echoing his word back at him. "You never say anything!"

"I don't know what we're doing here."

"You nixed my involvement in an interagency working group?"

He was going to kill Matt. "Not exactly."

"Whoa." She raised her hands in the air. "Not *exactly*? Don't play dumb."

Every fibre of his being wanted to stand up and tower over her, tell her to get out of his face and give him a minute to think. He couldn't keep his head straight around her, and she'd caught him off guard. Yeah, that was a stupid thing for him to have said to Matt, but he'd had his reasons. Not great ones. But he'd had reasons. Or at least one reason, and in the four months since he'd met her, he thought he'd done a pretty good job of burying the way she affected him, the way she scrambled his thoughts.

Maybe he hadn't.

Instead of surging to his feet, he rocked back in his chair and let her glare at him some more. "How'd you hear about the interagency working group?"

"Probably the same way you did. The health unit email loop. My senior partner forwarded the call for a representative from the middle of the peninsula, suggested we get a midwife in there because our client base is a vulnerable population, and affected by drug use in their homes, too. I rang them up and they said *you'd* be representing Pine Harbour and Lion's Head. I asked to sit on it as well, they called you, and you said no. Which I don't really think is your role, because who made you king? So here I am, demanding an answer."

Ah, so it wasn't Matt Foster he had to kill. That was a relief. Shame it was himself that was actually to blame. "Here's the thing…"

She waited.

He didn't elaborate. God damn it. He *had* blocked her. He hadn't meant that to be the impact, but—

Before he could fix his thoughts in any organized apology, she huffed and leaned in. "Look, I know you don't like me. That's fine. But this is my community now, too, and I want to be a part of things."

What?

No.

He meant, yes, of course it was her community too. God damn it. His mouth fell open, then snapped shut again. He could see her anger amping up, it was in her eyes, and her body language, and he needed to fix it.

———

KERRY WAS SO forking close to storming out of his office and following up with an email, because oh boy, was she steamed, and getting madder by the second. A paper trail would be smarter than a one-sided screaming match.

Why was he just staring at her?

His jaw worked, and then he leaned forward, his gaze guarded and careful. "I never said I didn't like you."

She laughed. That was the part he grabbed on to? "You don't need to say it. It's clear."

"Wait." He reached out and caught her hand, his fingers hot against her skin. As quickly as he grabbed her, his grip released and he dropped her arm. His eyes flared wide, his attention locked on her face. "I like you just fine, Kerry. There's a lot going on, that's all. And I didn't know it was you. The other person. I didn't know it was you when they called."

I like you just fine. Heaven help his friends and family if this was how he treated people he liked just fine. She was tempted to point that out. But she didn't, and he didn't elaborate. He didn't need to.

"I'm going to find out when that meeting is and just show up anyway," she said, trying to ignore the way she could still feel his touch on her skin.

I like you just fine. What the hell did that mean? He objectively did *not* like her. He didn't want to work with her, he didn't like the way she took care of his daughter, he didn't like the way she bought celery.

He grabbed a piece of paper and scrawled on it in black marker. "Good. You should be there."

"What?"

He stood up, slowly, and handed the paper across the desk. It had a date, time and location on it.

She stared at the paper, then up at him, then back to the paper. "Just like that?"

"I won't go." Was that an offer, or a statement?

Wordlessly, she reached out and took the paper. Then she swallowed hard. "We bring different perspectives. We should both go."

The tight, hesitant beat he waited before responding just about killed her. "All right."

Yeah. Relief flooded through her, bringing a delayed onset of hot, complicated tears to her eyes, so she spun on her heel and left before he could notice them.

She went back to the clinic, put the meeting on her calendar, then checked her schedule for the rest of the week. She laughed out loud when she saw that Becca had an appointment on the calendar for Saturday—but Jenna was going to see her, not Kerry. She hated that she felt relief at that, but after her run in with Owen right now, it was for the best.

But avoiding Kincaids wasn't that easy. That night, when she'd had enough of lying on her couch and watching the giant clock on her wall not move, she went over to the Green Hedgehog to find some of the soccer players.

Lore was behind the bar, but the only other person Kerry recognized in the place was Adam Kincaid, who was at a table with his friend Silent Stevie. He waved, and she returned the gesture, then took a seat at the bar.

"What's the drink of the day?" Kerry asked.

Lore gave her a wicked grin. "A Michelada. The Canuck Edition, if you will."

Kerry didn't know what a Michelada was, but she was in. Lore's concoctions were always worth the gamble. "I will."

When the bartender reached for the Caesar rim mix, Kerry thought she should warn her to make it not too strong, because she was driving, but as the drink building progressed, she realized it wasn't a shot of vodka that would be the base of the drink, but…beer from the tap.

"Just try it," Lore said as she pushed the cocktail across the bar. "It tastes like summer."

She was three sips in when Adam appeared beside her. "I'll have one of those, too."

Kerry glanced over her shoulder. Silent Stevie was nowhere to be seen. "How's it going, Adam?"

"You know. Work. Play." He winked.

She laughed. "In equal measure?"

"For now." He shrugged. "How about you? How's it going?"

I stormed into your brother's office and yelled at him. "You know."

"Work and play?"

She lifted her glass. "Mostly work. Although soccer practice is ramping up, so…."

Adam accepted his own drink from Lore, who leaned in. They chatted about the state of the soccer fields—still wet from the heavy spring rainfall—and the co-ed team Lore and Adam had tried to get going, and before Kerry knew it, she was at the bottom of her glass.

Lore tapped her fingernails on the bar top. "Do you want another?"

Kerry thought about her lack of a social life, and her light schedule for the next day. Then she glanced at the drive-home service number on the wall and nodded. "Yep."

Adam shrugged. "I'll take another, too."

"Maybe there would be more interest in a co-ed indoor soccer league come next winter," Lore said after she set their next round in front of them. "So we don't have to compete with the existing teams. What do you think?"

Adam shrugged.

Someone waved at Lore from across the room, and she excused herself.

Kerry took a long sip. "What don't you like about the indoor soccer idea?"

He paused.

Kerry held up her hands. "If it's none of my business, just tell me. I'm the new girl, just here to have some fun."

"It's nothing. It's a good idea, I just don't know if I can commit to it." Adam squeezed his lime garnish into the drink. "Who knows where I'll be come the winter."

"Nothing wrong with keeping things open," Kerry said lightly. "I moved here on a complete whim and it's turned out to be a pretty good idea."

Adam glanced at her sideways. "But it's mostly work."

"That's all right." The truth of that reply surprised her. For all her self-talk about needing to get out there and have some fun, maybe meet a new friend to take to bed, this was all the socializing she actually wanted right now. Friends to share a drink with so she didn't have to stew on being grumpy with Owen.

He was grumpy enough for the both of them, thank you very much.

The door to the bar swung open, and in walked Bailey Patel. Kerry waved her over, and Adam got up. "I'll give Bailey my seat. Nice to see you again, Kerry."

Bailey gave her a silent, raised eyebrow inquisition as the youngest Kincaid brother sauntered in the direction of the back room where there were pool tables.

"Look at you, hanging with the Canadian Hemsworths."

It was a mistake for Kerry to try to take a sip of her drink as Bailey got settled. The fizzy beer and clamato cocktail was not pleasant to snort. "What?"

"You know. The Hemsworths. Australia's finest."

"I'm familiar." Kerry wiped her face with a napkin.

"Adam is Liam, of course."

"And which one is Owen?"

"Luke. The bad boy oldest." Bailey paused. "There are more Kincaids, though. They don't map exactly."

Kerry was pretty sure that Owen wasn't that much of a bad boy. He was more like the stern, uptight dad type— who just happened to look like a darker Hemsworth, okay, she could see that now.

"Will is the one who isn't an actor," Bailey said confidently. "He's the elementary school principal."

Kerry frowned. "One of the Hemsworth brothers is a school principal?"

Bailey giggled. "No. One of the Kincaid brothers is. Will."

"Oh. Right. You said that. But then you called him an actor."

"It was a metaphor."

"I don't think that's a metaphor."

"A simile?"

Kerry snorted. She was definitely tipsy. "I don't know."

"If one of the Hemsworth brothers didn't act, is what I meant. Will is the one who is not like the others. The others are all your classic bad boys. Join the army, see the world. Come back occasionally to charm some of us out of our panties."

Kerry sat up straighter. "You?"

Bailey shook her head. "I've never had the pleasure, but rumour has it Adam has been having a good time since he's moved back. So you can see why I did the eyebrow wiggle."

Kerry shook her head. "It's definitely not that. He's cute, but not my type." Too young. Too flirty. "He moved me into my apartment. That's how we met. We're just friends."

Bailey looked disappointed.

"He's so young to be an Army veteran," Kerry murmured, thinking about Silent Stevie and Too-Charming Adam. Maybe they were two sides to the same coin. "You said they all joined the army?"

"Pretty much. One of them—Seth—he joined the Air Force."

"Interesting. Owen was in the army, huh?"

"Still is. He does the army reserve once a week. Have you seen him around town in his uniform?"

No, she hadn't. Kerry tried and failed to ignore the mental picture. She already had a robust catalogue of Owen images in her head, despite all conscious efforts to not be attracted to him. Owen in a t-shirt, revealing his tattoo. Owen in his paramedics uniform, sprawled out in his office chair, passively watching as she yelled at him. That last one was really weird, because it shouldn't be hot, and yet it was. And then there was the best/worst one, Owen holding her wrist and telling her he liked her just fine. She swallowed hard.

"I know, right? A Hemsworth in camouflage. Almost irresistible, if it weren't for Becca. With that salt and pepper in his beard…"

Kerry frowned. She knew what her friend meant all right. If it weren't for Becca, *she'd* go for Owen too, and it would be a terrible mistake.

But it didn't take much for her imagination to run away with the way his hand had felt on her wrist, the tight squeeze of his fingers, and the hot glare he'd given her—just for a second—before he announced he liked her. *Just fine.*

She shivered.

It was one thing to have a forbidden crush on the guy, because he was an asshole and she liked that a little in her fantasies. She liked his brittle crust, the way he wore it like a Viking going into battle.

She liked it—from a distance. She liked it in all the ways people usually liked bad boys. She could twist the way he'd said *I like you just fine* and give it a hard edge that made her wild. He could say it as he stroked his big, rough hands over her body, as he raked his gaze across her naked flesh.

"Oh, Kerry." Bailey's eyes were wide.

"No." Kerry shook her head vigorously. "Nope."

"Do you like Owen?" her friend whispered, but it was the kind of stage whisper Kerry worried people might hear. Nobody else was paying them any attention, but that could change in a heartbeat.

"I genuinely do not like Owen." Kerry could say that firmly because it was the truth.

She didn't like him. She might want him sometimes. That had zip-fork-all to do with liking a person.

CHAPTER NINE

OWEN FROWNED at the note on the calendar, which caught his eye as he slugged back his first coffee of the day. "Do you have an appointment today?"

Becca didn't answer as she moved around the kitchen getting ready. It was Saturday, but they both had to work.

She didn't usually have appointments on the weekend.

"Bec?"

"Uh...yeah."

"Do you want company? I can come with you after I check in at the station."

"No, I'm good. Thanks."

"All right." He pulled open the fridge. "Chicken for dinner?"

"If you can cook it while I'm at work."

"Slow cooker it is." He threw some sauce in with the meat, turned it on low, and put the lid on it. "I have to work some nights this coming week. Can you feed yourself?"

"Yeah. Or I'll go to Mom's, get a visit in. Between work

and school, suddenly weeks go by without seeing her, and she likes to rub the belly."

Owen laughed. Then he frowned. "Isn't she going to your appointment with you?"

Becca made a face. "Dad…"

"What?"

"Never mind." Then she sighed heavily. "No, not never mind. Look, I'm taking Hayden to the appointment. That's why it's today, so he can go and not miss school or work."

Owen dropped the lettuce on the counter. "What?"

"I told you we've been talking. He wants to be involved. A bit."

"That's not how parenting works."

She ignored that barb. "It's just an appointment. And he has a right to be a part of the pregnancy."

Owen grabbed his sandwich and shoved it into his bag. He'd promised to be supportive and have Becca's back, but the "a bit" grated at him.

"Dad—"

"Thanks for being honest with me," he said, stopping and looking right at her. Eye contact. "I appreciate it. I do. But that's all you're getting."

"Thanks for being honest," she parroted back.

He gave her a quick hug. "I gotta run. If he dodges the appointment, text me and I can meet you there."

"He won't." She said it with all the innocent confidence an eighteen-year-old could muster, her chin jutted proudly in the air.

Owen wanted desperately for her to be right.

But when she was, when she texted him a picture of her leg next to a skinny-assed eighteen-year-old boy's leg, sitting together on the couch in the waiting room at the clinic, the feeling that swept through him wasn't relief that she hadn't been stood up. It wasn't any kind of pain or worry that this would end badly for her, either.

It was regret that he didn't have an excuse to go and see Kerry, to maybe hang back and apologize if he could get the words out of his mouth in the right order. The need to see her and fix things pulsed inside him, thick and complicated. He'd wanted to use his daughter's appointment to get into the midwife's good graces. Ah, hell.

He would see her in a few weeks at the first interagency working group meeting. Somehow that thought didn't make him feel better. If anything, it chipped away at him. The chances of him making a good impression on her at that meeting were slim to fucking none and he knew it. He just couldn't get his act together around Kerry.

When he arrived at the station, he parked his truck around back, checked the schedule to see who should be in, and then went into the ambulance bay to keep an eye on the team hand offs from one shift to the next. On weekend shifts he tried to avoid doing the office admin work that often kept him behind a desk, so when the team was all set for the day, he hopped in his supervisor SUV and headed up the peninsula, putting himself in the field for a bit.

His loop took him into Lion's Head, and as he pulled into the centre of town, a call came in from dispatch. An unconscious woman, injury unknown. A soccer team practice near the lighthouse. He was the closest vehicle, and an ambulance was ten minutes out.

"10-4," he acknowledged, then flipped on his lights and siren.

He saw the group as soon as he turned the corner. He recognized one of them, Lore D'Angelo, a bartender and former troop of his. She was waving to get his attention, and he stopped right in front of her.

"Report?" He asked her as he hopped out and grabbed his gear from the back.

"Bailey fainted. We were running hill repeats, got to the top, and she keeled over. She's a good runner, Owen."

He nodded, listening to her, but his gaze was locked on the crowd, his focus on getting to the middle of it. The women parted for him, revealing Bailey Patel unconscious on the ground—and Kerry kneeling next to her, her fingers on the younger woman's wrist and neck.

What are you doing here? But it wasn't the time or place, and the answer was obvious. Becca's appointment must have been with Jenna, and Owen felt like an idiot for wanting to shove himself into the middle of that.

The midwife was dressed like the others, in running shorts and a long-sleeved technical shirt. She had one sleeve shoved up her arm, revealing her watch, and she only spared him a cool, split-second glance before she looked back at her wrist. "Pulse is strong and regular, skin is pale and cold." She rattled off a vital signs report that included observed respiration rate and a rough oxygen assessment based on extremities colour, which hadn't changed. "She's been unconscious now for three minutes without stirring. We called 911 right away because she's never had an incident like this before, according to the rest of the team."

Three minutes was a long time, especially for a patient who didn't have a history of syncopal episodes. The strong pulse was a good sign, though. Owen set down his bag and snapped on a pair of gloves, checked her pulse for himself to confirm Kerry's assessment, then grabbed his pen light. "Hey Bailey, can you hear me? What happened, kiddo?" He checked her pupils, and as soon as he flashed the light in her eyes, she stirred with a weak groan.

Kerry murmured encouraging words, and Owen sat back on his heels. Bailey lifted one hand, but it flopped back to the ground.

"Hey there, take it easy. Keep your head down for me, okay? Did she hit her head on the way down?" He looked across at Kerry, who met his gaze with detached professionalism.

"I don't think so. I was at the back of the pack, but Lore was right there, and I think she caught Bailey on the way down." She looked around, and the bartender stepped forward, her face worried and pinched. "Is that right, Lore?"

"Yeah. She fell back into me, and I couldn't hold her."

"Sounds like you broke her fall. That's great." Didn't sound like there was a risk of a neck injury. Owen hovered over Bailey, who blinked her eyes open, but then closed them again. "Hey, there. Take your time. But in a minute, an ambulance is going to pull up, very exciting stuff."

"Nooo," she groaned. "I'm fine."

"How does your head feel?"

She made a weak face. "It hurts."

"Anything else uncomfortable?"

"No."

He rocked back on his heels. "Let's try to sit you up, then. Careful."

Kerry took one side and he took the other, and they eased her up to sitting—just in time for Matt Foster and Dani Minelli to pull up with their lights going, too.

"Hey, boss," Dani said as she got out of the ambulance. "What do we have here?"

Bailey waved at her. "Nothing."

"We're still figuring that out," Owen said. "Syncopal episode, LOC duration of three minutes—"

"Three minutes and thirty three seconds," Kerry interjected.

He corrected himself, then finished giving his paramedics the report. Dani took over from there, getting a history from Bailey as the young woman adjusted to sitting, then standing.

Owen stepped away from the group and reported in to dispatch. He could leave now, and maybe he should, but he didn't. Instead, he went back to the circle, where Bailey was insisting she was fine.

"We can transport you to hospital," Dani offered. "Let the docs take a look at you. Or you can sign off saying you're good to go home, but you shouldn't be alone for the next few hours."

"I'll stay with her," Kerry offered.

Owen bit his lower lip, but Dani was on it. She listed the potential causes of a syncopal episode, quickly and without drama, and reiterated that if this was a first instance, it might represent a new medical condition worth getting checked out.

Kerry nodded, but she turned back to Bailey. "What do you want to do?"

"I just want to go home."

"How about we go back to your place, but we can call the hospital, too? Maybe they aren't busy."

The conversation went back and forth a bit, and by the time they were done, Bailey was in Kerry's car, and they were going to swing past the hospital on the way to Bailey's house.

Which meant Owen had to watch Kerry drive off—

without a backwards glance at him—and the apology still sat unsaid and heavy in this throat.

He followed Dani and Matt back to their ambulance so he could add a line to their report.

"That was slick," Dani said to him as he scrawled his signature. "How she convinced Bailey to go the hospital even though she was reluctant."

"Yeah."

"Isn't she Becca's midwife, too?"

"Yeah."

"She's good."

She was very good. And entirely professional, even when he was a jackass. He nodded. "All right, see you back at the station."

———

THE NEXT TIME Kerry saw Owen, he was in the army uniform Bailey had talked about. On her way home from a hospital delivery, she stopped to grab a coffee from the Tim Horton's in Wiarton, and he was at the head of the line.

Once again, she recognized him from the shape of his body, and heat raced through her. He made her feel voyeuristic and dirty in the strangest of places. The grocery store. The coffee shop. This crush could easily get out of hand.

Luckily, he was happy to douse it with cold water just by turning around once he had his coffee in hand. She was six people back, and his gaze—sharp, focused, critical— found her immediately.

It didn't surprise her at all when he stopped in front of her and gave his usual greeting—just her name, as curtly as possible. "Kerry."

"Hey," she said with a polite smile. *I like you just fine.* Then why didn't it feel like he did?

His jaw flexed, and silence stretched between them. Another rousing conversation, she thought to herself. But then he surprised her by stringing four words together. "I'll see you tomorrow."

"Why?"

Then he rocked back on his heels, his eyes flashing dark. "The interagency working group."

Oh. That. "Right."

Another heavy silence followed that, as he stood there looking like he was made of granite, and she wondered if this was how it would be tomorrow, and why had she insisted on being a part of this committee?

"I need to apologize," he said, his voice strained.

"Not if it pains you," she snapped back.

His eyes went wide. Really wide, and his mouth followed, stretching into an unexpected smile. "Not at all," he said softly. His gaze settled on her face, and that felt soft, too. "Not painful in the least, Kerry. I *want* to apologize. This isn't exactly the time or place, probably, but I should have said this weeks ago. I was out of line."

Her mouth flapped open, then snapped shut. Oh.

And then, because of course this was how her life would go, her pager went off. Owen glanced down to where she wore it on her hip, then back to her face.

"I'll see you tomorrow," he repeated, and she nodded dumbly.

From the counter, the coffee shop worker called for the next customer, and the line shuffled forward.

Kerry had to check her pager, and get a coffee, and move on with her day. But her feet didn't want to move.

They wanted to stay right where they were, pointing at Owen Kincaid and his wide, soft smile.

Behind her, someone coughed.

What she wanted didn't matter when she was holding up the line. "See you tomorrow," she said quickly, then moved ahead.

Glancing back over her shoulder, she watched as he headed out the door, coffee in hand. He used his shoulder, keeping his body sideways so he was looking at her until he was all the way out of the coffee shop.

"Sorry for holding up the line," she whispered to the older lady standing behind her.

That woman shook her head, a grin on her face. "Don't apologize to me, I think I enjoyed that as much as the two of you did. He's quite the looker. Almost like one of those movie stars."

A Canadian Hemsworth indeed. Kerry let out a shaky breath. Well, if the other woman liked what she'd seen, she must have missed the start of the conversation where it had been awkward as fork, but she wasn't wrong about the rest. Kerry had enjoyed the apology. And the smile.

If Owen smiled like that more often, though, things might get complicated.

CHAPTER TEN

OWEN HAD the shortest transit time to the interagency working group, because it was meeting in the new Pine Harbour library space upstairs from his office. The third floor of the Emergency Services building had been "under-utilized", and when the library was threatened with closure due to high operating costs in its former location on Main Street, the community rallied together. Owen organized the volunteer fire brigade to help move all the books to the new space.

But he hadn't actually been upstairs since it opened, so he headed up there with lots of time before the meeting so he could have a look around—and he had another reason, too.

Behind the desk was a very pregnant Chloe Dawson. She was typing on the computer, but looked up as soon as Owen approached.

"I'm not interrupting anything, am I?"

She shook her head. "I was just compiling a list of book recommendations for one of our patrons. What's up?"

He shifted awkwardly from foot to foot. "That's sort of why I'm here. As a patron."

She beamed at him. "What can I help you find?"

"It's been a while since there's been a baby in my house. And being the grandparent is different than being the parent, and I... I don't know what I'm looking for, exactly. But something that might refresh what I can do to be a good family member."

Chloe patted her belly. "I don't even need to look those up, and it's not from me doing my own reading. I'm in complete denial about what comes next here. But Tom has a stack of books on his bedside table, and as a librarian, I can't help but notice which ones he picks up over and over again." She grabbed a notepad and scribbled down three titles, then went to her computer. "We have one of them here in this branch, and the other two are able to be requested, if you'd like."

"I'll start with the one that's here." He picked up the piece of paper. "And I guess that means I'll need a library card, too. It's been a while since I've had one of those."

"I'll see if you're still in our system." She typed his name into the computer, then laughed. "The last book you took out was something called *Daniel Boom*, ten years ago?"

"The start of Becca's graphic novel phase," he said, memories washing over him. She'd been so little, but so grown-up at the same time. "Shortly after that she went to live with her mom more of the time for a year while I did a course out of town, and then she had her own library card."

Chloe gave him a thoughtful look. "Why don't you sign out something you might like to read or watch for yourself, as well as this book on being a good grandfather?"

Owen wouldn't know where to start. "Yeah, maybe."

She waved him toward the stacks. "Go find some books. I'll get your new library card ready."

That was how he found Kerry, nose-deep in a book, sitting cross-legged against the window at the end of an aisle in the mystery and thrillers section. Because he wasn't a small man and he hadn't been trying to sneak up on her, his footsteps probably sounded like a stumbling elephant came to screeching halt in front of her.

To her credit, she didn't look startled in the least as she stopped reading, glanced straight ahead at his boots, then slowly slid her gaze up his body until she made eye contact with him. Then she smiled. "Hello."

It wasn't much to go on, and there was definitely a part of him that wanted to turn tail and run, but he'd been doing that for months and it didn't get them anywhere. He didn't know how to navigate this, but they were about to sit down across the table from each other and talk about serious issues in their community, so that should probably be his entire focus with her. Not how cute she looked curled up with a book, her legs bare beneath a sundress. "Hi," he said. "I was going to grab a book to sign out before…"

"Me too."

"Is that one good?"

She glanced at the cover. "Yeah."

"Great."

"This is a pretty big library, actually." She climbed to her feet. "I'm impressed. When I first moved here, it was on Main Street."

"I helped move the books over," he offered. It sounded way less impressive out loud than in his head.

She nodded. "Great."

His neck flushed. This could only get more awkward, and he was floundering, so he grabbed a book at random off the shelf and held it in the air. "Found what I was looking for. See you in there."

Gripping the book tightly, he stalked back to the front desk and slid it across to Chloe. "I'll sign this out, too."

Her eyes danced as she took in the cover. *The Lady Loves a Necromancer*, read the title. Apparently the book he'd grabbed at random was a Gothic paranormal romance. Well, it probably wouldn't be boring, which was more than could be said for his conversation skills.

———

WHEN OWEN WALKED through the door at Mac's the next day at the end of the lunch rush, and he saw Kerry sitting alone in a booth, he promised himself he wouldn't grab a seat where he could watch her like a creeper.

In fact, he'd do her one better. Even though he'd planned to take a full lunch break, there was a stack of paperwork on his desk waiting to be done.

He nodded at the waitress behind the counter. "Can I get a souvlaki plate to go, please?"

"Sure thing."

He grabbed a newspaper someone folded up and left on the counter. He could read headlines while his food was prepped. He had no reason to turn around. No reason to look in her direction, no danger of making awkward small talk that made him look like an idiot.

So when Kerry crept up on him, and put her hand on

his arm, he didn't see it coming. So he leapt in the air, twisted around, and brought his hand crashing down onto the counter—eventually. First his hand went through a ceramic mug.

And part of the mug went through his hand.

"God damn it," he groaned as blood spilled fast and furious over the Formica countertop.

"Don't move," Kerry whispered. Her eyes were wide, her lips parted, just as shocked as he was, but she immediately took control, grabbing a stack of napkins and clamping them down and around his injury.

He wasn't going anywhere.

Kerry took a deep breath. "This is a bit outside my wheelhouse. But I want to look at it, okay?"

"It's fine," he said reflexively.

"Uh huh."

He hoped it was fine. But the napkins were wet and red. *Blood spreads like any other liquid.* And yet that knowledge didn't help him when he was the patient. He looked away from his hand, away from Kerry, and focused on a point on the wall.

The waitress was beside them now, asking what she could do to help.

"Can you get me some clean towels? Something more absorbent than these," Kerry said. The other woman pulled a stack from somewhere behind the counter. Kerry grabbed one and wrapped it around his hand tightly. Then she waited.

Owen could feel the swelling starting already. His hand hurt like a sonofabitch, but he could feel all his fingers, he was pretty sure. In a second, he'd look for the pieces of the mug and figure out how much of it was inside his hand.

God damn it.

"The bleeding is slowing down," she said. "Can you put pressure on this for a minute? I want to wash my hands."

The waitress squeaked in protest, clearly not wanting to get involved in the first aid directly, and Owen shook his head. "I can hold."

"You sure?" Kerry's face was tight with concern.

"Yeah." He replaced her touch, carefully avoiding the spot where he could feel a jagged piece of china stuck in his skin, and then stared at the spot on the wall again until she returned, her hands held high like a surgeon waiting to be gloved.

This was the exact opposite of a sterile operating suite, but he appreciated her efforts. She gestured for him to move his hand, and she carefully lifted the towel.

"Motherforker," she whispered.

"Do you always do that?" he asked through gritted teeth.

"Do what?" She was still examining his hand.

"Swear like a kindergarten teacher?"

She laughed. "Yeah. I guess so. Pregnant women are often in the presence of little people who will repeat any curse word that slips out."

"And you're a *Good Place* fan."

"That too." She bit her lower lip as she returned the towel. "I think you might need stitches. Do you want me to drive you to the hospital?"

"I don't need stitches."

Her eyebrow curved high. "No? You haven't even seen it."

He swallowed. "Show me."

She peeled back the cotton, revealing a wedge of ceramic jammed exactly where he thought it was, in the meaty muscle at the base of his thumb. Probably just missed the ligament, and hopefully wasn't deep enough to have hit the tendon.

Which meant it might be cosmetic damage only, but he wouldn't know that until the shard came out—and the wound was cleaned. He repeated her curse, although he didn't use the kindergarten version.

"Can I call 911 now?" the waitress helpfully offered.

"Nah, we're good here," Owen said with false bravado. He wasn't calling for a bus when he didn't need one.

Kerry nodded. "I'll take him in."

He made a face at her.

She raised an eyebrow. "Do you want *me* to clean it up? Because we can do this here or it can be done properly at the hospital. I have a suture kit in my car, I'm just saying."

She meant it as a threat, but he liked that plan better. "Pretty sure I'm bigger than your average patient."

"I don't do stitches on the babies," she said dryly. "And your palm isn't bigger than a perineum."

He deserved that, although he thought his hand was pretty damn big.

"Get your bag." His head was starting to spin. He nodded at the waitress. "Hey, can we use the back room for this?"

"Uh…"

Kerry cleared her throat. "You know what? If you want me to do this, we can take it outside. We don't need to be spreading any more biohazard risks around the diner. Health and safety complaints would mess with my preferred lunch routine." She gave the waitress a quick smile. "I'm going to take this guy off your hands. Can you box up my lunch and bring it out when his food is ready?"

"Sure thing, Kerry."

He got *uh….* She got *Sure thing, Kerry.*

His daughter's midwife was a walking, talking advertisement for the saying, *you catch more flies with honey.* And yet Owen still couldn't manage that shit when he was around her. Ironic.

She asked for a garbage bag, too, and carefully bagged up all of their biohazard waste—his blood all over napkins and tea towels he would have to replace—then got his hand wrapped up tightly again and gave him clear instructions on how to hold it, like he didn't know.

Except he was the patient now, and his brain wasn't working properly, so she was right to do that, and he appreciated it.

"I'm not a Neanderthal most of the time," he said to her as they walked across the parking lot to her car. He blurted it out to distract himself, maybe, but also to get it off his chest. He knew that's how he came off to her.

"No?"

He frowned. "No."

"Okay." She gave him a polite smile and unlocked her car.

"Do you think I actually am a Neanderthal?"

She shrugged. "You grunt a lot."

"Sometimes I don't know what to say."

Kerry smirked at that and gestured for him to get in the back seat of her too-small car. While he squished himself into the space behind her passenger seat, she went around to the other side, where she fit just fine. Deftly, she opened her medical bag and pulled out a couple of sterile pads, which she stretched out on top of a gym bag sitting between them on the back seat. A makeshift examination table. Then she pulled a headlamp out a side pocket, turned it on, and got down to business. "All right. Let's have a look."

He made a face as he unfurled his fist.

She didn't miss it. He saw the way she paused, looked at his face, and then changed the subject. "Is that what happened with the interagency working group? You didn't know what to say?"

Distracting someone from pain and discomfort with a jarring question was a good trick when he used it on someone else, but he couldn't say that he cared for being on the receiving end of it. He looked out the window, then back at her. Her eyes were focused down, carefully examining his wound. It was easier to look at her when she wasn't looking back. It didn't stop him from looking at her all the time, of course. But this was oddly nice. And for once, he wasn't stuck on the words. "That was mostly thoughtlessness. I was being selfish."

"Selfish how?"

"I…" In for a penny, in for a pound. "I don't know what to do about the fact that you unsettle me."

"I—" She jerked her head up. "I unsettle you?"

He grimaced. Classic Neanderthal move, he realized.

She sighed. "Hold tight. I want to clean this out a bit, get a better look." She grabbed more supplies. Just like with Bailey, her movements were spare and precise. An expert just doing her thing, effortlessly. Owen knew how much practice that took.

"Becca really likes you." And there it was again. The fact that Kerry was his daughter's midwife, and that needed to be their entire focus. He changed the subject. "Do you think it might be okay with some steri-strips?"

"To be clear, I'm not licensed to provide medical advice

to a grown-ass man, and I think you should go to a hospital and see a doctor."

"Advice heard, considered, and politely declined."

She laughed gently. "Politely?"

"I stand by that."

Touching his fingers again, one by one, she silently considered his request. "Do you care about a scar?"

"Nope."

"Then yeah, probably steri-strips are fine. I don't have any glue in my kit, but that's another option—"

"At the hospital, I know."

"Just had to get that in there."

"Seems to me that when Bailey didn't want to go to the hospital, you were just fine with that."

"And yet…" She tipped her head to the side and narrowed her eyes. "Where did she end up going?"

"Touché."

"The bleeding has basically stopped. I don't see any reason not to let it heal on its own. Off the record, I think you're fine to tape it up."

"Would you do me the honours? Not in any professional capacity, of course."

She laughed. "Of course not. How about as a friend?"

He jerked his head up. Her gaze was warm and locked on his face. "As a friend," he repeated. "That sounds pretty good."

"So…" Her touch was feather light as she tended to him. And she didn't elaborate on that single, trailed off word. *So.*

He could imagine a lot of sentences that started that way, and most of them weren't great. Instead of letting his imagination do its worst, he prompted her. Might as well get it all out on the table. "So?"

"I think I need to tell Becca about this, just to be completely transparent with her." She lifted her head. "Also, because I'm not a medical professional tending to your hand, just a friend, I want you to know you don't have any expectation of confidentiality here."

He laughed out loud. She was so damn earnest. "Okay."

"*And* if we're friends, I need to remind you that your daughter is my patient, and she *does* have confidentiality—"

"I remember." He barked it out, then his cheeks flushed. Why was he always so rough with her, so clumsy with his tone and his words, when she was just being nice? He ruined every conversation they had.

A knock on the window interrupted their conversation. Kerry rolled the glass down and accepted their lunch from the waitress.

"I think I've lost my appetite," he admitted.

"You might change your mind in an hour. Are you going home or back to work?"

"Work."

"My advice—as a friend—is to take it easy with that hand."

"Will do. I've got paperwork to get through, that's all."

She nodded. "Can I drive you over? Or at the least follow you to make sure you get there okay?"

He looked at his truck. Thought about how scrambled his brain felt at the moment. "You know what? I'd love a drive back to the station. I'll walk back at the end of the day, or get someone to drop me off."

It was the longest conversation they had ever had. It had taken a deep laceration to his hand to make it happen, but as Owen settled in at his desk, with his untouched lunch and his stack of work in front of him, he was calm and settled for the first time in months.

Friends. Maybe he'd been barking up the wrong tree before. What did he know about women anyway?

CHAPTER ELEVEN

JULY WAS a heatwave that never stopped, every day as relentlessly scorching as the one before it. Becca had a false alarm at early labour—Braxton-Hicks contractions that convinced him they needed to go to the hospital in a panic —at the start of the month, but then kept going. She worked through the rest of the month without complaint, and Owen made sure there were popsicles in the freezer for when she got home from her shifts at the golf course. As the weeks went on and her appointments with Jenna and Kerry got closer and closer together, it was clear that it wouldn't be long before everything changed.

And yet, like with everything else around his daughter having a baby, it still took him by surprise when his phone lit up on his desk on the first day of August.

"It's Rachel." Becca's mom sounded out of breath, and Owen's pulse jacked up. "We're on our way to the hospital. She's having contractions non-stop, and they're different this time."

In the background, he heard Becca crying, and his heart

tore in two. "I need to find someone to cover off the rest of my shift. But I'll meet you guys there as soon as I can."

"Thanks."

He paused a beat. "Rach?"

"Yeah?"

"Tell her good luck. And that I love her, and I'm proud of her."

"Yeah." He could hear the smile in her voice. "I will. Me too."

As soon as he hung up the phone, his fingers itched to pick it up again and call Kerry, to make sure she was on her way. But of course she was, and of course that wasn't what he wanted. He wanted to hear her voice, to have her tell him in her calm, confident way that this was going to work out just fine.

He rubbed the scar on his palm, the faint white scar evidence of her excellent care in the face of him being a terrible patient. Then he pulled up the schedule. Time to figure out who he could call in without disrupting the rest of the week. He had a waiting room to go and pace in.

An hour and a half later, he parked in front of the hospital. On his way through the front doors, he checked his phone. Rachel had sent him updates every fifteen minutes, and the latest one was that Kerry had arrived and Becca was waiting for an epidural. And Hayden hadn't replied to her texts.

Owen thought about sending Adam to pick the kid up and drag his sorry ass to the hospital, but one thing at a time.

He'd already done this trip to Labour & Delivery once before, on the Braxton-Hicks false alarm, so he knew where to go. He found Becca's room easily, and when he pushed the door open, he was relieved to see his daughter smiling—but it didn't last long.

Becca was in a hospital gown, sitting on the side of the bed, and half way through him greeting her, her face tightened up and her gaze lost focus.

Kerry set down the chart she'd been writing in and hustled to his daughter's side, giving her quiet instructions to slow down each breath and focus on the contractions doing good work.

Rachel curled up right behind Becca, his baby, their baby who was a woman now, but still so little to him, and something fractured deep in his chest. A crack in his heart that splintered and spread as Becca's whole life flashed past in silent memories. Her first cry, her first steps, her first words. The way she sprouted while he was gone, growing so much between his visits that it physically hurt to say goodbye, knowing he wouldn't see the same little girl two weeks later.

His desperate need to get back to her, to make a home for her half as good as the one her mother was making.

But in the last few years, he'd found himself itching for her life to speed up and fast forward? And now it had, suddenly.

Where had the time gone?

When the contraction passed, Rachel gestured for him to join her. "She likes pressure here," she said, pointing to the small of Becca's back. "You want to spell me off?"

"Damn straight." Owen washed his hands, then got into his station before the next contraction.

Becca leaned back against him when that one ended. "Hey, Dad."

He gave her a half-smile. "This is pretty real, eh?"

She laughed. "Oh yeah."

"You're doing great."

"They say it's too soon for me to get an epidural," she whispered. "First timer, I'm going to be here a while."

"We're all here for you. Do you want some music?"

They'd been working on a playlist for her labour ever since she found him with his CDs. They both had the list on their phones, but he didn't see hers anywhere. "I forgot."

"Where's your phone?"

That answer had to wait until after the next contraction.

Rachel held up Becca's bag. "In here?"

Becca nodded. Rachel found it, then plugged it in and set it on the window ledge. A Billie Eilish song was the first one—a Becca pick, without a doubt. That rolled into a Suzanne Vega song Owen had suggested, and then a song from the Lonestar album which Owen had added, but he was pleased and surprised Becca had kept on the final iteration of the list.

The next two hours rocked by with some laughs, and a lot of breathing. They were all relieved when the anesthesiologist showed up, and then Kerry and Jenna switched off so Kerry could go have a nap to be fresh for the night shift.

But even with the epidural, Becca found the contractions intense. As the light started to fade out the window, while Rachel was out in the hall calling her younger kids to say goodnight, Becca started to cry.

"Dad…"

He wrapped his hands around hers and let her squeeze the ever-loving shit out of his fingers as the contraction took over her body. "That's my girl. You're so strong."

"I wish Hayden was here," she whispered, like a confession.

He didn't want that to break his heart. He didn't want to want that for her, too, because he wanted to hate the kid. But he couldn't, because she was sharing her secret heart's desire with him. "I'll give him a call."

"You don't have to."

"No." He smoothed his hand over her damp forehead. "But I want to. As soon as your mom comes in, okay?"

Becca nodded.

He called his brothers first. Adam wanted to come and hang out in the waiting room. Will promised to corral him and only show up once their niece or nephew had made their debut into the world.

After Owen made the next call, he hoped he'd be kicked out of the birthing room because Becca had too many support people. That would be a gift he'd love to give to his daughter, but at the same time, he wouldn't be the best of company for anyone while he prowled on the outside looking in.

He didn't know if Hayden would pick up. He didn't know if the kid would even recognize his number. It's not like they were texting buddies. Owen only had the number because Becca had put it on call tree list—almost as if she was pretty sure he would be here.

And she'd been right to worry about that, but if Owen could talk some sense into him...

He hit dial while his heart was in that generous place, and listened to the rings. One, two, three—

"Hello?"

"This is Owen Kincaid."

"Yes, sir."

"Do you know why I'm calling?"

There was a long, uncomfortable pause. "Yes."

"Where are you?"

"I…"

"Hayden, now is not the time. Get your ass to the hospital. Becca needs you."

"I'm here." He sounded embarrassed. Good.

Owen blinked. "Where?"

"Outside." What the hell? "I—I've been here for a bit."

Owen swore. "Get inside."

Then he hung up and swore again before stalking to the elevators. It didn't take long for Hayden to appear, all six feet of him. He was wearing khaki shorts and a t-shirt that looked expensive. The kind Adam wore clubbing. "Where is she?"

Owen led the way.

Hayden cleared his throat. "Thank you for calling, sir."

Owen shrugged. "It wasn't for you."

"I understand." The younger man hesitated. "I got a job for the summer. Did Becca tell you that? I've been working as a line cook at Mac's during breakfast."

No, Becca hadn't said a word. And Owen rarely went there for breakfast anymore, since they'd leaned so heavily on Mac's for dinner due to her aversion to meat cooking in her vicinity. "Have you?"

"Yes, sir."

"What did your coach say about that?"

"He wasn't thrilled." Hayden's throat worked, like he was going to say something more about how important it was to focus on conditioning over the summer.

Owen didn't need to hear that, but luckily they'd arrived at Becca's room. "Shall we?"

Hayden almost pounced forward. "Yeah."

Inside, Rachel gave Hayden a hug, then got out of his way so he could sink down onto the bed next to Becca.

"Come on," she said to Owen. "Let's give them a minute alone."

"He dressed up," Owen muttered once they were in the hallway.

Rachel gave him a look.

"What?"

"If he'd shown up in his usual basketball shorts and a tank top, you'd have groused that he was underdressed for the occasion."

He snorted. "So he was just sitting outside, apparently. Waiting in his car."

She sighed. "At least he came inside eventually?"

Owen scrubbed a hand over his face. "Yeah. Listen, do you want a coffee?"

"Sure." She hesitated and glanced back at the room.

He pushed her back toward their baby. "Go sit with them. I'll go to the cafeteria and come back in a bit."

Rachel gave him a grateful look, then threw her arms around him. They weren't touchy-feely together, but Owen let out a rough exhale and sank into the embrace. "You should lie down and get some rest," he whispered. "It might take all night."

She gave him a *been-there, done-that* look.

He coughed. "Sorry. I know you know that."

"No, it's strange and surreal to see her go through it for me, too. I will get some rest. That's good advice."

He took the long way around the hospital to get coffee, stepping outside for some fresh air and another call to Will before his brother fell asleep.

"How's Bec?"

Owen grunted. "The same."

"Oh no, what's happened?"

"Hayden showed up."

"That's good."

Owen didn't immediately reply.

"Isn't it?"

"Of course it is." Owen rolled his shoulders, trying to stretch out the muscles along his spine. The freakout muscles, they could be called. "I know that in my head."

"And in your heart?"

"I don't want my baby to be hurt." Owen sighed. "Which we've talked about a hundred different ways. I know what you're going to say."

"Is it easier if I say it, rather than you saying it to yourself?"

"Fuck off."

"Happy to help." Will chuckled. "Can we bring you breakfast in the morning?"

Owen stopped in the shadows of the hospital and looked up at the lit up windows. He was turned around, and wasn't sure exactly which one was his daughter's, but it didn't matter. He'd been head-down in survival mode for too long, and he'd had this conversation with his brother more than once. Every single time, Will kept moving him forward.

Tomorrow, God willing, his brothers would show up and bring his grumpy ass a breakfast sandwich or two from Mac's Diner, and he'd be a grandfather.

Hell, he felt like crying in the worst and best way. "Will?"

"Yeah?"

"Thank you."

"For breakfast?"

"For everything. For prodding me along the last six

months, for kicking my ass constantly when I harp on Adam and Becca. For knowing my bark is worse than my bite."

Will made a noise that Owen couldn't decipher. Then he sighed. "You know we love you. To the moon and back, just like you say to Becca. But you can't lean on the bark is worse than your bite bullshit. Barks are bites."

Ah, double hell. "Yeah. Okay."

"Be nice to Hayden. And Becca. And Adam."

He wanted to protest that he was nice—at least to Becca and Adam. But nice wasn't enough. He didn't want his grandkid to think of him as the grumpy grandpa.

After thanking his brother again, he went inside and grabbed two coffees. He didn't have a text update from Rachel, but he still took the more direct route back to Labour & Delivery—until he spotted Kerry sitting at a table in a nook, halfway down an empty hallway. She was nursing a coffee of her own.

He stopped in front of her. "Can I join you?"

She gestured to one of the chairs. "Be my guest. I just got off the phone with the charge nurse upstairs. She says Becca's having a cat nap." She beamed at him. "She's progressing well. The baby will be here by morning."

"I just promised my brothers that, so that's good to hear."

"Everyone's excited."

Everyone *was* excited, even him. Especially him. But Owen also felt alone in his worry. Rachel had shared it in the early days, but then she'd gotten on board and was Team Baby the whole way. Why hadn't Owen been Team Baby?

Because he'd been Team Great Bachelor Plans, and full of

resentment. Resentment and worry took up a lot of space inside a human body, even one as big as his.

Kerry tipped her coffee cup at him. "How are you doing?"

"Hanging in there." He shrugged. "You know."

She shook her head. "I don't." He blinked in surprise, and she smiled. "Why don't you tell me?"

Emotion clogged in his throat. "Uh…"

"Come on, Owen," she said softly. Teasing. "Don't be a Neanderthal."

He grunted for effect, then shrugged again. "I think I worry too much. I'm excited, of course I am, but I'm scared for her, too."

"She's a rockstar."

"They're so young." It wasn't anything he hadn't said before, but this time it sounded to his own ears like more of a confessional moment.

Which meant, of course, that Kerry's pager had to go off in that moment. She glanced at it, then stood up. "She's awake again, let's go."

His heart pounded in his chest as he grabbed the coffee cups.

"I like the labour playlist, by the way," Kerry said as they got on the elevator. "I'm guessing the old school country songs are your influence?"

"She was humouring her old man. Besides, it's so easy now. Any song you want at the touch of a button, so I think the playlist is like ten hours long. Once upon a time, I agonized over the exact number of songs to fit into—"

"Forty-five minutes per side?" Kerry's eyes twinkled.

"Surely mixed tapes were before your time."

"Not at all." The corners of her mouth turned up.

"When I was little, my best friend and I would record our favourite songs off the top forty show every week."

Owen chuckled. "That takes me back. Listening for just the right moment."

"Had to catch the start of the song the *second* the intro stopped!"

"It took me weeks to get the perfect recording of 'Tears in Heaven'."

"For me it was *Livin' la Vida Loca*." Kerry sighed happily. "I had the biggest crush on Ricky Martin."

The elevator stopped and the doors opened with a soft ding. At the entrance to Labour and Delivery, Owen stopped Kerry and handed her the second coffee. "Can you give this to Rachel?"

"You aren't coming in?"

"There are a lot of… The two people rule…"

Kerry glanced over at the nursing station, then back at Owen. She stepped in close and lowered her voice. "It's a big room, and most of the time, I'm the only one around. Nobody will kick you out. If Becca wants all three of you in there, it's fine by me."

He gave her a grateful smile, and followed her. Inside the room, both Rachel and Hayden were holding Becca's hands, talking her through a contraction. Kerry took over, quickly and discretely checking Becca's progress.

"At this rate, it'll be time to push very soon. I'll go grab a second pair of hands, and then we can get started."

"Oh my God, really?" Becca burst into tears, and Hayden wrapped her in his arms.

From where Owen was waiting in the corner, on the other side of Becca, he couldn't hear their whispered conversation back and forth, but he saw his daughter nod and take a deep breath.

Rachel came over to join Owen.

He handed her the coffee. "I swear when I left to get this, I thought we would be in for a long night."

"Me, too. Maybe she was just waiting until he got here?" She took a sip. "Our bodies are strange things."

Kerry returned with Jenna, and together they got Becca moved around on the bed, sitting more upright with Hayden behind her, her feet in stirrups.

Seventeen pushes later—because Owen counted, it was the only thing he could do from the corner, although he wasn't sure his count was accurate, given that he was going by Kerry's instructions to Becca—Kerry lifted a tiny, wriggling bundle into the air just above Becca's blue hospital gown. "It's a boy!"

She delivered him to the new mom's chest and Jenna covered the baby with a flannel cloth. A little blue hat came out of nowhere for his head, and then Owen couldn't see anything for a minute because his vision was blurry.

Once the room had been cleaned up and Becca and the baby were bundled up together in the bed, they got closer to get a better look at the new little guy.

"It's a *boy*." Rachel leaned into him, and Owen swallowed around the lump in his throat. "Congratulations, Grandpa," she whispered. He jerked back in reaction, and she laughed. Over her head, Owen saw Kerry's eyes crinkled, too. She'd heard Rachel's comment, and now her shoulders were shaking. She gave him a quick, blink-and-you'd miss it sideways smile that said she'd seen him notice her laughing before she returned to writing in her chart.

Fucking hell. Fucking *eh*. "Yeah," he said shakily. "That's my name now." He dragged in a long, rough breath and addressed the new parents. "Speaking of names, what did you settle on?"

Hayden looked at Becca, who gazed back at him with far too much sparkling adoration for Owen's liking. Then she glanced down at their son, and her face dissolved into pure pleasure. "Charlie," she said softly. "His name is Charlie."

CHAPTER TWELVE

THE NEXT AFTERNOON, Owen drove Becca and Charlie home through a rain storm. It continued steadily all night, and the relentless drizzle hadn't let up by the time Kerry came over for the first home check up. Owen waited at the door, watching for her car, and when she pulled up he had an umbrella to protect her and her bag.

Inside, she stepped out of her shoes and then settled next to Becca on the couch.

They were all tired. Charlie was sleeping now, but he hadn't stayed asleep for more than twenty minutes all night, and neither had his mom. And because Owen's baby had been up all night, he had been as well. He was grateful that Kerry had shown up with her soothing voice and easy confidence. Becca needed some of that now.

He left them to their conversation and went to the kitchen to make coffee. He thought about whether or not he should take a week off work. The schedule was done, and he had a couple of senior EMTs who could cover the supervisor desk. Or hell, he'd still carry the damn pager. But the one thing he remembered crystal clear from when

Becca was a baby was the whole nap-when-the-baby-is-napping thing. Did it count if your baby had a baby, and nobody was napping properly yet?

It was early days, and she was in good hands. He knew that. But if the last forty-eight hours had reinforced anything for him it was that denying his feelings didn't help anyone.

Kerry appeared in the kitchen doorway just as the coffee finished brewing. "I got Becca tucked into bed with Charlie, nursing, and they both fell asleep."

Owen did a double-take. "That was fast."

"They both have a lot of rest to catch up on." She shrugged. "I'm just down the street if she wants me to come back. It's a treat to hang out with brand-new babies, especially one as cute as Charlie."

"I'm biased, but he's perfect, right?" Owen held out a mug of coffee, and Kerry came closer to take it.

She smiled. "He's perfect." She said it with tender wonder, a feeling Owen felt in his core. "And Becca's going to be just fine."

He let out a long, ragged breath.

Kerry raised her eyebrows. "How long have you been holding that in?"

"Eighteen years?"

That made her laugh. "I guess we talked about that at the hospital."

"We started to." He glanced at her hip. "Then your pager went off, because Charlie had decided to make his arrival."

"You're worried about how young she is."

"Of course I am."

"You have a unique perspective there. What it's like to be in your shoes right now?" She studied his face from behind her coffee mug. It was a probing question, but not an unwelcome one. Other than Will, nobody else had asked him that, and Will's questions were always a bit loaded, like he knew the path Owen *should* take. His brother always meant well, though, and the kicker was that he was almost always right. And when he wasn't, it was rarely that far off the mark.

Kerry's question felt different.

Owen was damn glad they'd decided to be friends. He needed this more than he knew.

"They aren't bad shoes," he said quietly. "I don't know how well I fill them some days, but I'm blessed and I know it."

"When did it get easier for you?"

"It took a while. Years. By the time she was in school, I had this house, and she came to live with me more of the time."

"I got the impression she lived here full-time."

"That came a few years later. When Rachel had her third baby, and bedrooms over there were in high demand. Until then, she went back and forth." He paused. "We have a good relationship. Rachel and I."

"I noticed that. That's good."

He nodded.

Kerry smiled. "And now you have Charlie here, too. Baby snuggles are a good thing."

"They sure are." He cleared his throat. "How about you? No kids, future kids?"

She laughed. "Future kids."

He nodded, and lifted his own mug to take a sip. Wrong move.

"I tell myself not to put the cart before the horse, and I don't even have a horse, you know?"

He snorted and inhaled coffee. Sputtering, he set the mug down and turned around, bracing his hands on the counter as he tried to fix his breathing and stop laughing at the same time. He grabbed a kitchen towel and swiped his face before turning back again.

Kerry's face was in her hands as she shook with laughter.

"A horse, eh?"

She laughed harder.

He pushed the envelope. "Not a bull?"

She doubled over.

Owen let loose with his own laugh. They should keep it down, because Becca and Charlie needed their sleep, but he couldn't stop. The laughter shook his whole body, it made his sides ache, and it warmed him from head to toe.

Slowly, Kerry straightened. She took a deep breath, wiped her eyes, and shook her head. She held his gaze as he settled down, too.

Then she bit her lower lip. "Bulls don't pull carts," she whispered, and they both started howling again.

It didn't even make sense, but that was what made it funny.

His insides hurt, and it felt good.

"Thanks," he said when they both stopped laughing. "I needed that."

"Any time." Her expression slid from friendly to serious professional in an instant. "How are you holding up, though?"

"You know."

She shook her head. "I don't, unless you tell me. Are you getting any sleep?"

"None."

"You should—"

"I know." He scrubbed his hand over his face. "I don't remember this part. The panic, the stress."

"Were you around in those first few days when…" She trailed off and waved her hand. "None of my business."

"It's okay. You can ask." He nodded in the direction of Becca's room. "I was there. Rachel and I, we got married. Not the right call, in hindsight, but I was doing the right thing. I was there every day. I didn't go away to school until we split up. Then there were two years when she was little that I wasn't around day in, day out. But that was it. But those early days…I was there, but it was a long time ago. I don't remember much of how we survived."

"It gets easier with each passing day. Tomorrow will likely be a bit teary, but by the day after that, her milk will start to come in and they'll figure this thing out."

He gave her a tired smile. "Never thought I'd be talking about my baby nursing a baby."

"You still haven't wrapped your head around it, have you?"

"I'm still sitting on that couch out there, processing her telling me she's pregnant."

Kerry moved closer and rubbed her hand against his forearm. "Earth to Owen. You've got that grandchild now."

Her touch unlocked a confession he hadn't shared with anyone else. "I'm happy for her. He *is* perfect. I just…I didn't think I'd have another baby in the house. There was supposed to be a golden age in there where I could date and have this place to myself."

She nodded and slipped her hand away, her fingers trailing through the crisp hair on his arm. Her gaze lingered on his face, though, her eyes thoughtful, almost curious.

In another time and place, he'd catch her wrist and bring her touch back to his body.

"I should go," she said.

But she didn't move away, and suddenly, Owen realized just how close she was. "Kerry…"

She blinked slowly as she tipped her head to the side. Her dark hair bounced, the waves baring a long stretch of her neck, and lust punched him straight in the face. Bam, sucker.

He reached for her, his fingertips brushing her cheekbone. She shivered, and maybe he'd have missed it if she were any further away, but she was right against him.

"We can't do this, right?"

He cupped her cheek anyway.

"No, probably not." She pressed into his touch, her eyelids fluttering shut. "Owen…"

"I waited a long time," he rumbled. "For it to be my turn again."

"You said that."

"It's going to be a while still. I can't—"

"And I can't, either," she whispered. "Not with a client's father. I'm sorry."

"Don't be sorry." He forced a smile he didn't feel. The heat swirling through his body demanded he kiss her, taste her. "You're good with her."

"Maybe in a few months. After she's discharged, and we're just neighbours and colleagues…" She trailed off, then a single word slipped into the air between them on a breathy whisper. "*Friends.*"

Could he pretend to just be friends after he'd had her so close to being in his arms?

Bam. Sucker.

Plus there was the not-so-small issue of her wanting a horse, and a cart, and he was long done with all of that.

So he rubbed his thumb gently along her jaw, then eased her away from him. "Thanks for the laugh earlier," he said softly. "That was the best thing that's happened to me in a long time."

Her eyebrows arched up.

He groaned. "Except for the whole grandson thing, of course."

"I knew what you meant." Her lips quirked, and he wanted to kiss her so much it hurt inside. "It felt good for me, too."

He dragged his gaze from her mouth up to her eyes, and held that connection for a beat. Then he nodded. "Good."

———

AS SHE SLID behind the driver's seat of her car, Kerry realized her fingers were shaking. *We can't do this, right?* Oh, but she'd wanted to.

Months of it's-fine, he's-off-limits-and-just-a-fantasy had collided with a very real, very tender moment of vulnerability and, maybe for the first time, she'd seen Owen Kincaid for all that he was. Not just a caring grump, not just a worried father, not just someone who carried the weight of responsibility like it was his own personal cross to bear. But also as a man, one stretched close to the limit, who needed to laugh. Who needed to be touched.

She'd seen him, truly seen him, and she'd liked him more than ever before.

Which was easy, she supposed. He'd done a very good

job of being unlikeable. How much of that had been a mask? And was it just for her, or for others?

A memory flashed through her mind. The first night she'd seen him, when he'd stomped through the Green Hedgehog. No, not just for her.

A movement in front of her broke her out of her thoughts. Owen had swung the door open. "Everything all right?" he called out after she rolled down her window.

"Fine," she hollered back, holding up her phone. "Just waiting for a text before I head on to the next appointment."

And then, so she wouldn't actually be a liar, she texted Jenna.

Kerry: SOS. But a personal one, not actually an emergency.

Her partner replied right away.

Jenna: Those are my favourite kinds of emergency. I'm at home if you want to come by for tea.

Tea. That sounded like an exceptional excuse to stop at the bakery and pick up butter tarts. When she pulled up out front, she was surprised to see a For Sale sign in the window. But it was business as usual inside.

She mentioned it to Jenna, though, who was more up on the local gossip.

"Apparently the Minellis are retiring. They want to travel and spend time with their grandkids."

"I hope they find a buyer for it. Losing these tarts would be the worst."

"True story." Jenna poured them each a big mug of tea,

and they settled into the breakfast nook that overlooked her forest of a backyard. Jenna lived outside of town, in a house her husband had custom built for her with his brothers. If Kerry had visited here before they'd looked at the clinic, she wouldn't have doubted Jake Foster's ability to do anything.

Jenna's house was a jewel, fit for a queen. Over the last few months, her partner had opened up more about what had brought her to Pine Harbour in the first place, and Kerry was in awe of Jenna's commitment—to her husband, who'd been injured overseas, and to her vision for their life together.

Sometimes, Kerry felt like she had zero vision for her own future. Other than her career, everything in her life had always been about the here and now, about living in the present. And she had a lot of fun doing that. It wasn't that she had regrets—not at all. But now she was full of weird and complicated, conflicting feelings.

Jenna had confided her secrets in Kerry. It was time for their roles to switch.

"I almost kissed Owen Kincaid," she said. "Just now. At his house. While my client was asleep in the other room."

Jenna's mug hit the table with a thud. Then she grinned. "Almost? How…almost?"

Kerry shivered again, remembering the feel of Owen's hands against her face, the soft way he'd touched her skin. "Just, uh, you know. He was right there, and we both wanted to. And then we agreed we couldn't."

"Right. It wouldn't be professional."

"Exactly."

"But it would be hot."

Kerry wanted to protest, but Jenna wasn't wrong. She smiled. "It would be."

"Do you want me to take over as Becca's primary?"

"No." Kerry inhaled sharply. She wouldn't put her personal interest in Owen ahead of a client's care. "I told him we are just neighbours and colleagues until she's out of my care."

Jenna wiggled her eyebrows. "Can I come to the next interagency working group session?"

Kerry groaned. That was next week. Oh boy. Of course, with Pine Harbour being the size it was, she was likely to run into him at the grocery store the next day, and at Mac's at least once before the meeting.

But a sustained two-hour session of trying not to notice the way his arms flexed when he moved paper? Not to watch how his fingers clenched a pen, knowing how tender they could feel against her skin?

The meetings would be torture.

And yet she was looking forward to them.

Danger, danger. She needed to burn off this energy in the worst way, so she changed the subject and proposed something she hadn't felt like doing since she moved to the peninsula. "I'm feeling antsy. Let's go dancing. We can get a hotel room in Owen Sound for the night."

Jenna made a face. "You know I'll go if you really want me to, but I'd rather crawl into bed with my husband and my baby and watch a baking show. But if you need a wingwoman…"

"I'll call Sarah." The receptionist at the main clinic had been her dancing buddy before she moved.

"Maybe some of the soccer players want to go?"

"Yeah." But Kerry heard the reluctance in her own

voice. She waved her hand and brightened up. "Yes, of course."

Jenna frowned. "Do you really want *me* to go dancing with you? Why?"

Kerry hesitated. "They're all so young!" she finally admitted. "I'm—" She cut herself off. She realized she had freely told Owen, without a second thought, that she wanted kids in the future. That was something she hadn't told anyone else, not even Jenna. "I guess I'm just feeling my age suddenly. Can I tell you another secret?"

"Of course."

"My biological clock started ticking six months ago. It's wild. I think that's why I've been so content to just settle in here and test out being a homebody, in case I decide to freeze some eggs for down the road."

"Oh, wow. So you're looking into options."

"Sort of. I've been doing my research in secret. I haven't talked to a doctor yet, but that's probably sooner than later."

"How do you feel about it?"

"I feel like I want a baby. Not now, because…"

Jenna howled. "They interfere with dancing."

"I'm painfully aware of that. Hence my equal and opposite urge to hit a club hard and do something stupid."

"Make out with a twenty-three year old?"

"Drunk text a thirty-seven-year-old grandfather," she confessed.

Jenna's face softened. "Oh, Kerry."

"I'm not going to do it, don't worry."

"I know you won't. But are you sure Owen is the guy you want, if you also want babies?"

Kerry blew a raspberry. "That's life, isn't it? Nothing ever lines up neatly. No, I know he's not a partner to raise kids with, don't worry. He's been there, done that, has the tattered t-shirt to prove it. The two things are separate for me, I promise." If she thought about it for a hot second, she could see how Owen could be a nice distraction from the tick tick tock of her biological urges. "And first things first...right now, my only burning desire is to cut loose for a night."

"All right. Let's go out. Life is short and your partying days might be numbered. We'll make it a big thing. Text Sarah, call Lore. We'll have a big ole girls night out in Owen Sound. Why not? And Sean and James will have a boys' night here at home without me. It might need to wait a few weeks, though, if we're going to find someone to cover both of our on-call shifts."

"I can wait." Kerry was surprised to hear how true that was when said out loud. She wasn't actually in any hurry to go out and party. If anything, she wanted it to test herself, to double check that she might actually be moving on from that stage in her life.

Where Owen and his searing gaze could fit into the next stage...that remained unclear. But until she figured that out, she'd probably enjoy bumping into him around town.

CHAPTER THIRTEEN

OWEN HEADED UPSTAIRS to the library thirty minutes before the interagency meeting. He checked the thriller stacks, but there was no sign of Kerry.

He hadn't seen her in a week. Seven days of unnecessary drives down Main Street, of popping into Mac's for coffee multiple times a day, and—once—even resorting to asking his brothers if they had seen her at the Hedgehog.

They hadn't, but that lead to a whole heap of uncomfortable follow-up questions he immediately regretted opening himself up to.

His phone vibrated in his pocket, and he pulled it out. Speak of the meddling jerks.

> **Adam: Kerry's just arrived at the fire station.**
> **Owen: We have a meeting.**
> **Adam: Is that why you wanted to know if she was at the bar the other night? A "meeting"?**
> **Owen: You're grounded.**
> **Adam: If only you still had that power over me.**
> **Owen: If only.**

Then he frowned.

Owen: Hey, why are *you* here?
Adam: I've said too much. *poof*

Owen pivoted around, searching for a window that overlooked the parking lot. Sure enough, there was Adam's truck. And just a bit closer to the door, Kerry's car. He should head downstairs and giving his baby brother a dose of his own meddling medicine. It was the Kincaid way.

But on the other hand…

His pulse thudded heavy at the base of his neck.

Whatever Adam was up to, he was going to get away with, because Owen wasn't going anywhere if Kerry was on her way upstairs. He grabbed a book and leaned against the end of the stack, in plain sight. Just acting casual.

He'd touched her.

She'd been in his kitchen, and he'd touched her face. Need burned inside him, made worse by the fact that she was off-limits, at least for the time being.

Never before in his entire adult life had he wanted anyone quite like this. It was consuming and dangerous and it felt very good, deep in his chest. Like *good things come to those who wait* kind of good.

Everything else on his Great Bachelor Plan list faded away, and *get Kerry in his bed* pulsed in neon letters instead. Of course there was still a crying baby in the room across the hall. A baby she had delivered just two weeks earlier. But in time. *Soon enough.*

It couldn't come soon enough.

But when her dark curls bobbed into sight, Owen

remembered that there were two of them playing this waiting game, and where he might be tangled up in his unholy desire to taste every inch of her, Kerry seemed completely composed as she stopped at the return slot and deposited her books, then checked out the bulletin board before slowly making her way in his direction.

"Early again," she said by way of greeting. Her eyes danced, a lovely sparkle as she held his gaze, but that was it. No other outward indication that this was anything other than two colleagues catching up before a meeting.

He held up the book in his hand. "I've been waiting for this one to come out."

She glanced at the cover, then burst out laughing. "Really?"

He groaned. "No." Then he glanced at the cover. *Iron Curtain Stealth.* "I need to start actually looking at books before I pick them up around you," he muttered under his breath.

"Oh?"

"Last time we were in this stack, I accidentally signed out *The Lady Loves a Necromancer.*"

Her eyes went wide. "And?"

"It was pretty good."

She laughed again. He'd been craving that sound and he didn't even know it.

"I returned it a while ago. You should see if it's available."

"I will." She reached into her bag. "On a professional note, I drafted some points I'd like our committee to consider making a public statement about. Do you have a few minutes now to discuss them in advance? If we have common ground, it might be easier to get buy in from everyone else."

Kerry was, by far, the most progressive member of their committee. Owen was glad she'd pushed to be included on it. He might lean more conservatively in terms of resource allocation, but he couldn't fault her optimism or commitment to public health.

He took the note, their fingers brushing for the briefest of split-seconds, and read it over. They were more than solid ideas—they were brave and fearless, but each bullet point was carefully constructed to focus on patient safety. "These are great. You've got my support."

"Excellent." She glanced past him. "Now, where did you find that necromancy book?"

———

WHEN OWEN GOT HOME from work Friday night he immediately noticed something was up with Becca. She was acting a little strange, a little distant, and someone was blowing up her phone. He hoped to hell it wasn't Hayden. The kid had come around twice for brief visits, but pre-season training had started, and well, there were only so many commitments a nineteen-year-old jackass could juggle at once.

"How did Charlie nap today?" he asked, rocking the sleeping baby as she bustled around the kitchen.

That she had dinner sorted out was also strange.

"Fine."

"Did you nap?"

She didn't answer him, because she was buried in her phone again.

"Becca, did you hear me?"

"Yeah, Dad." She blinked at him, set her phone face

down on the kitchen counter, and crossed her arms. "I heard you."

"What did I ask?"

"Probably something you didn't need to worry about."

He shook his head. "I don't think you heard me."

She sighed. "Yes, I napped."

He laughed and threw his free hand in the air. Charlie didn't stir. "So you did hear me."

"I told you that I did!"

"But then—"

"It's called boundaries, Dad. We need them. You don't need to worry about my every waking second, you don't need to check on me and see if I'm parenting exactly the way you did."

"Is that what I'm doing?"

She made an exaggerated thinking face.

He glanced at her phone. "What is this really about?"

"Nothing." She rolled her eyes. "*Nothing.* Go take Charlie into the other room and let me finish cooking."

"You don't need help?"

"Helicopter grandparent," she snapped at him. It was a mock-complaint, meant to distract him from whatever she wanted to pay attention to on her phone, but he let her push him out of the room.

If she wanted him to lie on the couch and watch a baseball game with Charlie, he wasn't going to complain.

This had been his greatest joy with Becca, too. Eighteen years later, he was once again overwhelmed by how good the top of a baby's head smelled, how warm and perfect their little bodies felt when perched on his chest. And Charlie seemed to like it. He stayed asleep for almost an hour, waking up just as Becca joined them on the couch with two plates of food.

She took the baby, and Owen dug in to his dinner. She was still off the smell of meat cooking, so she'd made an oven-roasted pasta sauce that was amazing.

"I'm going to have to go for a long run or something tomorrow," Owen said, patting his belly. "That was a carb-loading feast."

"You'll find some way to burn it off." Becca handed him his grandson back. "And I'm eating for two, so…"

"Hey, I'm not complaining. It was delicious."

"I've been watching cooking videos whenever I'm stuck in a cuddly Charlie nap. That was one of them."

"It's a real winner."

The game he was watching hit the seventh inning stretch, and he got up to do the same thing when there was a knock at the door.

When Owen answered it, he found Will and Adam on his doorstep. They were both dressed like they were going out for the night, in dark jeans, polished boots, and matching black shirts.

"This is an intervention," Adam said, a wicked gleam in his eye adding a dangerous glint to his already cocky grin.

Owen glanced from his brothers to his daughter.

Becca shrugged. "What? You needed to get out of the house and you wouldn't listen to me."

"You haven't told me to get out."

"Would it have worked if I did?" She didn't wait for him to answer. "So I called in reinforcements."

Adam grinned and flexed his arms. "That's me."

Will gave him a backhanded slap on the chest. "Us."

"Sure. Mr. Tough Guy Principal here is going to force your stubborn ass out onto the dance floor."

Owen looked back at Becca. "Are you sure you want me to be gone all evening?"

"Dad. Seriously. I'm going to be fine. And…Hayden might come over for another visit—with Charlie, don't freak out—and that would be easier if you weren't here. You keep scaring him off."

He sat back down. "I knew something was up. I'm not going anywhere."

As one, Adam and Will descended on him. "She's a grown-up, you ass." Becca giggled when Will said that. "And he's the kid's father. Plus we need a designated driver, so get your butt in your truck."

He didn't want to go. But he didn't want to stay, either, and deal with the awkwardness of Hayden and Becca. She was right—he probably did scare the kid off, and if they needed some time alone to get used to being parents together, so be it. He stood, sighed, and scrubbed a hand over his face. "Fine," he muttered. Then he glowered at Becca. "I'll leave the nanny cam on, so nothing inappropriate."

She rolled her eyes. "We don't have a nanny cam."

"That's beside the point."

"Go put on something nice."

He didn't own anything that even came close to that description. Nothing like the black buttoned down shirts his brothers wore. But he had black t-shirts. He bought those every time they went on sale, so he pulled on one that had hit that sweet spot of being broken in enough to be soft to the touch, but not yet stretched out and worn.

In the bathroom, he glowered at his face in the mirror. Should he shave? He ran a hand over his five o'clock shadow. No, he was fine. He needed to get past the bouncers, but he didn't need to actually impress anyone. The stubble could stay.

When he returned to the living room, Will was giving his boots a quick toe polish, and Adam was making cooing sounds at Charlie. "Your grandpa's going to have a good time tonight," the traitorous uncle said in a sing song voice. "Yes he is. Oh yes he—"

Owen cleared his throat. "Let's get this show on the road."

But once they were piled into his truck and driving down the highway toward the city, he not-so-grudgingly admitted to his brothers that Becca's instincts had been right. He should have realized sooner she needed an empty house in order for Charlie and Hayden to bond properly.

"Remember when you caught Josh with a girl in his room? How old was he?" Adam laughed.

Owen's neck burned at the memory. "He was seventeen. Fuck, that was embarrassing for all of us. But don't bring that up now, God damn it, Adam. She gave birth two weeks ago. Do *not* put that shit in my head."

"She's not going to do anything with Hayden."

From beside Owen, Will did a slow turn to the back seat. "You know this how?"

"We talk," Adam said. "What? I'm the cool one. And I'm closer to her age than Owen's. She grew up with me in the next room, remember? I'm her big brother."

"No you're not," Owen grunted. "But if you've got reassuring intel that she can barely stand Hayden and is being a mature co-parent, I'm all ears."

"No dice, bro. She loves him—sorry, but it's true, and you know it. That's no secret. But she doesn't trust him, and she's holding him at arm's length. So yes, she's being a mature co-parent. That part is bang on. She learned that from you and Rachel. You can't blame her."

Owen rubbed the back of his neck. "That feels like a backhanded compliment."

"That's because it was," Will said dryly. He pulled out his phone. "Changing the subject, some people from the unit are going to be at the club tonight."

Owen made a face. As a senior army reservist, he didn't always like to hang out with army people. The rank stuff got blurred during social events, and he didn't love that. Of course, as he was being forced to examine more and more these days, when did he love anything other than holding his grandson and watching a baseball game?

Will waved off his bad mood. "Don't worry. It's 90s Throwback night at the club, so not the younger guys. Some senior NCOs, their partners. Rafe Minelli and his wife."

"Stevie's coming," Adam piped up from the back seat. "And some of the crew from Warriors Moving."

"Should be a good night," Owen murmured.

When they arrived, they had to park down the street because the lot was already full. At the door they paid their entrance fees, had their ID checked—always amusing for Owen, who had felt too old to be ID'd since before he was even of age to buy booze. Having a kid early did that to a guy. He'd been old before his time, and now… well, at least the bouncer didn't kick him out for not wearing a nice enough shirt.

By the looks of some of the people in line with them, the boot shine hadn't even been necessary.

Have a good time, he repeated to himself. A good challenge.

After their eyes had adjusted to the dark, Will gestured

around the space, which Owen had never been in before. "The bar is over there," he yelled, pointing to the left, and around the dance floor. To the right, where he pointed next, was a stepped up seating area, darker and hard to see in, but just as full of people as the dance floor was. "I'm going to look for the guys from the unit. You two hit the bar, then let's meet over on the far side."

Even though the music was from the 1990s and the crowd was more mature than the average club-goer, Owen still felt older than dirt as he followed Adam. His younger brother elbowed his way toward the bar like a pro.

When was the last time Owen had bellied up to any bar, let alone one surrounded by scantily-clad nubile bodies? Did going to the Hedgehog a couple of times a year even count if he just played darts and Lore brought him beer like he was some kind of antisocial ogre?

He winced.

He *was* an antisocial ogre. And everyone was having a great time. He could learn something from them. Scanning the crowd, he forced himself to keep an open mind about the evening.

That was when he saw her, in the middle of a pack of women.

Dark bouncing waves, and a lot of skin.

Kerry twisted to the music, a little halter top shimmying around her torso as she moved. It was metallic, reflecting the light. Her skin sparkled too.

So much skin. Bare shoulders, bare abs, and when she turned all the way around, a very bare back. Her halter top tied in two places, at her neck and in the middle of her back, and that was it.

She couldn't be wearing anything underneath it, and Owen's brain flatlined.

He turned on his brother, standing behind him. Adam's mouth was hanging open, and Owen thumped him hard in the chest. "Is this a set up?"

"Oh, fuck. No." Adam snapped his mouth shut and turned, jerking his gaze away from the women. "Dude, I didn't know they would be here."

———

"THIRSTY?" Kerry hollered in Jenna's direction.

Her friend nodded, then mouthed the words, *water bottle*.

Kerry left her friends on the dance floor and wiggled her way through the crowd, heading in the general vicinity of the bar. She was too short to see clearly on the dance floor, but as she hit the edge of it, the density of the bodies gave way and she burst out of the crowd.

Owen stood right in front of her, his arms crossed and a weird look on his face.

She skidded to a stop, breathless and slightly confused. Her mouth opened and some small sound came out, maybe *hey* or *hi* or *what?* Whatever it was, it was too quiet for even her to hear herself. Her brain wasn't really processing either words or the large, sexy man in front of her. Owen wasn't alone, either. Behind him, trying very much to get in front of him, was Adam, who was shooting her a look that was trying to say *it's all cool* but also a little *he's not comfortable here, help a dude out*.

No kidding Owen was out of his element in a dance club. But he looked good, in a black t-shirt and faded jeans that hugged his solid thighs and tight hips.

Eyes off the hips. She looped her gaze back up to his face, and pointed to the bar. Adam led the way, Owen stepping to the side to let her sweep past him, and then he closed in behind her as they waited their turn to order. It was easier to talk here. Everything was still loud, but Owen's body made a very good sound shield.

"I saw you out there," he said in her ear. "Dancing."

That gave her a thrill, the thought of Owen watching her dance. She twisted her head and glanced up at him. "Did you?"

From beside her, Adam chimed in. "I tried to push him out there, but he wasn't having any of it."

"We just got here," Owen groused. "I'm getting my bearings."

"Do you dance?"

He shrugged. "Sure."

"This is his first time ever coming here," Adam offered helpfully. He was clearly enjoying this, and Kerry didn't blame him. She was enjoying it, too, but on a whole different level. She tried to read Owen's expression. Did Adam know they had almost kissed? How much did Owen share with his brothers?

The bartender swung past them, and they placed their orders. Adam wanted a Red Bull and vodka and a beer— one was for their brother Will, he explained—and Owen asked for a Coke. Kerry ordered two bottles of water, and tried to put money for them on the bar, but Adam waved her off as he handed over a credit card.

"It's Will's," he said with a grin.

The music changed, sliding from Britney Spears to C+C Music Factory, and Kerry wiggled her hips. Owen stepped up to the bar, giving her a bit of room to dance as they waited for their drinks. She grinned at him. "What are the chances we show up here on the same night?"

He smiled back, but didn't answer.

The drinks arrived, and Adam grabbed the two he'd ordered. "Pretty good chances, actually. This is the only nightclub within a hundred kilometres of here and we're all hot-blooded—"

"I will pay you a hundred dollars to leave us alone," Owen growled.

Adam winked at her—oh *God*—and disappeared onto the dance floor, leaving them alone.

"So..." Kerry said, now breathless for a whole new reason. "You're here with your brothers."

Owen did something halfway between a shrug and a nod. "He won't say anything."

"Adam?" She glanced over her shoulder. He was long gone. "I'm not worried about someone seeing us together, if that's what you mean."

He visibly relaxed. "Right."

She leaned in. She couldn't help it. "We do work together, you know." Teasing. Cajoling. A little closer. "And we are...friends, right?"

All the relaxation left his body as he shuddered. It had been too long since she'd had this effect on a man. It was heady and fun. And in a few more weeks, it would be entirely above board. For now, she would have to walk the line carefully.

Someone bumped into her from behind and she collided with Owen, his hands wrapping around her body as he shielded her from the pulse of the crowd. Strong, warm fingers slid over the bare skin on her back, and that line she'd been worried about walking carefully got very hard to see.

Electricity arced between them as he held her close for the second time, as she breathed in the scent of his nice clean shirt, and the skin on his arm that was right there.

She had an up-close view of his tattoo for the second time, and it reminded her of bumping into him in the grocery store and the way he stalked off.

A lifetime ago. Since then, they'd shared laughs, and secrets, and forged a tentative friendship that put a lot of weight on pretending they didn't want each other when obviously they did.

She wanted Owen so very much. It had been too long since she'd had a no-strings-attached fling.

Against her back, his hand shook for a second, then he skated it down her hip in a surprisingly sure move, landing his electric touch on her upper thigh. Her head swimming, she glanced up and found him staring intently at her, his eyes glittering in the dim club lighting. She found the rail at the bottom of the bar and she hoisted herself up with his help so she was leaning against him, closer to meeting his impressive height.

His one hand was hot and steady on her leg, and the other started to roam up and down her back. Neither of them said anything. He touched, she held still, and inch by inch, he explored all the bare skin her halter top revealed. When he got to her shoulder, she shivered, and the groan he made was dangerous. She knew the risk of tangling with him. But she also knew she wouldn't get him out of her system any other way.

It was the t-shirt, she told herself. The way it rode up on his arms, baring too much of his biceps. Showing off that damn tattoo, that delicate ink that was nothing like the rest of his personality. She'd been tricked by worse in the past. And Owen was the opposite of the worst—he was, underneath that gruff exterior, a lovely, funny man.

But he was the father of her client, and this was inappropriate. She fought through the cloud of desire and pressed her hands against his hard chest. "Owen, stop."

He dropped his hand from her thigh like she'd just burst into flames, and stepped back. Not far—he kept her shielded from the rest of the club. They were both shaking.

"Jesus," he rasped. "I'm sorry."

"Me too. I'm—I—"

"I don't know what came over me."

Lust. It had consumed her as well. "I wanted you to hold me." Want. It was a present-tense desire. She wanted him to still kiss her right now, right here, again, even as she told him no, as she insisted they couldn't. "But we can't do this here. Or now."

His hands tightened on the edge of the bar and he nodded.

The music changed again. "Livin' La Vida Loca" started pulsing through the air, and Kerry wanted nothing more than to slide against Owen, get his hands on her bare hips, and dance as close together as humanly possible.

Instead she grabbed the bottles of water from the bar and swallowed around the lump in her throat. "I have to get back out there," she whispered. "See you later."

CHAPTER FOURTEEN

THE CRY WAS tiny and ragged, but it still woke Owen from his sleep. The creak of floor boards in the hallway told him he wasn't alone in being woken up, either.

Pulling on a t-shirt and a pair of sweatpants, he quietly eased open his bedroom door—and came face-to-face with his daughter's wide-eyed ex-boyfriend. Hayden had a fussing Charlie up against his chest and was trying to awkwardly calm him.

"What are you doing here?" Owen rumbled.

Hayden's mouth flapped open, then closed again. He visibly swallowed hard, then turned and bounced his way into the living room, where Becca was passed out on the sofa. Next to her, the empty baby swing was still moving back and forth, the tinny rainforest music a bizarre but perfect soundtrack to this three-in-the-morning party they were having.

Owen turned off the baby swing arm, leaving the music playing. He quietly moved past Hayden. "You want coffee?"

The kid followed him into the kitchen, Charlie protesting the whole way.

"How about you make it, and I'll take him." Owen reached for his grandson.

Hayden didn't move.

"I won't—" Owen cut himself off. "What's wrong?"

Hayden gave him an embarrassed look. "I don't know how to make coffee."

He didn't know how to soothe a crying baby, either. Owen sighed. "Turn Charlie over and hold him with your arm against his belly. It's probably gas, and that feels good."

"Thanks."

Owen grabbed the carafe from the coffee maker, filled it with water, then poured that into the reservoir before trying to make conversation again. "When did you…" He choked back *sneak into my house* and went for the more diplomatic question— "come over?"

Hayden sighed. "Becca texted me an hour ago. She got up to feed him and couldn't find anything to watch. I walked over to keep her company."

"Don't you need to work tomorrow?"

"If she's not sleeping, I shouldn't get to sleep." The kid jutted his jaw out. His bravado only lasted a minute, though, then he sagged back against the counter. "It's harder than we thought."

"I'm familiar."

"She's really good with him."

Owen nodded. "She is."

"I want to be better."

"That comes with time." Owen stopped before he put the coffee grinds in the filter. "*Do* you have to work in the morning?"

Hayden's face fell. "Yeah."

"Give me Charlie. Go lie down in Becca's room. I'll wake you up in a few hours. What time do you need to get going?"

"Seven."

"Shit, son. Next time, you guys wake me up." Owen shook his head.

Hayden still didn't pass over the baby. "He's quiet now."

Owen finished measuring out the coffee, then sighed and added more grounds. "I'm not going to tell you to put him down, then."

"I did get some sleep before she texted. I'll grab a nap in the afternoon. I'm only working the breakfast rush."

"How's that going?"

"Good."

But Owen could do the math. A couple of hours over breakfast rush at Mac's didn't pay much. Still, he nodded. "Good."

There was a lot loaded into that single word. There was no love lost between them, and Owen wouldn't—couldn't —change that. He didn't want to. But he hoped for Becca's sake this could be a bit of a truce.

It was time for him to start seeing Hayden as Charlie's dad. Hell, now Hayden was walking Owen's own path. They had more in common than probably either wanted to admit, but it was what it was.

His resolve to be open-minded and kinder to Hayden lasted almost ninety-six hours, until he found Becca in a puddle of tears on the couch, surrounded by piles of baby laundry.

Charlie was asleep in his bouncy chair at her feet.

Owen carefully found the only free real estate in her

vicinity and lowered himself quietly into a squat beside her right knee. "Bec?"

"I don't want to talk about it. I'm an idiot."

"You're not."

"I texted Hayden earlier to see if he wanted to go for a walk with Charlie. He's sleeping longer in the stroller or baby carrier, so I thought Hayden could take him for a couple of hours and I might get some sleep. Or I don't know, just stare at the wall. Anything."

Owen didn't want to jump straight to bloodlust, but he saw red. He couldn't help it. "What did he say?"

Becca's face crumpled again. "*Nothing.* He didn't even bother to reply. I thought maybe he was sleeping, because he's been working a lot of mornings, but I just saw that he was tagged in someone's picture. He's at a bonfire tonight. He's out partying, and I'm home with our baby, and that is not the life I want." She choked on the last word. "I mean, I want Charlie. Of course I do. But I can't do this hot and cold thing with Hayden. He needs to be in or out, and if he's out, he can be *out.* I'm not going to make...offers...like that."

She hesitated around *offers*, and Owen knew it was because she'd exposed herself by making a request. She wasn't just making time for Hayden to see his son, she was asking for some time to herself, and Hayden didn't seem to care about that.

Owen did. But that wasn't the same. "Can I take Charlie out for a walk?"

Becca shrugged listlessly. "Sure."

"Take that time for yourself. And ask me for more of this, okay?" He frowned. "Have you talked to Kerry about any of this? Or your mom?"

"Yeah. Yes, to both. Kerry made me take a whole screening test for postpartum depression."

Owen fought back a smile at the sullen tone Becca had around *made me*. "She was doing her job."

"I know."

He took a deep breath. "I'm going to grab a sweatshirt, then I'll take the little guy out for a while. You grab a hot shower, make a TikTok that makes it look like you're having the Best Time Ever, and show Hayden you don't need him."

She didn't reply.

"Becca, you *don't*—" Owen stopped. He looked at his daughter, who was staring down at the tiny, soft pile of laundry. He remembered the way Becca had gazed at the kid after Charlie's delivery, and what Adam had said the week before. "You love him."

Her profile tightened. "That doesn't matter."

"It does, though." He sighed. "We can't lie to ourselves. That never works."

"Yeah, well." She shrugged. Then she gently lifted up the baby and bundled him into the bucket carseat. Owen's cue to put on a sweatshirt and give his grown-up kid a bit of space.

The stroller—a *welcome to the world, Charlie* gift from Rachel and Hudson—was a lot more complicated than they had ever had for Becca. It was a beast of a machine with giant wheels, that needed to be carried off the porch first and unfolded on the driveway before the tiny bucket seat could be clipped into it.

But once they were rolling, Owen had to admit that it was a smooth ride, and Charlie didn't stir the entire time. That gave his grandpa some time to chew on the fact that Becca's heart had been bruised, again.

As he cut across the edge of the residential neighbour-hood and headed for the hill down to the harbour, he called Adam.

"What's up?"

"I'm out for a walk with Charlie in the stroller. What are you doing?"

His brother made a clattering noise. "Nothing."

"Do you want company?"

"I'm not at home." There was more clanging in the background.

"Where are you?"

"Working out."

Owen didn't miss that Adam pivoted to saying what he was doing, and not where he was doing it. He stopped at the top of the hill. Ahead of him stretched the dark edge of the lake, disappearing in either direction behind thick stands of trees. He and Charlie didn't need to head down there and be all alone. He turned the stroller around, pointing back up Main Street. If he walked fast, he could be at the Emergency Services building on the edge of town in fifteen minutes.

"Gotta go," his brother said.

Owen rolled his eyes. "All right. Talk to you later."

He stopped at Mac's first to pick up coffee, because who knew how long he'd be waiting for Adam to finish his workout, and then he texted Becca to let her know that he was still on a big loop around town but her baby was fast asleep and all was well.

When he got to the station, he didn't bother going inside. Charlie was having a good long sleep, and Owen liked the quiet of the evening. Bright fluorescent lights would ruin both of their vibes. It didn't take long for Adam to appear, his hair and shirt damp with sweat.

He waved. "You figured out the mystery."

"What's going on?"

His brother gave him a disarming grin, one that almost certainly worked on people he wanted to sleep with. It didn't work on Owen.

"Adam."

His younger brother's eyebrows snapped together to a more honest frown. "Yeah?"

"You've been here an awful lot."

"We've been over this."

"Have we?"

His brother tossed his bag into his truck. "I dunno. Maybe you've been deliberately obtuse and ignoring all the signals I've been clearly sending your way so you aren't surprised when I get into fire school."

Owen expected that kind of snap back from his other brothers. Josh would toss a few f-bombs in there, Seth would use only the first five words and let Owen sort the rest out himself. Will would say it all in a diplomatic gloss.

But Adam?

He scrubbed a hand along his jaw, painfully aware he'd turned into a tension ball on the way over. "Try me again."

"Nah, it's fine."

"I'm all ears."

Adam's eyebrows shot up. "No disrespect, but you don't listen to me."

Ah, fuck. "I want to. I get tangled up in *you* not listening to *me*, that's all."

"My life," Adam said. "Remember?"

"Sometimes I worry it's you that doesn't remember."

"Was that a shot about Mom and Dad? Because I do, and you're a jackass. But you're a jackass who cares, so listen up, big brother. You can't protect me from life."

"I can try." Owen heard the futility in his own words. "I want to try, God damn it."

Adam leaned against the back of the truck. "Do you want to stop me from doing something I want to do?"

Owen swallowed hard. Why had he charged over here? He should have kept walking, down to the lake. "I want to influence what you want to do."

"Ah, man. You do, every day."

Then why did he feel like if Adam got hurt, it would be his fault? "That doesn't make me feel better."

"What are you afraid of?"

Owen glance down at Charlie. He'd spent far too long being afraid of what this sleeping, perfect child would mean for Becca's life. "I'm afraid of risk," he finally admitted.

"Me, too." Adam huffed a hard laugh. "I hated the army. You know that?"

No. Owen hadn't known that. "Tell me about that."

"I hated how it messed up Stevie. How it turned out to be bullshit on the inside, just like everything else. Sometimes I worry that firefighting will be the same. That's why I'm hanging out here a lot. To try and see it from their eyes, to make sure this is a good idea. Because you warn me that it's not, and I listen to you."

Owen stopped the gentle push-pull on the stroller and dragged his brother in for a hug. "You're a good kid."

"Not a kid."

"You know what I mean."

Adam squeezed him tight. "I do."

Owen wiped his eye. "All right. We should talk about something else."

"We could talk about you and Kerry at the club last

week. You looked cozy when I left you at the bar. And then you seemed…happy for the rest of the night."

Dazed had been more like it. Happy? His feelings about what had almost happened were a lot more nuanced than *happy*. "Pick another topic."

"Why?"

Because she was Becca's midwife for another two weeks and three days. "Because it's private, and complicated."

"Like my desire to become a firefighter?"

That was a direct shot. Owen winced. "Yeah, I guess that's fair."

"Does Becca know that the two of you…"

"Are friends? Yes."

"You're more than friends."

Owen stopped and gave his brother a pointed look. "We've never kissed. Do I like her? Hell, yes. I'm not going to deny that. But we're just friends."

For now. For another two weeks and three days, and then however long it would take him to ask her out, and given his track record of stringing words together in a nice and persuasive way around her, it could be a lot longer than that. *No.* It *wouldn't* take longer than that. He was done chewing on words he should say out loud.

So he cleared his throat. "We're just friends for now, anyway."

Adam pumped his fist in the air.

The back of Owen's neck was going to burst into flames, but it was good to see his brother didn't judge him for his not-so-secret crush.

———

KERRY WAS late for the September interagency working group meeting because her clinic ran late that day. But she wanted to fit in her last client appointment, even if it created a schedule conflict. She didn't want to shortchange her client, but she didn't want to rebook, either.

She slipped in the door as someone launched into what sounded like the third agenda point. There was only one empty chair left, two past Owen on the same side. She slipped him a note on her way to sit down, then tried to catch up on the discussion.

She failed miserably, but nobody called on her for input, and she only had a teensy-tiny remnant of guilt when Owen stood up and gave her an intense, tight-jawed, hard-eyed look. "Kerry, do you have a minute?"

"Sure." She gathered up her notepad, waved goodbye to the other committee members, and followed him out of the meeting room. She expected him to head through the library to the stairs that would lead down to the lower level where his office was located, but instead he cut to the left. Ahead was a door marked *Authorized Personnel Only*, although she figured that included the EMT supervisor. On the other side was a quiet office corridor, and an elevator.

Owen tapped the button to call it. He used his thumb, and she realized his hand was tightly fisted around her note.

Her pulse jumped as the elevator arrived and they quietly stepped on together.

Owen leaned over and jammed the door closed button. Then he pulled a key from his pocket and inserted it into a slot on the panel.

"So did you—"

Before Kerry could finish the question, Owen had her in his arms, pressed against the wall.

Her heart pounded in her throat as he grazed her skin with his thumb. Her jaw, her throat, and then the back of her neck as he hovered his mouth just above her lips. "Becca's last appointment was today?"

"She called earlier to change it and I told her I had time at the end of the day," Kerry whispered. "Sorry I was late."

The corner of his mouth jerked into a half-smirk. "I was wondering if I would see you."

"Maybe I should have texted."

"Do you have my number?"

She licked her lips. "Sort of."

The other corner twitched now. "From her chart."

"Yes."

He groaned and moved closer. Another fraction of an inch, and they'd be kissing. Why weren't they kissing yet?

"I can't stop thinking about you." The raw confession tore loose from his body, his voice grating like he tried to hold it in, because it was an admission that violated everything they had previously agreed to.

"It's been a long month," she agreed. She could play this cool, even though her heart hammered against her rib cage as if Owen was offering to go down on her right here, right now.

He smiled, a little wild, just on the edge of control. "I have a question for you."

The answer was yes. Yes, here in the elevator. Yes, whatever he wanted. Her head swam and her knees threatened to buckle.

The elevator made a sound, a small beep, and then another one. Louder, more persistent this time. Kerry's hammering heart desperately wanted Owen to ignore it, but that wasn't his style. And in a building full of first responders, maybe it wasn't wise to have alarms going off, she could see that ending badly—and publicly.

He stepped back, leaving her pressed against the wall and shaking. He glanced over at the panel, swore under his breath, and pulled the key out. Then he tapped the first floor button.

What? Every cell in her body shrieked in protest. He needed to do the key trick again. They needed more time. She straightened up. "You were asking a question?"

He dragged his hooded gaze down her body.

Yeah. The answer was definitely yes.

"Have dinner with me tomorrow night." The doors opened and he stepped halfway out of the elevator, leaning his hand against the door to pin it open while she stared at him.

Dinner.

She had been prepared for a hot night of no-holds-barred sex. Not dinner. Not after that scorching pin against the wall, and the grind against the bar at the club, and even the way he'd touched her for the first time at his house. Their connection was dangerously combustible chemistry. She didn't need to be wined and dined to invite Owen into her bed.

"That's not a question," she said, buying herself some time.

Weren't they about to kiss?

When could she tear his clothes off?

Those were questions. *Have dinner with me* was a command.

He smiled, all the way to his eyes. "Would you please have dinner with me? Let me take you out, Kerry. Let's do this right."

Her heart liked that a lot. Too much, but whatever, the answer had always been yes. Since the first moment she laid eyes on him, big and grumpy and not looking at anyone as he stalked across the Green Hedgehog. "Yes," she said in a rush. "Will you pick me up? Do you know where—"

His eyes glittered as he nodded. "I know where you live."

"Okay then." She hitched her bag over her shoulder and moved to leave the elevator.

Owen stopped her, his hand grazing down her arm before catching her wrist. He glanced back over his shoulder, then moved them both back into the elevator again. "Fuck it," he said, closing the door. "I can't wait another minute."

Her breathless gasp was lost this time as he covered her lips with his. Her bag hit the floor, he tangled his fingers into her hair, and finally—finally—she learned what the press of his mouth against hers felt like. *Warm magic.* Like flames appearing from nowhere to gobble up dry kindling, and then perfectly settling into hot, glowing embers. Tender, questing magic, his lips caressing hers as his fingers flexed in her hair. Restraint shook through his entire body.

She softened into his embrace, and by the time he eased back, she was melting in all the right places. She smiled up at him. "I wasn't sure you were going to kiss me."

He flushed. "I wanted to kiss you as soon as the doors closed, but I want to do this right."

She touched her fingers to her lips. "You did. You are."

He rubbed his thumb against her jaw, and she reached for him.

"My turn to kiss you," she whispered. She brushed her lips against his, parting just a bit. A tease and a promise of more to come.

When they broke apart, he pushed the door open button. "I need to…"

"Yeah. Me, too."

He took a deep breath. "Hey. So, maybe I could give you my number the proper way now?"

She let out a shaky laugh and pulled out her phone. "Please."

By the time she got home, there was a text from him confirming their date.

Owen: I'll pick you up tomorrow at six, if that works for you?
Kerry: It does. I'm looking forward to it.
Owen: Me, too.

CHAPTER FIFTEEN

OWEN CHANGED his shirt three times. He fixed his hair twice, and on his second stomp back to his bedroom from the bathroom, Becca wandered into the hallway with Charlie asleep in a wrap on her chest and gave him a curious look. "What's going on?"

He hadn't been subtle about the nervous energy. He gestured for her to follow him, and pointed to the two shirts on his bed, both button-down, one blue, the other dark grey. Then he waved helplessly at the black Henley he was currently wearing. "What's better for a date?"

"You have a *date*?"

"Yeah."

She glanced at the clock on his bedside table. "Is it a date for *tonight*?"

"I'm picking her up in fifteen minutes."

"Oooh, a secret date."

"I was going to tell you."

"Really? When?"

"At some point between now and thirteen minutes from now when I leave the house."

"So she's local." Becca's eyebrows wiggled. "Interesting. Do I know her?"

Warmth crawled up his neck. "Yes."

"Is it someone from the army?"

"I'll tell you if you stop asking questions."

"But this is fun. Is it—"

"It's Kerry."

Becca blinked at him. She stood there, her mouth hanging open, and she just stared. Then she rocked back on her heels. "My Kerry?"

That tripped him up. He frowned and thought twice about pointing out that technically, Kerry wasn't her midwife anymore.

Becca matched his frown. "When did you ask her out?"

"Yesterday." He held up his hands. "Bec, if you have a problem with this—"

She shook her head violently. "No, that's not… You like *Kerry?*"

"Yeah."

"I didn't see that coming. Has this been happening right in front of me?"

He gave her a rueful smile and gestured at Charlie. "You've been busy. And it wasn't a thing that was actively happening. We've been very appropriate."

"Oh my *God.*" She made a face. "That means you thought about being inappropriate and had to keep it together. *Dad.*"

"I—" Owen swallowed hard. He'd gone eighteen years avoiding this exact conversation.

She waved her hands. "Let's move past that. You want shirt advice?"

"Are we okay?"

"Sure. Please don't break her heart."

"I—" Owen was having conversational whiplash. "Why do you think I would break her heart?"

Becca paused. "I don't know."

"I don't know how to take that."

"Well, I don't know why I said it, but I think it tracks." She pointed to the blue shirt on the bed. "Wear that one. And maybe pick up flowers on the way."

"From the non-existent Pine Harbour Flower Shop?"

"From the front yard, Dad. Jeez. She'll love that they're handpicked. That's a very Kerry thing to like."

She wasn't wrong. Owen promised he would pick flowers, then changed his shirt.

———

HE ARRIVED at her front door carrying tiger lilies wrapped in newspaper.

Kerry's first thought was, *careful, you're going to fall for this guy.* Her second thought was that she'd be so lucky. It wasn't meant to be, of course. They were at two very different places in their lives. But for a little while, if tonight went well, maybe Owen could be hers. She found herself holding her breath and hoping the date would meet the ridiculously high expectation she'd accidentally built in her mind.

Crushing on a guy for months was dangerous like that.

She'd tried to temper those expectations, texting him to suggest he could just come over with a bottle of wine, but he wanted to go out for dinner first. *Call me old fashioned,* he'd said. Now there were flowers.

He'd shaved, gotten a hair cut, and he was wearing a button-down shirt that stretched very nicely across his chest and hugged his arms.

"Well, hello," she said, taking in all of him again. "You look good."

"So do you." His eyes darkened as he looked her up and down, and the corner of his mouth twisted into a tempting, sexy smile.

She'd dressed for exactly that reaction. Tight black pants, a loose, off-the-shoulder blouse that ended an inch above her waistband. Dressy but fun, with lots of skin showing. She stepped back, every cell in her body tingling. "Come on in, we can put those flowers in water."

Which was absolutely code for letting him brush against her as he came into her apartment, and when she caught the faintest whiff of the scent of his soap on his skin, any thought of finding a vase was abandoned. She pinned him against the inside of the door, grabbed the flowers with one hand to keep them from tumbling to the floor, and swallowed the *oof* sound he made as she pressed into the *very* solid front of him. When she pulled back, she was pleased to see that the kiss she'd laid on him had given him twin bright spots high on his cheekbones.

"You look really good," she murmured.

As soon as she turned to deal with the flowers, he caught her around the waist and pulled her back against him, dropping his head to kiss the side of her neck in a slow, agonizing tease.

"I give as good as I get," he growled in her ear, and the electric tingles sparked dangerously hot beneath her skin.

Tilting her head back, she bared more of her flesh for him as he tasted her, then traced the curve of her throat as he turned her again in his arms so he could capture her mouth.

The flowers may have been a forking ruse.

"Do you really have a dinner reservation?" She mumbled as his hands slipped under the hem of her shirt.

He shook against her in silent laughter. "Yeah."

But his fingers didn't slow down, and then his palm was flat against the skin on her side and she really wanted to drag him to her bed.

"Owen?"

The flex of his fingers digging deep into her flesh said a lot. The deep, ragged breath he sucked in before stepping back filled in the rest of the story, but the way he dipped his head and looked her right in the eye was the surprise. "I want you so much. More than I thought." A muscle in his cheek flexed. "But I want your company first. So…dinner."

"Dinner," she whispered.

She didn't move. He was so close, and smelled so good, and had felt *amazing* up against her.

He leaned in again, but instead of kissing her, he brushed his fingers over her hand and took the flowers from her.

Her heart thudded against her rib cage.

He glanced around her open concept space. "This place is very cool."

"I like it." She gave him the ten second tour with her index finger.

"The clock doesn't work, eh?"

"Apparently not. I like it anyway. It makes up for the fact there's no bathtub in the washroom."

"What!" Owen feigned mock horror on her behalf made her laugh.

She pivoted away from him and grabbed a large mason jar for the flowers.

He helped her put them in, then took her hand and rubbed his thumb across her knuckles. "Ready to go?"

"I'm all yours."

They took his truck, which was delightfully clean, and fell into a conversation about music as soon as the radio came on—and Owen promptly turned it down, but not before Kerry heard the latest country hit playing. She teased him about bro country, and he teased her back about Ricky Martin and liking retro dance music.

"I saw you dancing that night," she said. After their second almost-kiss. "You like that music just fine."

"You watched me?"

"A bit. I was busy dancing myself."

"I know. I saw you, too. Somehow you were always on the other side of the dance floor from me."

"It was safer that way." She shot him a coy look across the cab of the truck. "I mean, look at last night and tonight when you picked me up."

He grinned. "That was quite the nice kiss you laid on me at the door."

"It would have been terrible if I'd done that in the middle of the dance floor."

"Awful." He winked and reached across the cab, giving her his hand to hold. She liked the warmth of his palm and the strength of his fingers here just as much as she did when he held her. "I told Becca about the date."

"I was wondering if you would."

"I almost didn't. It's our business, and we're just seeing where things are going, right?"

She nodded. "But then…"

"But then I was wearing the wrong shirt." His face went soft, as it did any time he was thinking about his daughter. "And Becca caught on to the fact I was a bit flustered."

Kerry laughed, then covered her mouth. "Sorry," she mumbled from behind her fingers. "That's cute." She threw him a bone. "I changed twice."

"Yeah, but you have more dating experience than me."

"When was the last time you went on a date?"

He didn't answer her.

"Owen?"

He was a big beast of a man, and the way his nose flared only made the image that much more complete. And right now the beast was at a loss for words.

The way he was overprotective of Becca, it made her wonder... "Have you ever dated?"

He laughed. "That's a complicated answer."

"It usually isn't." But Kerry could see how it would be for Owen, Mr. Conflicted, who shook when he wanted to kiss her.

There was nothing conflicted about the way he glanced sideways at her, though. He gave her a warm, confident smile. "Now we have something to talk about over dinner."

He'd picked a steakhouse with a view of the Tobermory harbour, at the northern tip of the peninsula. They weren't the only customers in the restaurant, but it wasn't busy, and they were seated well away from anyone else, in a booth in the corner.

"What do you like here?" Kerry asked as she perused the menu.

"I don't know. I've never been here before." He gave her another of those bashful but confident smiles that felt warm and deep and very addictive. "I guess that's me bringing up the lack of dating thing again."

Tell me more. Tell me everything. "So..." She wanted to ask what was different about her, or now. But there was something fragile about Owen that she wanted to protect. So she tip-toed softly. "You said it was complicated."

"Yeah." He played with his water glass, frowning in a thinking way. "There was a period in my life when I was young and stupid, and I couldn't connect what felt like a good time in the moment and what still felt like a good time the next day. That was while I was away at school, and only home every other weekend with Becca. It was a dark period in my life for a lot of reasons. My..." He swallowed hard. "My dad died while I was gone. My mom died soon after I got back. I had time to make up for with Becca, and four younger brothers to take care of, too. It was a lot, and even after my brothers left the house..."

Kerry tried to do the math. "Adam's ten years younger than you?"

"Yeah. So he left home just as Becca hit pre-puberty, and..." He laughed. "I love her so much, but that was a roller coaster. And then Rachel had more kids, and Becca didn't want to spend more than a few nights a month there—she goes there a lot for dinner," he hastened to add.

"It's okay. I understand complicated family dynamics. My parents are divorced and re-married, both of them, and they both had more kids. I went back and forth."

"Siblings on both sides, eh?"

"They're all much younger than me."

"Are you close?" Owen was watching her attentively, and Kerry hesitated. "Sorry, I don't mean to pry."

"It's not prying," she said softly. "It's complicated, as you say. I don't have much in common with them. Or my parents, for that matter. I think my situation is different than Becca's."

The waiter arrived and Owen ordered a steak with a side of grilled vegetables. Kerry followed suit. When he asked about drinks, Owen deferred to Kerry. "Would you like wine?"

She shook her head. She wanted to be clear-headed and sober when she invited him in at the end of the night. "I'm good with water tonight."

"Sounds good," the waiter said, picking up their menus. "Can I tempt you with some flatbread and dip to start?"

"Oh..." Kerry said at the same time as Owen nodded. They both chuckled.

"Yes, please," she said. And once they were alone again, she shifted a little closer to Owen. "I'm having fun."

"Me, too." He paused, then leaned in all the way and brushed a soft kiss across her lips. "What else do you want to know about me?"

The answer pulsed heavy in her bloodstream. *Everything.*

————

DINNER WAS AMAZING, but filling, and they both passed on dessert—at the same time, again.

Owen wasn't in a rush to end the date. The exact opposite, in fact. When they stepped outside, he gestured to the harbour. "Do you want to take a walk?"

Kerry slid her hand into his and squeezed. "We could. Or..." She caught his gaze with her own. "We could go back to my place."

He wasn't going to say no. "I'd love to."

They held hands to his truck, their arms brushing, awareness zinging through him of what might come next.

He wanted to taste her, make her feel good. Hold her without having to let her go for a good while.

The conversation on the drive back to Pine Harbour was different. Just as easy, but the pace changed. Less about exploring what they had in common and where they came from, and more about who they are now. Work. Friends. Dating, again, this time about Kerry.

"My career has always come first," she said. "The midwifery program was so intense."

"How long was it?"

"Four years, pretty much year round. And on the job training for a lot of it, all over the province. I think I moved six times, and then another three times after graduating."

"Is that how you see it going in the future?" Owen didn't like the way his chest tightened up. She'd already been here nearly a year. If she moved that often, how long until she headed on to the next place?

But she shook her head. "I think I'll settle here. Jenna's a great work partner, and we've already ramped up to full client loads. She wasn't sure we would, but it was worth it to her to work closer to home. And I'm glad I took the leap with her."

"I'm glad, too."

"Now," she teased.

He shook his head. "I've liked you from the very start, Kerry Humphrey. I promise you that."

"Maybe it was for the best I couldn't see that back when we met." She bit her lower lip and smiled. "You would have been hard to resist if the door was open to friendship from that first meeting."

"That's a hell of a compliment." He laughed. "You were hard to resist even when you didn't like me."

"I liked you," she whispered. "Too much."

Ah, hell. He cleared his throat. "I'm glad we're getting to know each other now."

The last ten kilometres dragged until the turn for Pine Harbour came into sight, his pulse thumping at the promise of being alone.

He followed her up the stairs to her apartment like she was leading him into a dream.

"Do you want something to drink?" She asked as she opened the door and stepped inside, turning on the lights.

Owen waited until the door closed behind him and she'd turned around to look at him, then held out his hand. "I want you."

Instead of coming in for another doorway kiss, she hooked her fingers into his and led him forward, through the narrow and long living room to the bedroom she'd pointed to before. She kicked off her heels, and Owen followed suit, taking off his boots. He should have done that at the door, but she had him in her thrall.

Kerry came to stand in front of him and ran her fingers up and down the line of buttons on his shirt. She was extra little in her bare feet, and he stood still while she explored him. "How do you want me?" she murmured. "Naked?"

A groan ripped from his throat. "Yes."

"All the way naked, or do you want to peel my clothes off little by little?"

She was killing him. "Yes. Both."

She laughed gently. "You have to pick one for the first time."

The first time. He let out a rough breath, relieved there would more of this together. "Let me undress you."

"Can I do the same for you?"

"Please."

Her fingers slid around the top button, touching his bare skin for a split second before moving to the next one. Again and again, she grazed his chest with her nimble touch, undoing him in more ways than one. He stayed where he was until she had his shirt off, then reached for her. His turn, now, and he savoured the act of baring her flesh. He traced the hem of her shirt as he gathered the delicate fabric in his hands, bringing them around her body to carefully lift the shirt up and over her head. Then he held it between them, leaning in for a slow, exploring kiss.

Kerry's kisses matched the way she looked at him. Teasing, curious. Sexy in a way that seemed to have no limit. Each slide of her tongue was erotic in a whole new way, making him bold. He wanted to look at her, spread her out and feast his eyes, but he couldn't back up enough, couldn't let go of her for even a second. His hands drifted to her pants, and she helped him. The fabric gave way and he felt the shape of her. Curves and muscle, dips and valleys of warm skin. Her bottom fit perfectly in his hands, filling his spread wide fingers as he lifted her up and somehow got them on to the bed together.

He lost himself in the taste of her, the sweeping, head-spinning arousal sparked by each deep open-mouthed kiss. She touched him, too, all over. Her fingers lingered on his jaw, then his chest, and headed for his belt when he halted her.

Soon enough. But he needed to slow down, or he'd be inside her and it would be over before he even got a good look at her. "It's been a while," he rasped, stilling her hand with his. He rolled her onto her back and pushed himself up so he was above her. He put his hands on her hips, and she lifted so he could peel off her panties. "Let me just have a minute with you here. God, look at you. You're so pretty."

He liked the way her eyes went warm and soft at the compliment. It was true, though. She was pretty. He liked everything about the way she looked spread out beneath him. The soft flutter at the base of her neck, the deep pink of her lips, flushed and swollen. The bright gaze looking up at him.

It was always her eyes that got him the worst. The way she'd looked at him, really looked at him, when he took Becca to her first appointment. The way she'd watched him through meetings, and every damn time they bumped into each other.

The way her gaze had lingered just long enough in his kitchen to know she was twisted up the same way he was —it had been an invitation then, and it was again now.

"What are you thinking?"

"I like the way you look at me," he murmured. "I always have."

She reached up and pulled him down on top of her, colliding them together for another searing kiss. He chuckled. "I'm trying to take my time here."

Her eyes crinkled. "And I'm trying to get you inside me."

He couldn't resist that. "I have condoms." He grinned and hopped off the bed, which made Kerry laugh. "What?"

"You have the energy of a man who hasn't been laid in some time."

"That's an understatement."

She smiled wickedly. "I know the feeling."

"Has it been a while for you, Ms. Humphrey?"

He crawled back on top of her, protection now in hand.

"Since I moved here," she whispered. *Since they'd met.*

Raw, animalistic hunger surged through him. He kissed her mouth until her lips were swollen, then kept going, tasting her neck, her breasts plump in his hands. She took off her bra and he swirled his tongue around her nipples until they stood proud, then gently pulled on them with his mouth until she was shaking beneath him. He'd planned to fuck her first. He needed to be inside her something fierce, but she'd waited a long time for this, for him, and he didn't think Kerry had been in the habit of denying herself pleasure in the past.

He had months of pleasure to make up for.

He kissed down her belly, loving the way it quivered as he got closer to her thighs, to the lovely, warm centre of her. Her scent made his mouth water, and when her legs fell wide apart, when he saw the dark, tight curls give way to a soft, pink pussy, glistening for him, he forgot all about the condoms and bowed his head for his first taste.

She went taut as soon as his tongue slicked against bare skin. He reached beneath her, bracing his arms under her legs, his hands finding her hips and the curve of her waist. Her back arched as she spread herself wider for him. Inviting him to lick more, suck more. He did. He explored first, then settled in where she seemed to like it best. He went from soft to firm and back to soft. Slow licks. Eager pulls on her clit as she seemed to get closer.

If he could make her come like this, he'd feel like a king. If she came first, it would be okay if he didn't last long once he got inside her, if he lost control. But God, he wanted to feel her come on his cock, too. He wanted it all. He wanted this feeling to last all night, wanted her pleasure to last all night.

He lifted his head. "Tell me what you need."

"Fingers," she said, her eyes dancing. "Put your fingers inside me."

He held her gaze as he touched her. Watched her face as he slid one finger, then two into her tight pussy. Her expression shifted, her eyes got more hooded, and then unfocused, as he found the spots inside her that pushed her closer to the edge. Ducking his head again, he added his mouth. *Come for me*, he thought. He wanted that. It was selfish. He wanted it for her, of course, but he wanted it for himself, too.

It was primal and elemental. The kind of egotistical feeling he might be discomforted by later on, but right now made him feel ten feet tall.

When her thighs shook on either side of his head, he stopped changing it up and stuck with what was working, letting her grind against his face as she got to that peak. Her body clenched up, froze for a beautiful moment, then shuddered back to earth, twitching against his tongue and around his fingers. He stayed with her as her limbs fell wide against the bed, until she sighed and ran her fingers through his hair, and finally spoke. "Wow."

Yep. A God damn ten-foot-tall king, that's what he was.

He pushed himself up to lie next to her. She leaned in and licked his mouth, tasting herself, and his cock surged to extra-hard with a new rush of blood.

"You taste so good," he murmured.

She made a happy sound. "I bet you do, too." Leaning in, she licked his neck, a long, luscious swipe that ended just behind his ear. "Can I taste you, Owen?"

How had he gone thirty-seven years without knowing what it was to have her mouth, wet and hungry against his skin? He would never be the same. What did he taste like to her? "Lick me again," he whispered, his voice hoarse, his plea desperately honest.

"I'll lick you all over."

That thrilled him to his core. The thought of her tongue on his belly, her mouth on his cock. The wicked smile she might flash before she swallowed his length. She moved over him, her hair tickling his body as she used her mouth on his chest, his nipples, his lower belly. When she finally got to his belt, he didn't stop her this time. She undressed him, then perched between his legs and wrapped her lips around his erection.

He'd never felt anything so lovely in his entire life. He'd never *imagined* anything so good as the playful way she used her tongue around his crown. It was hyperbole and truth at the same time. Owen liked sex all right, it felt good. But this wasn't that. This was more, this was steeped in play and mischief and it felt profoundly, deeply intimate.

Warning bells should have been going off in his head. Instead there was a ticker tape parade.

But he didn't want to come like this. Not right now. And Kerry must have read his mind, because she lifted her head. "Condom?"

He took care of it, under her careful and therefore erotic observation, and then she climbed on top. There was a moment just before she took the aching tip of him into her body when she paused and just looked at him, where she locked her gaze on his and held his attention. *Ready?* Oh yeah.

Then she sank down an inch, and Owen's eyes rolled back in his head. Slowly, Kerry rocked her hips, easing him into her. She was tight and hot, and took her time. Her breasts swayed as she rode him, and he reached for her.

Her chest arched into his touch, her nipples hard as diamonds. She clapped her hands onto his, holding on to him as she sped up the pulse of her hips. The soft push of her thighs against his sides was driving him mad in the best way.

As tension built, he eased her down, so she could brace her hands on his shoulders, so her nipples were closer to his mouth—yes—and so he could hold on to her hips, still those soft fucking thighs, and take over.

He thrust into her from below, driving up off the bed as she trembled in his arms. His orgasm suddenly threatened to take over, no stopping it. "Touch yourself," he growled. "Get yourself there."

"I'm there," she whispered, her breath panting to match his. He clamped one hand on her hip, buried the other in her hair, and swallowed her cries as he slammed his cock all the way into her one last time, burying himself deep in her gorgeous pussy as his climax spurted out of him.

Sex would never be the same.

Owen would never be the same. And he wasn't fucking complaining. "Holy hell," he rasped. "That was amazing."

She kissed him, then kissed him again, before sliding off his body and nestling into his side. He grabbed a tissue and dealt with the condom, then hauled her back on top of him. The top of her head fit perfectly on his chest, and he breathed in the scent of her hair, fruity and vanilla. The heavier scent of sex hung on the air, and the two merged together, burning into his mind.

Her fingers slid over his skin, tracing the moon on his arm. He waited for the question—what's the story here?—but it didn't come. When she looked up at him, she smiled, a wild, joyous look. "I like the feel of your skin," she said. "You're strong."

"Strong enough to hold you up in the shower."

She sucked in a delighted breath and he rolled out of bed, then reached for her. She squeaked his name as he hauled her into his arms.

"Strong enough to carry you there, too," he muttered as she buried her face in his neck. God, she felt good against him. Sweet and soft and warm.

Her shower was built for one, so round two was a lot of kissing and touching and being pressed against the wall. Kerry sank to her knees and brought him back to full strength immediately. Once the stars cleared from his eyes, he eased his fingers into her and she rode his hand.

"I don't want you to be sore," he whispered as he pumped into her slowly.

"Worth it," she murmured back.

When she came for the third time, he watched her right up close, savouring the way her lips trembled and her throat worked on her wordless gasps.

He called her beautiful and meant it in the deepest way possible.

But once they climbed out of the shower, he couldn't ignore the time on the clock—not when Kerry glanced at it, not when his internal Dad alarm went off, either. He dried her carefully with a towel as he sat on the edge of her bed.

"This was amazing." She kissed him, soft and lingering, before swaying to her closet and pulling on a t-shirt that barely covered anything. He wanted to drag her back into bed.

But she was getting dressed, a clear sign he had to go.

He had to go. He knew that. He had to go for his own reasons, too. He didn't want to.

"Thank you," he said gruffly.

She came back and touched her fingers to his mouth, tracing the shape of his lips and sending a shiver down his spine. "That was for both of us. I needed it, too."

CHAPTER SIXTEEN

KERRY WOKE UP BEFORE DAWN, thinking about the night before. She rolled over in her bed and imagined Owen's big, warm frame there beside her. She thought about the way he'd kissed her goodnight at the door, at least the tenth kiss between him leaving her bed and actually departing.

He had caught her wrist and kissed the palm of her hand. "I want to see you again. Tomorrow."

"I have indoor soccer practice," she'd said regretfully. "And then an early morning the next day. But soon. I want to see you again, too."

She was positively giddy over him. She was right to say no to a repeat tonight. They needed a little bit of space to absorb how good it had been, and then they would hook-up again on the weekend. Or early next week.

Grabbing her phone, she sent him a quick good morning message. He replied almost instantly.

Kerry: I woke up thinking about last night.
Owen: I'm thinking about it right now.

Kerry: Really.
Owen: Yeah.
Kerry: Are you alone and thinking about it?
Owen: All by myself in bed.
Kerry: Me, too.
Owen: Thinking about what I want to do next
time, too.

She fanned her face, bit her lip, and dove under the covers.

Kerry: Tell me.
Owen: I want to see you strip for me. I want to
come over when you're already naked, too. A
hundred different variations of you undressed are
racing through my mind.
Kerry: Wow.
Owen: It's a nice way to get the day going, that's
for sure.
Kerry: I might stay in bed a little longer. Do some
thinking of my own.
Owen: That's so hot. I want you to show me what
that's like when I see you next.

What had she been thinking, they needed a little bit of space? Bonkers talk. And Owen was *filthy*. Did he know how dirty he was being right now?

Kerry: Hard to text and ... think at the same time.
Owen: You're killing me. Go ... think. Have a beautiful start to the day.

She did just that, and afterward, as her hand lingered

between her legs, she looked up at the ceiling and wondered just what sort of affair she might be getting into with this man. A wonderful one, she knew that already. But what other surprises lay beneath the surface of Owen Kincaid?

That question bounced joyously in her mind all day. By mid-afternoon, she knew she was going to bail on soccer practice. She texted Lore with an excuse, then messaged Owen.

> **Kerry: I've made myself available tonight, if your inquiry as to my company still stands.**
> **Owen: LOL. It stands all right. I can be there at seven.**

She flew through the rest of her clinic work, and once the space was locked up for the night, she danced her way upstairs and into a hot shower. She shaved, and pampered her skin, and then thought about Owen's fantasy. A hundred different variations of her undressed. She could deliver at least one of them tonight.

When he knocked, she raced to the door. The grin on his face and the knowing, heated look in his eyes as he took the fact that she was wearing a barely-buttoned shirt over her bra and panties—and nothing else—made her feel very good about her decision to invite him over. "I thought you had soccer practice," he said as he stepped inside.

She shrugged. "I told them I had a big work project and I had to take a rain-check."

"A big work project?"

"We work together." She paused a beat. "And you're—"

His mouth crashed against hers as he hauled her into his arms. The kiss was wild, all restraint lost as she climbed into his embrace, as he pushed her against the wall. As his hands—those hands, oh, she loved them so much, his strong fingers, *yes*—slid under the fabric of her shirt and up her back.

He had her bra undone before their first kiss broke apart. Her shirt slid to the floor as he tasted her a second time, and by their third kiss, he had one of those beautiful hands in her panties, cupping her pussy.

She *really* loved his fingers. Heat made her head swim as he stroked her, featherlight and teasing at first, then more deliberate. Getting her ready to be fucked, because they both knew what this was.

"Are you sore from yesterday?"

She smiled as she shook her head. Not at all.

He pulled a condom from his back pocket, and she laughed out loud. It was on the edge of hysterical, but she didn't care how she sounded. Owen could know how much she wanted him. That was okay.

She pulled at his shirt, and he got the clue. He peeled it off as she worked on his belt then unbuttoned his jeans. She worked her fingers into his boxers so she could wrap her hand around his heavy, warm length.

"I needed you all day," she admitted, her pulse pounding. They needed to lose the rest of their clothes and maybe find a flat surface. The floor would do. They'd made it all the way to her bed the first time, they didn't need to pretend to be polite anymore.

He worked one finger into her as she stroked him, then he added another. "I want you," he whispered. "Right here. Is that okay?"

What kind of a question was that? "Uh huh."

He yanked her panties down her hips, and she let go of him to help. By the time the scrap of cotton was on the floor, he had the condom rolled on and was looming over her.

She shivered as he reached for her, as he cupped her face and kissed her with bruising intensity. She shook as he wrapped his arm around her hips and hoisted her into the air, up against the wall.

"Owen," she gasped, his name a plea and a question wrapped into one. So by *right here*, he meant literally, against the wall.

Oh, yes.

"I've never done this," he growled. "Hold on tight."

If he hadn't said that, she wouldn't have known. He was strong and sure as he found her slick and ready for him. He notched his cock against her entrance, then pushed in, finding space inside her body that hadn't existed a moment before. Not enough space, of course. He was big and needed to work his way in, but he did that as he held her against the wall. Sure, even thrusts, his thighs working beneath them to make her gasp over and over again.

She clung to him—her arms around his neck, her legs around his waist—but she didn't need to. He had her. She held on tight for other reasons. Because he hadn't done this before, because it was a gift how much he wanted to take her right here inside her door, up against the wall.

Because it had never been this good, this raw, with anyone else. He did things to her she couldn't even properly name.

She closed her eyes and rode him like the worked-up bull he was. Her fiery, fierce man, all pent up and needy. She didn't usually orgasm from penetration alone, but the mind was a powerful aphrodisiac, and that image—of need, of Owen being so much bigger than her, the way he was holding her against the wall, the desperation of *right here*—propelled her toward a climax with shocking ease. The coil tightened and her clit throbbed, getting harder and more sensitive each time Owen bottomed out, the push of his body amping up the sensations triggered by the thick drag of his cock inside her.

How many ways could she make this happen? What magic words could she text to him and he would just appear for her, hard and ready to bury himself in her body? *I've been touching myself, I'm wet already. The door's unlocked, let yourself in and see if you can find me.* It could be a gloriously playful winter ahead of them.

What else hadn't he done?

His mouth opened against her neck, his lips silently whispering her name. *Kerry.* She felt it as much as heard it. Breathing his name back, she let her mind fracture into pieces of desire. His cock inside her. Her need. Fantasies. The hard grip of his hands. Secrets. Falling, spiralling. The heaviness of her breasts against his chest, the way his mouth had felt there the night before. Owen's head between her legs.

With a cry, she came, her climax surprising her even though it had been right there already. Owen followed with a guttural cry, his body tensing up as he pinned her against the wall. He twitched deep in her belly, and her clit spasmed again in response.

Right there, up against the wall.

She closed her eyes and dragged in one breath, then another. Holy shit.

Owen's arms shook as he braced her against the wall. He pulled out, then set her down. He exhaled roughly and braced his forearm next to her head, then gave her a bashful look. "That was fun. Sorry I didn't buy you dinner first."

She giggled. "I wanted this first. But I was going to make myself a sandwich. Do you want to join me?"

He tugged up his jeans. "Let me get cleaned up and then I'll help you make them."

THE THIRD TIME they had sex it was another booty call, this one in the late afternoon. "I swear to God, I want to take you on another date," he said as she let him into her apartment.

"Two busy schedules." She shrugged. "Take off your clothes, I want to see you touch yourself."

"I am the luckiest man in the world."

Forty-five minutes later, as Owen lifted his head triumphantly from between her thighs, Kerry was pretty sure *she* was the lucky one. He'd given her the show she wanted, then gave her a bonus second orgasm for being such a good masturbation buddy.

Kerry had never had so much fun in a single week. Dates could come in time, as their schedules allowed. She was happy they could squeeze in this time together wherever it fit.

Owen sprawled back in her bed, the sheet tangled loosely over his legs, Kerry tangled over the rest of him. Her hair was spread over his shoulder as she rested her cheek on his chest. Her fingers traced up and down the landscape of his torso.

"Tell me something fun," she murmured. "Something else you want to do."

"What?"

"You said, uh…" She squirmed around so she could look up at him. Her mouth curved into a joyful smile. "Right before you came, you said, 'Cross *that* off my list.'"

"I did not." Owen frowned. "Did I?"

"Oh yeah. You growled it, right at the peak of abandon." She winked at him.

"What is that wink for?" He laughed. "Peak of abandon." Then his eyes went wide. "*The Lady Loves a Necromancer.* You read the book."

"Of course I did," she said brightly. Then she slid her hand lower down his belly, making him shiver. "Anyway, back to the topic at hand. What is this list, and what else can we cross off it?"

He shuddered as her fingers skated down the sensitive crease between his leg and his balls. "You're not a bucket list score."

She paused. "I wouldn't mind. I take that as a compliment."

He caught her wrist and flipped her onto her back, dragging her hand up the bed so her arm was safely where he could see it—and also revealing all of her delicate spots for him to reciprocate the intimate teases. She squirmed, and he let go. "Stop distracting me, and I'll tell you. It's not a sex list."

"Ooh." She was so intrigued. "But you do have a list?"

"Sort of. It was more of a general plan than a list. I, uh, called it my Great Bachelor Plan. For life once Becca moved out, but then that didn't happen. Wild, happy sex was on it. What we've been doing definitely qualifies. But that was the only sex thing on it, I swear."

"It's okay, I have a sex list."

His eyebrows shot up. "You do?"

She laughed. "Of course. I kind of thought everyone who likes sex did."

"I don't."

"Do you maybe a little, and you put other stuff on it to cover up what a filthy, dirty, amazing romp in the sheets you are?"

He groaned. "No. Although…amazing?"

"Truly exceptional."

"Wow."

She poked his chest with her finger. "What else was on it?"

"Tell me one of your things, first."

She thought about it. Something on her x-rated wish list. "I've never been skinny dipping. And if there was a way to safely have sex in public, but not actually risk violating someone else's right to not see me have sex…" She laughed. "That kind of ruins it as a point on the list, but I can't help it."

He tangled his fingers in her hair and gave a gentle tug. "Never apologize for being thoughtful."

"It wasn't an apology," she pointed out, sticking out her tongue. "There, I gave you two."

"You've never been skinny dipping?"

"Nope."

"The lake's too cold now, but if you're still speaking to me next summer…" He trailed off.

She bit her lip. Next summer was a long way off.

"Never mind," he said.

"No." She pushed herself up to sit. "It's okay. Should we talk about…whatever this is? I mean, are we…are you…do you…"

He joined her in sitting, and set his hands on her upper arms. "I'm good. I'm happy just being with you. But if you want to talk about…"

She laughed. "Neither of us can say the sentence out loud. That's probably a sign that we're both focused on the here and now, right?"

"Right."

"Can we make a deal?" She straightened her spine and tried her best to look serious, and not nervous, but they were both naked and they'd tripped into a Relationship Talk far too soon into their fling. "I want to know more about your Great Bachelor Plan, and I think we can talk about my wish list, too, and we agree that everything could happen on a hypothetical timeline separate from however long we're sleeping together."

He held out his hand. "Deal."

She slid her fingers over his and shook. "Skinny dipping next summer. That's my share."

"I've never unplugged for an entire weekend. No pager, no phone, no kid responsibilities. Maybe camping or a trip to the city, but phone *off*."

His was so wholesome compared to hers. And also something he should have been able to have already. "You've never done that?"

"No. Time away from Becca was time for work."

"Vacation?"

"Becca time."

"Oh, wow." She pumped her arm. "Let's make that happen for you. What else?"

He grinned. "I want to smoke a joint."

She giggled. "Good. I was worried your list was too wholesome for me to handle."

"Have you ever?"

"Oh yeah. College. Whew. But not in many years." She thought about her list. "All of mine are variations on the exhibitionism theme. I want to record myself having sex, but I don't want that video out there, ever. You know?"

He nodded solemnly. "Masks."

"What?"

"Masks are the obvious solution there. I'm game."

"You are not."

He shrugged. "Sure. You use a burner phone, not hooked up to the cloud in any way, put the masks on before you start recording, and wear clothing over anything identifying."

"Like your tattoos." She blinked at him. "This plan sounds like it's been tested."

He shook his head. "Not by me. But some of the shit I hear about at work lands and I file it away. Just in case." He cleared his throat. "A lot of my list is big boy toys. Don't judge me."

"I would never. Like what?"

"A home gym. As long as I've been an adult, every room in my house has been filled with growing people. One day, they'll finally be gone, and I want to have a room that's nothing but weights and a treadmill, and I don't have to workout with young guys who drop weights with horrible clanging sounds that make me think they're breaking my building."

She giggled. "You work out at the station now?"

"Yeah."

"Sounds horrible," she said solemnly.

"I warned you my list is selfish."

"It's not."

"I haven't even gotten to the truly extravagant stuff yet. Like, I sort of want to buy a four-wheeler."

A place to pump iron in peace and quiet. A giant machine to ride around. Really good sex, a weekend to himself. It was the wish list of a college kid, looking forward to the independence a full-time job would bring him. Almost two decades delayed, and now delayed again. Kerry's heart ached for that kid, this man, who still worried he shouldn't want anything fun in his life. "That's amazing," she said softly. "That sounds like a really good time."

"I want to clarify, that the wild, happy sex on my list was specifically, a weekend spent naked with a woman. So we haven't done that yet."

"Not yet." She kissed him. "But we will."

From her bedside table, his phone vibrated. He sighed. "Real life calls. Would you grab that for me?"

She handed it over. He didn't roll away as he checked it. He stayed where he was, like it had better be pretty important if he was going to get out of her bed, and she liked that feeling a lot.

"One of my brothers," he rumbled, looking at the screen. He tapped into the message app. Right above the most recent message was a photo she recognized—Owen holding Charlie in the hospital, right after the delivery. Her heart did a funny ping-pong thing as he read the newest message, but all she could see was Owen and his grandson, the wee little brand-new person she had just delivered.

"Huh," Owen said. She snapped her attention to the message he was showing her. "It's Josh."

Josh: I've got big news. Coming into town tomorrow. Owen, can I crash at your house for a few weeks? Bought a place but it'll take some work to be habitable.

Kerry didn't know much about Josh, but this sounded exciting. "Which brother is this?"

"Josh is a mechanic. He's worked on the racing circuit for a decade, down in the States."

"That's cool." If Kerry was remembering correctly, the other brother who left home was a pilot. She wondered how Owen felt about the adventurous careers of his brothers, and if that had any impact on his secret desire for a more adventurous personal life. "He bought a place, sight unseen?"

"That's a very Josh thing to do. It's probably a terrifying shack, but he's real good with his hands. He'll fix it up."

As they talked, more bubbles appeared.

Adam: Way to keep a secret, bro! My place or Will's might be better. Owen's guest room was turned into a nursery.
Will: What Adam said. This is exciting!

Owen let out a sigh of relief, which made Kerry laugh, and added his own message.

Owen: My couch is available, always, but yeah, Will's house might be more comfortable.
Josh: Cool. Thanks. I'm in Ohio for the night. See you in the morning.

"I guess you're going to be busy over the next few days," she said as he closed the messages app. "We better get in a little more quality time before you leave."

"I'll sneak away," Owen promised. "With Josh in town, they won't even notice that I'm gone."

CHAPTER SEVENTEEN

OWEN COULD NOT HAVE BEEN MORE wrong about his spending time with Kerry going under anyone's radar.

The first thing Becca told Adam after he arrived was that her dad had gone on at least three dates with the midwife. Owen willed himself not to burst into flames as his internal narrator corrected her. One date and two sex-filled visits to Kerry's apartment, but it was best for all of them if his daughter thought he was keeping things wholesome.

"You've been spending a lot of time with Kerry, huh?" Adam went in for the high-five, which pained Owen to the core. He held up his hand reluctantly, and his brother hooted. Out loud. "Way to go. I thought that was all secret still."

"You knew?" Becca turned on Owen. "He knew?"

"He had guesses, which I told him were none of his business because Kerry and I were just friends."

"Were." Adam waggled his eyebrows. "Past tense."

"Shut up."

The rumble of Will's car out front was a blessed change

of subject. And then, right on his heels, there was another rumble. Becca squealed and bounced Charlie in her arms. "That's Uncle Josh, I bet! Let's go see what he's driving, it sounds deadly."

She wasn't wrong. And sure enough, behind Will's Duster was a burly '71 Cutlass sedan. The rebuilt car gleamed. Adam whistled. "Holy shit. Look at that."

The last time Josh had come home, a few years earlier, he'd had an ugly vintage Mustang, which he sold on his way back south. This was a sweet upgrade. It looked like he'd done some serious customization on it, too.

By the time they got to the cars, Will was already under the hood.

"Man, it's good to see you," Owen said, holding out his hand to Josh.

His brother took it and pulled him, clapping him on the back. "Will says he's still having trouble with his car."

Owen laughed. "That's not the only reason we're happy to have you home."

Becca came in for a hug next, which made Charlie cry, and that made Adam laugh. "He likes his mom and his grandpa, and that's about it."

"Grandpa," Josh said, looking Owen up and down. "That's kind of wild."

"I'm getting used to the name." Owen gestured to the house. "You want to come in?"

Josh glanced at the watch on his wrist. "Actually, I want to show you something. Can we go for a drive?"

Adam hopped in with Josh, Will drove himself—just in case he broke down—and Owen took Becca and Charlie in his truck.

Josh led them on a merry chase through the neighbourhood, slowing on Main Street before speeding up again and heading down the hill to the harbour. He parked in the abandoned lot across the road from the water and rolled down his window. Will parked and got out of his car, and Owen pulled up next to Josh to find out what the heck was going on.

His middle brother glanced at his watch again, then pointed out to the water—and then higher, to the sky, where a plane appeared from the north. A float plane, and Owen's heart swelled at the surprise.

"We're just waiting for one more person to join us," Josh said.

Seth.

They all piled out, Becca putting Charlie in the stroller because he'd fallen asleep on the drive, and after crossing the road, they watched as the plane circled the harbour, then came in for the landing.

Pine Harbour had a much smaller marina than neighbouring towns, just a few slots. Seth taxied to the end of the row and tied up there. Owen glanced at Will, who looked just as surprised as he was. Will grinned at him. "Sometimes the kids are okay, eh?"

"What a good surprise." He cleared his throat and lifted his voice. "Adam! How long have you known about this?"

"Only as long as you," their youngest brother hollered back. "This is all Josh."

Something in Owen's chest shifted. It was more than just having all of them home at once, which was a truly rare event. It was Josh, the rebel who ran away, organizing a family reunion out of the blue. It was Seth walking down the dock like something out of Top Gun North. It was his brothers coming back, without cajoling or bribing, to this town they'd both flipped the bird to many years before.

He strode ahead of the others, meeting Seth at the entrance to the marina.

"You had to make an entrance," Owen said.

"You love it."

Owen laughed. "I really do. The plane's looking great."

"Yeah. She's getting her miles in, too."

"Work good?"

"Great. Busy. Thinking of hiring another pilot, too. How about you? Keeping busy?"

Seth was Owen's original secret keeper. His middle brother had been the first person he'd told when he found out Rachel was pregnant. Fifteen-year-old Seth had pulled a bottle of vodka out from under his bed. Owen didn't even bother to try to give him shit for it. They'd each done a shot, Seth had told him it would be okay, and the next morning, his wild but loving brother crossed the parking lot at school and gave Rach a big, tight hug.

Owen still carried guilt for that shot of vodka to this day. Big brother feelings were wild like that. But he couldn't wait to tell Seth about Kerry. About how wild she made him feel, and how good *that* felt. If anyone might understand, it would be Seth. Now wasn't the time, but soon. "We'll have a drink tonight and I'll fill you in. I've met a woman."

Since there were no secrets in their family, everyone arrived right behind him as he said that. Becca clearly wanted to spill all the dirt. He gave her a Dad Look, and she brought Charlie forward instead. "He's sleeping," she explained to Seth. "He does that a lot right now, at least during the day. If you stay at our place, be prepared for middle of the night company on the couch."

"They can both stay at my place," Will interjected. "All right, Josh. Where to next on our caravan of surprises?"

Josh turned and pointed. They all followed the line of his arm, to the old convenience store and gas bar at the corner of Main Street and Harbour Road, shuttered for at least five years. "That's mine. I bought it last week."

Everyone erupted.

"What are you going to do with it?"

"What do you mean you *bought it*, like you're going to live there?"

"Are you opening a store?"

"What—"

Owen put his fingers between his lips and let out a piercing whistle.

Everyone stopped talking.

He gestured to Josh. "Go on."

"I'm not re-opening the convenience store, or opening a gas station again. They took the tanks out years ago. But it is still zoned as a garage, and there's an apartment in the back. I'm going to do custom commissions on hot rods and muscle car rebuilds. Pine Harbour Custom Garage has a certain ring to it, don't you think?"

Owen loved it. "Amazing. But what happened to the racing circuit?"

Josh shrugged. "It got old."

There was more to the story than that, but maybe that too was a story for later.

Owen looked at his brothers, all home just a couple of weeks before Canadian Thanksgiving. What a gift. "This calls for a celebration. Let's go back to my place and fire up the grill."

———

THEY SPENT the afternoon at Owen's, soaking up the sun in his backyard. Another week or two and the leaves would start to change colour, the nights would get cold, and they'd start to batten down the hatches for winter. It turned out Charlie liked Seth a lot, and he had his fourth nap of the day on his great-uncle's chest.

They took turns talking about work. Adam didn't bring up fire school, which surprised Owen and he made a mental note to ask him about that later. Becca dug up her old art kit, and Josh sketched out some of his ideas for the garage.

"I want to be in there before it gets cold, so the next couple of weeks are going to be a lot of hustle to get the apartment safe for occupancy."

"Just how uninhabitable is it?" Will asked.

Josh made a face. "It was cheap, let's leave it at that. It's not condemned, if that helps."

It did—barely. Owen thought about the money he'd set aside for the home gym and the four-wheeler. He thought about Kerry, and how it had felt to confess his secret wish list to her—and how, maybe, now he didn't care about it quite that much.

He could rent a four-wheeler for a weekend. "Are you open to investors? Maybe we could hire Jake Foster to help you get it cleaned up real quick."

Josh shook his head. "I appreciate the thought—I do —but I've got some money saved up. Enough for a couple of cars to get started, and I think I might be able to barter some work, too. I'll find guys who can help. Adam, I bet you've got some army guys looking for work, yeah?"

"Yeah, probably do."

From behind a pair of sunglasses he'd donned on the

drive back, Josh lifted his eyebrows at Owen confidently. "I'm good. But thanks."

Owen raised his beer in salute. His brothers had been grown for a good long time already, but every time that was underscored, it still took him by surprise. It was time for him to stop assuming they needed him.

After dinner, they left Becca and Charlie to a quiet night in with Netflix while the brothers headed over to Will's house. He lived closer to the edge of town, in a new build home, with a big basement and a spare room. Owen and Adam caught a ride with Josh, so they could walk (or stumble) home at the end of the night.

Probably the last time Owen had had more than two drinks in a night was the last time they were all together for Christmas a few years back. He talked about Kerry a bit to his brothers. But there was no opportunity for him to talk to Seth one on one, and every time the topic of relationships came up, Josh changed it to cars, travel, or music. Anything but women, and they all got the message loud and clear.

Owen didn't mind. He had someone else he could share his new thoughts with. He left before Adam did, and he called Kerry on his solitary walk home.

"Hello, stranger."

"It's been twenty-eight hours," he said.

"A lifetime," she teased. "How are your brothers?"

He filled her in on the day's news.

"That's so cool! How long is Seth in town?"

"Two more days. We're all going to work on the garage tomorrow, and then he flies out the next morning."

"Do you want to come over then?"

"I have to work that day…" He trailed off, trying to picture his calendar in his head. "Beer's making my brain a bit foggy. I'll check when I get home. I think I'm on four straight days, so I could do a late dinner?"

"Sounds nice. Where do you want to go?"

"I was thinking Mac's. Would that be okay with you?"

"Sure. Less driving time, more talking time."

He let out a sigh of relief. "And then if you don't mind company..."

She laughed gently in his ear. "Oh, Owen. I never mind that kind of company. It's a date."

CHAPTER EIGHTEEN

TWO DAYS LATER, the brothers all crowded into a booth at Mac's at six in the morning for one last breakfast together before Seth flew north again.

Owen spotted Hayden in the kitchen, his bandana-covered head bopping back and forth. Owen had thought Hayden would have quit, as the summer was over and hockey season had begun again. His coach couldn't be happy about the split focus. One thing for a junior hockey player to grab a job in the summer, another to take their focus away from training and playing during the winter.

When Hayden brought a plate of food to the pass-through window, he caught sight of the Kincaids, and his mouth pulled tight.

Owen's last thought before he was pulled into a conversation about the garage was that the little shit better not spit in his food.

After dropping Seth at the marina and waiting for him to take off, Owen headed to work. One of Kerry's suggestions at the interagency working group had been to create simulation cards health workers could use for micro-training sessions on the job. He wanted to carve out time in his morning to work on that.

But the schedule came first, so he plowed through that. Then he grabbed his notebook and headed into the garage. He thought if he maybe sat in the back of a bus, he might be able to sketch out what kind of conversations he wanted his paramedics to practice more.

He was nearly done when Dani poked her head around the door. "Hey, boss. You've got a visitor."

Owen hopped out of the ambulance and stuck his head around the side. He scowled when he saw it was Hayden. He jerked his head to the side of the garage bay. "My office."

To his credit, the kid didn't flinch. He nodded stoically and followed Owen.

Once they were at his office, Owen kicked the door shut, because he wasn't in a mood to be nice to the little shit. Not that he ever was. "What do you want?"

"I saw you at the restaurant this morning."

"Yeah. I saw you, too. I was surprised. I thought it was just a summer gig."

"That was the plan."

"What happened?"

"I f— I messed up."

"With the team?"

Hayden shook his head. "With Becca."

Owen sighed. "This isn't the place, son. I'm not the person you need to talk to about this."

"I think you are. I want to show you that I mean it when I say I want Becca. And our baby."

"The thing is, that's easy to say. Harder to show in your actions."

"No." Hayden's voice cracked, but he didn't move. "No, sir, it's not. It's scary to say, to be honest."

"You've jerked her around all year. I thought when you showed up in the hospital, and then I found you *in my house* in the middle of the God damn night, that meant you got it."

"It did. It does."

"You're running hot and cold on my daughter, and I don't like it."

"Not any more. I'm all in now."

"Is that why you came here? To make empty promises? And you'll do it again, if she gives you another chance. When you do, I'm going to remind her that you've done this before."

"You should. But you won't need to."

Who the hell was this man child to be so sure of himself? "Why are you *here*, talking to me, instead of talking to my daughter?"

Hayden swallowed hard. "It's not instead of. She comes first. Charlie comes first, I mean." His face threatened to crumple, but he pulled it together. "For me, that's true. Becca and Charlie first."

"You have a funny way of showing it. You blew her off for a bush party."

"She told you that." Hayden nodded. "Of course she did."

"She tells me other things, too. She tells me how important your hockey career is." Becca hadn't said that in months, but Owen was feeling righteous now.

"I'm leaving the team."

Owen's mouth fell open. "What?"

"Hockey is not more important than her, than Charlie. I

made the wrong choices for a while there because of some misguided sense of being a certain kind of man. But that's not why I'm here. I'm here because I *did* talk to Becca first, and she told me to come and see you. She said, if I could stand here and take your shit, she'd hear me out." Hayden paled. "I don't think what you're saying is shit, sir. That's—"

"I recognize my daughter's words, don't worry," Owen said dryly. Confusion twisted inside him. "She told you to come here?"

"No." Hayden's Adam's apple bobbed up and down. "She said I should talk to you. She meant asking to talk to you at home or something. I decided to come and see you here because you were in your uniform this morning and I didn't want to put it off another day. Don't get her in trouble—"

"Son, you have a wild misunderstanding of my relationship with my daughter if you think I'd get her in trouble for encouraging you to be bold. I'm a bear, not a monster. And Becca's a grown-up now. So are you. Your *getting in trouble* days should be behind you."

That shut Hayden up, which gave Owen a moment to think.

Becca wanted Hayden to come in front of Owen and say a few things. Why? He didn't love the answer that immediately came to his mind. He needed to talk to his daughter—and he had a date with Kerry tonight. Something in his schedule would have to give, and it would be his social life.

He took a deep breath, hating the way his neck got tight and his back teeth clenched down. It was what it was. Kerry would understand. And maybe his conversation with Becca wouldn't take long.

Hayden shifted awkwardly in the silence. "She thinks you hang the moon in the sky," he finally said.

Owen's throat tightened up. That had been a thing when she was little. He wore it on his skin, because he wanted so badly to be that man for her as she grew up. He would do anything for her, provide anything she needed. Hang the moon in the sky and decorate it with diamonds. "Won't be long before Charlie thinks the same of you," he said gruffly. "If you hang in there with him."

What he wanted to say was, *I've been in your shoes, kid. I've done the right thing. There was nothing right about it in the end.* But Owen wouldn't have heard that back then. Hell, he couldn't bring himself to think there had been another option. He would have married Rachel even if present-day Owen had travelled back in time and showed him it would end badly.

He didn't regret his marriage.

He regretted that he couldn't find enough love in his heart to make it work. That he had to watch her be happy without him, happier still with another man, while he twisted with worry and self-doubt, and his own efforts to find happiness had left him feeling empty time after time.

Empty and dangerous.

Would Hayden leave Becca in a few years, go away to school to better himself, and take a stranger home every night to try and make himself feel something?

Would it take him another fifteen years to be open to a real relationship?

God help him if he did. But Owen had never had to stand in front of Rachel's father and prove himself, either. They may be walking in similar paths, but they weren't the same person. Owen hadn't had a bunch of dickheads making life hard for him, for one thing.

"Hayden."

"Yes, sir?"

"Don't call me that. I don't deserve that. Call me Owen." He cleared his throat. "Just be honest. With yourself, with my daughter." He took a leap. "With your coach, too. Be honest. If you need backup for that, I'll be there. I bet your dad would, too. I hope he would. If your teammates are being dicks to you about having a baby, that's on them, and I think your coach will want to know. Am I reading too much into the situation?"

Hayden's mouth tightened up. "No. That's accurate."

"Son, if you're done with hockey, that's one thing. If you're leaving it against your true desire, that's another. Has Becca told you to give up hockey?"

Hayden hung his head.

Owen knew the answer was no. His daughter wouldn't. She was stubborn and fearless, and as Rachel had said almost a year before, she was also Hayden's biggest fan. "I have to get back to work, but I'm glad you stopped by. I hope we can talk again."

As soon as Hayden left, Owen texted two people. First, his daughter to let her know he'd had a visitor and wanted to talk about it over dinner. Then he glanced at his watch. It was lunch time. Maybe...

Owen: What are you up to today?

Kerry: I'm in the clinic. Currently having lunch in between appointments.

Owen: Are you alone?

Kerry: Why Mr. Kincaid, what are you suggesting? (That's a yes, by the way)

Owen: I'll swing by for a few minutes.

She met him at the back door, and as soon as she saw his face, she let out a sigh. "Are you okay?"

"Do I look as twisted up as I feel?" He huffed and pulled her in for a hug. "Yes, I'm okay." He pressed his forehead against hers. "Can I take a rain-check on dinner tonight? I need to talk to Becca about something."

She kissed him on the mouth. "Of course. Was that all you wanted?"

Not at all. "I have twenty-three minutes." His fingers tangled with hers, bringing her hand to his chest. "I thought we could spend at least seventeen of them making out."

———

BY FOUR IN THE AFTERNOON, Kerry was done with her day. And hungry, because her lunch had been abandoned for something even better than a salad. Since she was suddenly on her own for dinner, she headed to Mac's. Apparently late afternoon was the time to come. The parking lot was nearly empty and inside she had her pick of booths.

In the corner was Adam Kincaid, brooding over a cup of coffee. The twisted look on his face reminded her of his oldest brother, and her heart softened.

"Do you want some company?"

He glanced up, ever so quick, then glared back at his coffee. This wasn't like him, at least not any version of Adam she'd ever seen before.

"Sorry for interrupting."

But before she could step back, he jerked his head up again. "No, stay." He dragged in a long, sobering breath. "I'd love company."

She slid into the opposite side of the booth and grabbed a menu. "Can I ask what has you all out of sorts?"

"Can I swear you to secrecy?"

That made her pause. Could he? "Secret from whom?"

"My brother." Adam held her gaze. It was a knowing look, but also an understanding one. It wasn't a secret that she was seeing Owen.

Just how tender her heart was towards him, though… that might be a secret still. But if she read between the lines correctly, it was one Adam had her number on. She took a deep breath. "It depends. Is it about Becca?"

Adam shook his head vigorously. "Hell no."

"What's going on?"

He shoved a folded piece of paper across the table at her. When she opened it, it took her a minute to process what she was reading. "You've been accepted into an accelerated fire school program?"

"It starts in January. I applied late, and was sure I was way down the waiting list. But…" He wiped his hand across his mouth, then gave a shrug, his expression incredulous. "I guess I got lucky."

"Adam, this is great." She set the letter down and looked at him, really looked at him. "Isn't it great? Does Owen not know that you applied?"

He made a face. "No. He knows I want it, though. But I didn't think I'd get in until next year, and now suddenly it's around the corner, and…"

"Ah." She wasn't sure she should get involved in Kincaid business. The old Kerry wouldn't have. But if this was yet another thing Owen would be dealing with, she wanted to know. "Are you going to tell him soon?"

"As soon as I work up the courage." He slid the menu

over to her, ending that part of the conversation. "I've already ordered."

She flipped it open, but her thoughts were stuck on all the different worries Owen had to juggle. It was a minor miracle they'd had so much time together in the last week, but that wouldn't be standard.

I miss you during the day. He'd said it, but she was thinking it at the same time. He'd stirred up feelings she didn't know she was capable of having. This fling was already deeper and more intense than she usually allowed her dating life to get, and it had happened in such a short time—if you didn't count the months of longing when he'd been off-limits and grumpy.

Maybe she needed to shift her perspective on the start and end dates of their relationship. It wasn't like they started at zero when he asked her out. That had been a culmination in and of itself—taking their relationship to the next level, a healthier, happier one to be sure.

"Do you know what you want?"

Kerry snapped the menu closed. Not only did she not know what she wanted, she was terrified to look at that question too closely just in case she didn't like the answer. But the waitress wasn't talking about Owen. Food—she needed an answer about food. "What's the soup of the day?" Kerry asked, trying to buy some time and play it cool.

"Tomato bisque."

"I'll take a cheeseburger—Swiss cheese, please—and a Greek salad on the side."

"Sounds good. Anything to drink?"

"Lemonade?"

"On it."

The waitress left, and Kerry glanced across the table at

Adam. "Is that why you weren't all over Lore's plan for a co-ed indoor soccer team for the winter? You had high hopes you wouldn't be here?"

He looked impressed. "You have a sharp memory. I said that once, months ago."

"Soccer has become the central tenant of my social life, what can I say?"

He nodded. "That was why. But you might be able to convince my brother Josh to play." He paused. "Or Owen?"

The thought of Owen negotiating the politics of a team sport made her giggle.

"No, not Owen," Adam said.

She shook her head. "He's got a lot on his plate, anyway."

Adam frowned. "Not that much. Don't be scared off."

That surprised her. "I'm not."

"You're good for him."

"I'm—" She was speechless, that's what she was. She hadn't really been prepared for the conversation to go there. It was very small town, and she suddenly felt naked.

Adam read that immediately, and leaned back. "He hasn't said anything. It's just an observation."

"One that maybe you've talked about with others?" She asked it lightly, but she wanted to know.

Adam grinned. "In passing."

In her head, Kerry heard Lore telling her it was never boring on the peninsula. That had certainly proven true.

She glanced toward the kitchen. "My cheeseburger could arrive any minute now, I'm just saying."

Adam laughed, and at least that was better than the tight, sad face she'd seen when she walked in.

CHAPTER NINETEEN

WHEN OWEN GOT HOME, Becca was in her room. It smelled like dinner was under way, something warm and fragrant, and he could hear his daughter talking to her son.

"Yes, you show me how you can stretch. Just like that. Kick those legs. Can I get a smile? Can I make you smile? Awww. I love you, too. Yes I do. Yes I—" Owen didn't want to interrupt the cuteness, but Becca sensed his presence in her doorway. She glanced over at him. "Hey."

"Dinner smells good."

She nodded. "I think it will be."

"You've been making some amazing things lately." Why did this conversation feel so awkward? Owen hated how the words clogged in his throat. *You're all grown up. Suddenly. I see you.*

"I paid attention last year when I was working banquets. Some things stuck."

"You think maybe you'll want to try cooking as a career?" Even as he asked it, Owen knew it was the wrong question.

Becca gazed down at Charlie. "I don't know."

A polite answer, or a deflecting one, because he was pretty sure she did know—she had hopes for Hayden to carry the load.

No point ignoring the elephant in the room. "Hayden came to see me today."

She nodded. "He told me."

"You didn't tell me you wanted me to talk to him."

"And have you charge over to his parents' house and cause a big thing?" Becca shook her head. "No. And he needed to do it on his own. He's really struggling, Dad. But he's being honest about it, and I dunno, but I think that's worth something."

You don't know. That's exactly the problem. But Owen didn't want to shut down the conversation even before it got started. "Tell me more."

"He wants to get a full-time job and give up hockey."

"He doesn't want to give up hockey, Bec."

Her face twisted. "He feels like he should."

Owen knew that feeling well. "He could. But he will always wonder what would be."

"If he gets a job, we can get an apartment together." There was so much hope in her voice, it killed Owen.

"Is that what he's told you he wants?"

Another nod.

"It'll be hard."

"I know."

"Is he going to try to get more hours at Mac's?"

"No." She played with the blanket as Charlie squirmed. "That was a temporary thing. He has to get out of his contract with the team first before he starts job hunting."

"How temporary? He was there this morning when your uncles and I went in for breakfast."

"Frank is letting him work a few more weeks. I don't know exactly. We haven't made a firm plan yet, it's just talk. I told him, I wouldn't make a plan until he got things straight with you."

It wasn't for Owen to give the green-light to their relationship, though. It couldn't be his responsibility, even if he wanted it to be. He always wanted to shoulder the risk others took, that was a hard lesson he'd had to learn. But this was Becca and Hayden's call to make, not his. "It was good of him to come and talk things out with me, but you two need to be clear on what you want. I told him that, too. I told him he needed to be honest with everyone. Have you thought about what might happen if he doesn't get a job? What if he focused on hockey until it ran its course?"

"He won't pick hockey over Charlie." Her chin jutted out, her eyes glittering. "He's Charlie's father."

"He's hurt you more than once."

That stopped her, but only for a moment. "Maybe Charlie and I need our own space either way."

"I would understand that, if that's what you want."

"It is. For me, and Charlie, and Hayden."

She was so steadfast in her support of him. Owen shook his head gently. "That kid doesn't deserve you."

"That *kid* is the father of my child, so enough with the growling." His daughter's voice sharpened to a knife point, and Owen froze. "He came to you and told you he fucked up. He's doing the work to be there for us. But more importantly, I want to live with him. I want to give him that chance, and I don't need you to judge me for it."

Owen had never been more uncomfortable in his over-sized body than in this moment.

"You wanted more than this for me." She looked at him, square in the eye, as she said that.

He couldn't lie to her. "Yeah. I did."

The right corner of her mouth lifted in a sad smile. "This is all I want for myself right now."

"That might change in the future."

"Did it change for you?" She might as well have asked him if she wasn't enough for him.

His inhale was rough and ragged. He didn't want to answer that question.

"Dad, I don't feel shortchanged by this life we have. For a while now I've wondered if you thought I did, if you thought maybe you didn't give me enough of something. But... Do *you* feel shortchanged?"

He couldn't breathe.

And he couldn't tell her to stop. This was her life to examine, too. His life was her life. Fuck.

"It's okay."

A tear slid down his face. Fuck. "No it's not."

"Yeah." Her voice went quiet. Impossibly soft. "You're free now. You can do whatever you want."

"Becca, I like having you and Charlie here." It was the God's honest truth, and it took him by surprise. He didn't doubt she wouldn't believe him. He hadn't given her any reason to.

"But you also want your own space. You've never had that. I see you." Her soft words were an echo of his own observation when he got home. For so long, it had been just the two of them, a dyad surrounded by a larger, loving family. But when it came right down to it, day in day out, Owen had been the role model for Becca. He'd taught her to watch and take note, and she'd used it to see right through him.

Regret filled his mouth, his throat. "I never wanted to make you think…"

"You didn't." She smiled softly. "You taught me that it's possible to be very happy with a compromise in life."

"You aren't a compromise." His heart was breaking. Actual, shattered pieces fell apart in his chest, spearing him sharply in the most random of places. "I'm so sorry I ever gave you that impression."

"Life is nothing but compromises, because we can't have everything we want. That's just not how it works. We can't gorge ourselves on happiness. There are costs, and they are worth it. *That* is what you taught me. Right?"

He nodded numbly.

"You've always been there for me. Don't stop now."

Fuck. That was the thing, right there. He didn't get to pick when he was on Team Becca. "I'm sorry, kiddo. You're right. If Hayden makes you happy, then I'll deliver you to him myself."

"I'm not moving out tonight."

"Oh, thank God." He heaved a rough exhale in relief and hauled her into his chest. "Come here."

"Already here," she mumbled against his shoulder.

"I love you so much," he whispered into her hair. "I'm always on your side. Whatever you need."

———

A FEW HOURS LATER, Owen was lying alone in the dark, not sleeping but not worrying—exactly—when his phone lit up.

Kerry: How'd your evening turn out?

He'd told her he needed to talk to Becca and then…
nothing. Should he have updated her? But there was a
different relationship there because of the midwifery, so
maybe boundaries were better.

> **Owen: My daughter is all grown up. We had a good
> talk. She amazes me.**
> **Kerry: Yay.**
> **Kerry: Are you in bed now? Was it too late to text?**
> **Owen: Never too late. And yeah, trying to sleep.
> Sort of. I was wide awake, though. How
> about you?**
> **Kerry: Getting ready for bed now. It was nice to
> see you at lunch.**
> **Owen: Any chance you might be alone again, say,
> midday tomorrow?**
> **Kerry: I hoped you might ask that…**

OWEN PACKED a lunch for two this time. The day before
he'd taken up Kerry's entire break with kissing, and that
had been nice, but a bit selfish. This time, he was prepared.
He left the station five minutes before the time she'd told
him she would be free, and had to hold himself back from
running to his truck.

He was a kid all over again, single-mindedly focused
on a big, fun thing. When he pulled into the parking lot
behind the clinic, Kerry's car was the only one there. He
parked next to it, and as soon as he hopped down, she
opened the door. She was wearing a sweater to ward off

the cool fall weather, her feet shoved into knit slipper boots, and he wanted to toss her over his shoulder and carry her upstairs and show her how touchable she looked.

Instead, he followed her into the clinic's kitchenette and set the brown bag lunch on the table. "I brought sustenance," he managed to get out before she collided against him, her lips hungry.

"That's the sustenance I really need," she whispered against his skin. "But lunch is nice, too."

Curving his hand over her shoulder, he traced the shape of her. Soft curves, firm muscle. He wanted to trace every inch of her, explore every rolling plane, but there wasn't time for that. Settling his fingers on her waist, he tucked her right in against him and lowered his head so their faces were pressed forehead to forehead.

"I miss you during the day," he whispered.

"Owen," she breathed. He rubbed his hand back and forth under the hem of her shirt, over the soft skin on her sides. "Oh…"

He wanted to take her to bed. But more than that, he wanted to hold her and talk to her, and show her that he was her friend as well as her lover.

Of course he was drawn to her, aroused by her, and wanted her desperately. The way she made him laugh, and the way her body folded softly against his when he darkened her doorstep. He showed up with a frown, and she moved into him, giving him a hug every God damn time.

He probably didn't deserve her sweetness. She had the brightest shining star of a personality and he was the town crank—or at least his family's resident grump. He knew that, deep down, he had to try extra-hard to be worthy of

Kerry, so he'd planned to bring her a picnic lunch. And it had still turned into making out.

He wasn't trying to seduce her here. She was at work. He had to get back. They both needed to eat, and his craven wants were secondary to all of that. Loud, pulsing, but secondary. With a frustrated growl, he released her from his embrace and—gently—shoved her back.

She laughed and buried her face in her hands.

"Sorry about that," he said roughly as he pulled out the sandwiches he'd made for them. "I can't help myself."

"Who said you should stop?"

He sat in one of the chairs and tugged her onto his knee. "Eat some food so I don't feel bad about monopolizing your lunch hour."

Her curls bounced around her face as she reached for a sandwich half and brought it to her mouth. "Please don't feel bad. I miss you, too, and if you're just down the street, I don't know why we should deprive ourselves of a kiss or two." It had been more than two. "But if you want to feed me, I'm not going to say no." She took a big bite of the chicken salad. "This is delicious. Are those dried cranberries? Yum."

"Secret ingredient." He watched her eat, then joined her. "Hey listen, speaking of feeding you... How would you feel about joining us for Thanksgiving?"

She paused mid-bite, then took her time swallowing before she answered. "Who is us?"

"My brothers. Becca and Hayden and Charlie."

"The whole family." She hadn't stiffened up or pulled away from him, but she was clearly reluctant.

Owen smoothed his hand over her back. "Never mind, it's okay if you don't want to do that kind of public thing."

"It's not that." Her brows pulled together, like she was

picking her words carefully. "It's more like, are we there yet? We haven't really talked about what this is and what it isn't. But on the other hand, this is a really good sandwich, so I'm probably going to say yes."

He laughed, because she was both earnest and funny, but also damn, that level of honesty was refreshing. "I want you to say yes, and if we need to talk about what this is—and isn't—first, I'm fine with that. I like you so much, Kerry. I want to spend an obscene amount of time with you, and I'm happy for my family to know that I'm rolling out the good cranberry sauce just for you."

"Tell me more about this sauce." Her eyes sparkled as she leaned in for a quick kiss.

He told her about the entire meal. How Becca and Will usually did the sides, but the main elements were all Owen. A free-range turkey from a local farmer, dry-brined with spices. Sausage and apple stuffing. A special cranberry sauce this year, from scratch, since Kerry liked the chicken salad sandwich so much. The world's best gravy.

"It all sounds amazing. I'm on call that weekend," she warned. "But if I'm not with a client, I'm there."

He floated back to work as if he'd won the lottery, and didn't bark at anyone for the rest of the day.

CHAPTER TWENTY

OWEN LOVED THANKSGIVING. Seth always flew south for it, and this year the plan was to make a whole weekend out of it. Seth would fly in Saturday morning and they were going to rent four-wheelers for a brother-bonding day that Adam kept threatening in the group chat to "make epic." Owen worried that meant it would end with them rolling up at the strippers in Owen Sound.

Adam: Chill. We know Kerry has you on lock.

Owen couldn't argue with that.

Owen: I invited her to Thanksgiving.
Will: I should hope so.
Owen: It's a significant step!
Adam: For emotionally stunted people, maybe.
Seth: Shots fired.
Owen: Shut up. I don't see any of you cooking your women a feast for the ages.

All the dots on the screen appeared then, all three of them writing at the same time.

Seth: Your woman?
Will: Your what?
Adam: YOUR WOMAN!

Why couldn't he erase text messages? But he'd said it, and he wasn't taking it back. He grinned, grateful he was alone in his office so nobody could see just how wide his smile spread. His heart thumped heavy in his chest.

Owen: I have to get back to work.
Adam: Epic, I say.

But before the epic-ness could commence, Owen had the pre-holiday week to get through, and it was a busy one. The week before Canadian Thanksgiving saw a big turn in the season. The nights got colder, the leaves started to change colour at a rapid pace, and after the quiet of September, suddenly the peninsula ramped back up for tourists. One final rush full of retirees doing day trips to see the colours and then, on the long weekend, cottagers flooding back to their weekend homes to close everything up for the winter.

Which meant emergency services had to work over-time to keep everyone safe and respond to the greater volume of accidents that inevitably happened.

On the Thursday, Owen spent the last of five twelve-hour shifts in a row helping police untangle a traffic jam of more than eight hundred people all trying to get into a picture-perfect corn field for some social media challenge. So when he handed off the weekend supervisor responsibilities to Dani, his newest recruit for the leadership stream, he was damn glad to be done with people.

He already had everything he needed for the family feast on Sunday. He was going home for some much needed peace and quiet. And the house was actually going to be all his. Hayden's parents had just left for a two-week Mediterranean cruise, so Becca and Charlie were staying with him at their house—a trial run of them living together.

Owen had even driven the baby swing over there himself the night before. And then he'd arrived on Kerry's doorstep unannounced, and she'd taken him to her bed. They didn't talk. He had an early morning for his final shift in a row, and she was on a baby countdown for a client. Time was a precious commodity.

And then the corn field happened. Idiots with drones and tripods and a complete lack of safety comprehension.

Owen was bone-fucking-weary by the time he pulled into his driveway. Absolutely done with the world. He headed inside, got the laundry sorted, and then threw himself into a hot shower. As the steam worked its way into his muscles, he thought about the night before. How good Kerry tasted. His cock thickened, his balls pulled tight, and he closed his eyes. His fist wasn't the same as her body, his memory of her laugh not the same as actually hearing it. The joyous way she giggled at the funny parts of sex, the husky note her voice took on when she got really serious about his pleasure.

If he didn't think he would fall asleep mid-act, he'd invite her over. Maybe tomorrow…

He stroked himself a little harder, enjoying the squeeze of his fist. But even coming by his own effort sounded like, well, too much *effort.* Fuck it. He was going to bed—and that was a good call, because his head had barely hit the pillow before he was asleep.

The next thing he heard was a knock at the door. He bolted upright in bed and blinked in confusion at the window—it was sunny out.

How the fuck long had he slept?

The clock told him at least twelve hours. And the knock sounded again. Annoyingly chipper. Definitely Adam. He rolled out of bed and stalked through the house, stretching and shaking off the stupor he'd apparently been taken over by last night. He was mid-yawn when he opened the door and found Kerry standing there instead of his brother.

"Oh!" Her eyes went wide as she took in the sight of him standing in front of her in nothing but his boxer briefs. His hand went to his head, his fingers shoving into his hair, and her eyes zoomed wider still. Then her sweet, sexy little mouth split into a big, wide grin. "Uh, good morning."

It most definitely was with Kerry on his doorstep. She looked good enough to eat, in black leggings and a soft, touchable tunic sweater in a dark orange that made her eyes look like they were flecked with gold.

"Coffee?" She had two travel mugs in hand.

He stepped back. "Absolutely."

"I won't stay long, I know this is your first day off all week, but I made myself a latte for the road and thought I'd drop one off for you, too." She gave him a sly smile. "I didn't realize I'd get such a nice show for my effort."

Owen felt himself blush, and since he was mostly naked, there was no hiding the way his neck went red and it crawled onto his chest. "Come here," he said gruffly as she laughed. He kissed her forehead. "Tell me again where you're going? Did you already tell me about a road trip? I'm still waking up."

"It's not a road trip. I overstated the 'for the road' bit, probably. There's a farmer's market down the highway, but I've learned I need to take my own lattes with me."

Owen knew the farmer's market well. It was popular with the same people who had flocked to the corn field the day before.

"You're welcome to come with me if you want."

"Yeah," he heard himself saying. "Of course. Let me go brush my teeth and maybe put on clothes. You want to follow?"

She kicked off her boots and set the coffee mugs down on the little table in his vestibule. This was the first time she'd been in his house since those home visits after Becca gave birth, and now they were alone. He gestured to his bedroom as he headed into the bathroom to wash up.

When he came back, Kerry was looking at the photos on the wall. It had been a project he'd done a couple of years ago, although he'd recently added a picture of Charlie, too. Every picture was in a black frame, but that was the only rule. It had started with a cluster in the middle—him and Becca, a photo of his brothers when they were younger, and an even older picture of his parents. Since then he'd added photos of him in his uniforms, both army and paramedic, and Becca featured heavily, too.

Kerry pointed at one of the army photos. He was in the field, all "cammed up" with scrim on his helmet and green and black paint distorting his facial features. "Where was this taken?"

He laughed. "The training base in Meaford."

"Oh!" She looked surprised. "I thought maybe you went overseas. It looks so intense."

"That's the point. But no, I've never gone away. I had too much going on here at home."

"Lore says you're still in the army?"

He nodded. "The reserve, and I do the bare minimum these days. But it's good to have a medic on staff, so I try to make as many weekend exercises as I can. It works out to once every other month most of the time, and a few ranges to stay qualified on the various weapons."

"Wow." She turned, her gaze following him as he went to the dresser and pulled out a long-sleeved shirt and a pair of jeans. "Have you ever been to this farmer's market before? I've heard good things."

"Nope." He popped his head through the neck hole of his shirt. "First time. Can't wait."

"Really?"

"Yeah. Why?"

"I don't know." She scooted closer as he stepped into his jeans. "It was on a list of the top ten not-to-be missed places this fall."

"For locals, those lists are places to avoid," he said dryly.

"Oh!"

He hooked one arm around her hips and pulled her in close. "But to spend a bit of time with you, I will brave the hoards of tourists in search of artisanal honey."

"How did you know that's what I wanted?"

He laughed as he kissed her. "That's what everyone wants. Wild leeks, smoked rainbow trout—"

"The trout was mentioned in the article!" Kerry groaned. "Is it going to be very busy?"

Distressingly so, Owen was sure. "It'll be fine. We're armed with the best lattes on the peninsula, right? And it looks like a beautiful day out there. Let's do this."

They went in her car, which would be easier to park in a crowded lot, but they lucked out. The crowds from the city hadn't arrived yet, and they found a spot. And the look of glee on Kerry's face when the very first stall was selling artisanal honey made Owen genuinely happy.

"It's single source," she whispered.

Owen doubted the bees stuck to one kind of flower, but he kept that to himself. It probably meant something else. Instead he focused on how much fun it would be to lick a drop of the honey off Kerry's finger. Or her—

"Ooh, these are cute!" She picked up some beeswax food wraps and did a little happy dance.

He could definitely enjoy the farmer's market if Kerry kept making sounds like that.

After she made her purchases from that first stall, she slid her fingers through his and they wandered down the main aisle. He bought some fresh herbs for his turkey and stuffing, Kerry bought locally-grown apples, and then they went into the barn, where stalls that needed refrigeration were located.

There was a good-sized line at the counter for Great Lake Fisheries's smoked trout, so they headed the other way. Kerry stopped at every cheese counter, and Owen filed that away for a date night idea. Just the two of them and a big-ass cheese board.

And then, in the corner, was a familiar face. "Hey, man!" Owen held out his hand for his turkey guy to shake. "I didn't know you came here." He gestured to Kerry. "Kerry, this is Duncan. He was going to drop a fresh turkey round to my place later today, but maybe I can pick it up now?"

"Absolutely," the farmer said. He went over to the tablet that was attached to the debit machine. "I don't have one here that's exactly the same size as what you ordered, but I can size you up and that should be the difference for the delivery fee you paid, does that work?"

"Sounds good." Owen slung his arm low around Kerry's waist as they waited.

"Artisanal turkey," she whispered to him. "All the rage, I hear."

He shook with laughter. "Yep."

It was genuinely better tasting, though. That was his defence, and he was sticking to it.

———

THE NEXT DAY, after prepping his artisanal turkey to be dry-brined in the fridge while he was out, Owen headed over to Will's place. Josh arrived next, with Seth in tow, and Adam showed up last. Because he was the last to arrive, they told him he drew the short straw for seating in the truck on the day of epic brother adventures.

They piled in Owen's truck, Adam squished in the middle of the backseat between Will and Josh, while Seth rode shotgun. They stopped at Mac's on the way out of town to pick up sandwiches and cold drinks, packed up to go, then headed north to the rental store on the edge of the provincial park.

After a day spent on the trails, Adam directed them even further north, to a craft brewery in Tobermory for dinner and drinks.

"Pretty good day," Owen said as their plates were being cleared.

"It's not over yet." Adam glanced at his wrist. "Another surprise coming our way in about ten minutes."

Will leaned back in his chair. "Ten minutes sounds like

just enough time for you to tell us why you've organized such a big day."

Adam flashed his best charming grin. "Ah. That."

Owen was genuinely caught off guard. It wasn't out of character for Adam to want to make a big deal out of brother bonding time. "What's going on?"

"I got some news a couple of weeks ago, and I wanted to tell you all together. Remember, we're in a public place, and we have nine minutes, so if now's not a good time—"

"Spit it out," Seth said. "I'll hold Owen back if need be."

Owen protested that with a sputter.

Adam took a deep breath. "I've been accepted to a firefighting program, starting in January. I'll be back at the end of the summer if all goes well."

January.

Shock roared in Owen's ears. Adam had warned him this was coming, in every way he could, and yet he still felt blindsided. Denial was a hell of a drug. But as his mouth flapped open, as he watched Will shake hands with their baby brother, as Josh pumped his fist in the air and Seth looked sideways at Owen in concern, the tingling subsided and he was left with a warm, unexpected feeling.

Pride.

"Shit," he said. "I didn't think you'd actually do it, and then you went and did it like a boss anyway."

He stood and held out his arms. Adam came around and gave him a bone-crushing hug.

"You're going to be great," Owen said his voice rough with emotion.

"Thanks." Adam squeezed him back. "That means everything. I'll be safe, too, I promise."

He better.

Owen cleared his throat as Adam moved on to Seth, then Josh.

Adam's timing had been bang on, because as soon as they finished congratulations, a pretty young blonde woman wearing snug khaki pants and an Eco Guide hoodie came in through the double doors. She glanced around and raised her voice. "I'm looking for the Kincaid party for the owl prowl."

Adam waved his hand. "That's us."

An owl prowl? Owen rolled his eyes. His brother had fallen for the pretty guide, he'd bet money. But this was better than strippers. It wouldn't stop him from pointing out that the army usually paid him to do this in night reconnaissance exercises, though.

"Come on, boys. Let's go find some nocturnal animals." Adam flashed the guide a wicked grin. "We're all yours."

Owen just hoped he wouldn't twist a damn ankle.

CHAPTER TWENTY-ONE

KERRY SPENT Saturday night and Sunday morning at the hospital. She sent Owen a text mid-morning warning she might not make his Thanksgiving dinner, but soon after she sent it, her client's labour sped up.

Bodies were wonderful, mysterious things. She helped bring a sweet, tiny slip of a little girl into the world just after one in the afternoon. After getting mom and baby settled into the postnatal ward for the day, under the watchful eye of a nurse, Kerry headed for her car, and drove north.

She would never tire of deliveries. She liked every part of her job, except saying goodbye to patients at the end of their time in her care, although even those had a note of celebration. But the rush of labour and the triumphant success of deliveries were by far her favourite. They made the long nights and weekends spent on call worth the sacrifice.

When she got to her apartment, she made an emergency espresso, threw herself into the shower, and changed into something pretty but comfortable, because Owen had warned her there might be some touch football played. Then she grabbed the bottle of wine she'd bought for the occasion, took a really deep breath, and headed to Owen's house.

Cars lined the street. Two vintage cars, one of which she recognized as the beater Owen and his brothers worked on sometimes. *That's Will's*, she reminded herself. The black shiny one would be Josh's. She'd seen his garage coming together on her walks down to the harbour, but they hadn't met yet. Two pickup trucks completed the parade of vehicles, and she pulled in behind one that had a custom H0CK4 license plate.

She could bet money that would be Hayden's. She'd never gotten much of a bead on him in the few appointments he attended with Becca, but he'd shown up for the birth and she knew the young woman loved him. For both of their sakes, and Charlie's, Kerry hoped he wasn't as one-note as he sometimes appeared.

When she knocked on the front door, it was Becca who answered. In the last month, the young mom seemed to have aged a couple of years in a really good way. She looked all grown-up, and in her arms was a bright-eyed boy who had changed so much.

"Charlie!" Kerry exclaimed. "Look at both of you, oh my goodness."

Becca gave her a hug, then traded the baby for the bottle of wine. Charlie was easily twice as big as when he was born, and he followed Kerry's face very carefully as she made cooing faces at him. "I have been thinking of you, little man. It is so nice to see you."

He burbled and blew her a spit bubble. The highest of compliments. She held on to him as Becca introduced the uncles Kerry hadn't met yet—Josh, the mechanic, and Seth, the pilot.

"Owen's in the kitchen," Adam said. "He was just threatening to kick us all out into the backyard because we take up too much space, but now that you're here, he's going to be nice again."

"Is that right?" She laughed as she carried Charlie into the kitchen. "Let's go find your grandpa, shall we?"

"I heard that," Owen said when she appeared in the doorway.

"Which part?"

"The part where you called me grandpa."

She wiggled Charlie at him. "I remembered how much you liked it in the hospital."

He leaned in and bussed his grandson's cheek, then shifted and gave Kerry a softer, welcoming kiss on the mouth. "I do like it," he whispered. Then he straightened his apron—clearly a present from Becca at some point, because it said *Dad Cooks It Best* on it. "You're just in time. I was about to carve the turkey."

"Ooh, lucky me. Can I help?"

"You can keep me company while the boys finish setting the table." He raised his voice. "Hayden!"

The young man appeared promptly in the doorway, his broad shoulders filling it. His gaze went straight to Charlie, who burbled happily. Someone loved his daddy, that was for sure. "What can I do?"

"Take the stuffing and potatoes to the table, please."

Kerry and Charlie went to the far side of the kitchen and got out of the way as the counter was cleared of bowls mounded high with food. She watched as Owen carefully carved the turkey and arranged it on a platter, issuing directives to his daughter's boyfriend like the drill sergeant she knew he sometimes was. Before she knew it, everyone was gathering in the living room again, where the couch had been pushed up against the window to make room for an extra long table extension. Becca sat at one end, Hayden beside her and then Seth and Josh finishing that side. Owen was at the other end of the table, next to Josh, and Kerry sat next to him. Adam took the seat next to her, and Will sat beside him, stealing Charlie on his way to his chair.

They played musical baby as the bowls of food were passed around, and once everyone had a full plate in front of them, Owen raised his glass in a toast.

"Happy Thanksgiving," he said, his voice rich and warm. "I say this every year, but I am grateful for this family, and I mean it more this year than ever before. Each and every one of you is special to me. Now eat up."

Kerry pressed her lips together, unexpectedly emotional. That wasn't the plan. The plan was cranberry sauce and artisanal turkey, and being grateful for the sweetest, sexiest friendship she didn't see coming. Nothing more. "Here here," she said as they clinked glasses.

After they'd all made the right noises, because every single bite was delicious, the conversation went from the formal toast to little noisy pockets of conversation at every corner of the table. Owen asked Kerry how the delivery went, and she gave him the briefest of highlights. She asked about the dry brine, because holy cow did that make a difference to the taste of the bird, and then he shared that Adam had gotten into fire school.

"Really," she said, turning to give Adam a big *yay, you told him!* smile.

Adam grinned. "Kerry already knew."

Owen laughed. "What?"

She made a face. "Yeah, he told me a week ago. I caught him at the diner, stewing over the admission letter."

Owen scooped her hand in his and kissed her fingers. "And you kept his secret?" She nodded as Owen smiled at her, the corners of his eyes crinkling in approval. "Good girl."

It was the kind of thing she might have bristled at from another man, in another setting, but from Owen, knowing he appreciated her respecting his brother's personal space, it warmed her to her core.

At the other end of the table, Seth was telling Becca a harrowing tale of a rough landing, and she just kept shaking her head. "Nope, nope, nope. That's insane, Uncle Seth! I can't believe you."

Hayden said something about it putting the risks of hockey in perspective, and then Kerry's attention was dragged back to Owen.

That's how the whole meal went. Snippets of conversation, and then she'd find herself staring at the host, the patriarch of a misfit family. A big man with bigger feelings, she thought.

They took a backyard break while Becca and Hayden cleaned up before dessert. Kerry gamely joined in as they played three on three touch football. Owen was on the opposite team, the quarterback, and she did her gamest best to cover him despite the fact he was twice her size. In the end, she resorted to dirty tricks—dirty talk, muttered under her breath, about the fact she was free for the night and all the things she planned to do to thank him for the delicious meal—to distract him from his goal.

He still made the throw, and Josh scored a touchdown for their team.

Kerry's team came back, though, and it was tied up when Becca called them back in for dessert.

"The best possible finish," Will said diplomatically.

Owen caught Kerry with a big bear hug from behind. "We'll continue this later," he whispered in her ear.

She looked forward to it.

———

OWEN'S FAMILY left in waves. The brothers first. Josh, because he had work to do in the garage, and he took Seth and Adam with him for free manual labour. Then Will, after he helped pack up leftovers for everyone.

And finally Becca and Charlie in his bucket seat, being carried by Hayden.

"I didn't really get enough Charlie cuddles," Kerry said once everyone was gone and Owen had pulled her onto the couch for a grown-up cuddle of his own. "He's very cute. And everyone got along…"

Owen chuckled. "Is that a sideways observation that I didn't growl too much at Hayden?"

"Maybe. I mean, I noticed *some* growling, but…" She giggled at the look on Owen's face.

"He's all right. He's trying."

She nodded.

He searched her face. "Is it okay if I talk about Becca stuff with you?"

"Sure. I'm not her midwife anymore."

"It's not like therapy, where there will forever be a complicated relationship?"

"You weren't my client, Owen. Tell me about you."

"Okay." He scrubbed a hand over his face.

"Was today hard?"

He considered the question long enough Kerry wondered if he wasn't sure. "No," he finally said. "It's not hard to see her with Hayden. And the kid is trying, I give him full credit for that. If anything is hard, it's trying to mind my own business. Which I know that's what I need to do, now." He took a deep breath. It filled his entire body, his shoulders lifting and spreading wide before he exhaled. "It's hard to be rational as a parent, especially when your kid suddenly grows up."

"You're doing a great job."

"You know I don't always, though. I worry that I've fucked her up."

"What do you mean?"

"Did I teach her that men aren't always open about their feelings? That it's okay if they're gruff...?" He shrugged. "Or, you know, a straight-up rude asshole."

"You?"

"Me." He caught her hand as she tried to poke him. "It's okay. I know you thought I was a jerk." She bit her lower lip and tried not to smile. It was hard, because he was so earnest, and he kept going. "You called me a Neanderthal."

"If I recall correctly, you opened that door by declaring yourself *not* a Neanderthal, and I found that funny. You aren't a jerk. And I think with the people closest to you, you're very open about your feelings. I bet Becca sees that more than you think, because you're so gentle with her. You're a hard nut to crack, Owen Kincaid, but once someone gets in, you're pretty soft on the inside."

"That sounds like a compliment."

"It is. You have become such a special friend. More

than a friend," she hastened to add. She wriggled closer and lowered her voice. "A lover. I'm so happy, and you've been a big part of that. So take the compliment, please. This fall has been exactly what I needed. I was in such a weird place over the winter and spring."

"Anything you want to talk about?"

She made a face. It was easier to listen than to open up.

He laughed. "It's fine."

No, he'd shared. She took a deep breath. "Are you sure?"

"God damn it, woman, yes. I just bared my heart to you. Bring it on."

"I feel like I need to put some content warnings on what I'm about to say. Hear me out, okay?" She rolled away, just to have enough space between them. "Like a lot of people, I sort of tripped over my biological clock as I entered my thirties. It took me by surprise, but I'm rolling with it. I'm not in a rush to have kids or anything like that, but they're on my mind now. That pre-dated moving here, to be clear. But dating stopped being fun. It was a wild ride that veered between looking for a partner to raise kids with and feeling like I needed therapy to debrief on why I was clearly choosing people I would never *have* kids with. So moving here was a bit of a break from all of that, but I spent probably the longest celibate period in my entire life wondering if I wanted to freeze my eggs and how I felt about raising a child by myself."

He took her hand again. She liked the warmth of his skin against hers, the safety in his big fingers reaching for her when she was vulnerable. "And here I am talking about how I fucked up my kid."

"You didn't, though," she reminded him. "Anyway,

that's my baggage. It's been a lot of fun to ignore it this past month."

"That's what it is, isn't it? We all have baggage. I have a whole mess of feelings around what shoulda, coulda, woulda happened if Becca hadn't gotten pregnant with Charlie. I told you I had a little countdown clock in my head to when she'd move out and go away to school."

She nodded. "Your plans to live a wild life."

"The Great Bachelor Plan. Yeah. Because…and this isn't my finest hour, so don't judge me. I—it never really worked out well, me and dating, while Becca was little."

Kerry thought back to their first date, when they'd talked a bit about that. "You've said that before."

"I guess I wanted a re-do on that. Just in an older, wise kind of way."

"What am I, chopped liver? You're doing that now, and I have to say, as the recipient of your older, wise attempt at dating, I think it's going very well."

"You're more than dating," he confessed. "You're—this —I jumped into the deep end. I was going to wade in, get my toes wet."

"Keep it casual?"

"When you say it like that, it sounds shallow." He slowly shook his head. "I don't know if what I wanted was legitimate, or if that was fear talking. But I had a plan, and it got blown out of the water. That rocked me for longer than I like to admit, because I was so afraid."

"Afraid of what?"

"Watching Becca repeat the hardest years of my life."

"What was the worst that could have happened when you were her age?"

He barked out a cold laugh. "Losing custody of her.

That was my greatest fear, you know, right up until her eighteenth birthday. Losing her."

"She's a grown-up now."

"Barely." He dragged in a breath. "I don't know. It's hard to explain. I just felt like once I moved back here and Rachel and I split custody—and then once she got re-married, and she and Hudson had more kids—everything felt constantly precarious. Like any second they would decide they wanted Becca to live with them full-time, because it would be a better home life. Even though Rachel told me over and over again that she appreciated how much time I wanted with Becca, it never really sank in."

"And Becca adores you."

"Being worshiped by your kid doesn't make you a good parent. Letting your kid party as a teenager doesn't make you a good parent. Your kid getting knocked up just the same way you did definitely doesn't make you a good parent." His voice cracked. "I am not a good parent, Kerry, and I've known that since the minute she was born. I spent eighteen years waiting to be called on that shit."

"That's a huge weight."

"I never said any of that out loud. Not to anyone."

"I'm glad you told me." She climbed on top of him, straddling him, and presssed her forehead against his, trying to show him with her body how much she liked him, exactly the way he was. How much she wanted to be close to him, always, but especially when he shared scary stuff. That none of his fears were scary to her.

"I'll be a better grandparent," he said softly, and it broke her heart.

"You are a great dad, Owen."

"Eh," he said. "Anyway, it doesn't matter now, I guess. Can we pretend I didn't just dump all of that on you?"

She shook her head with a smile. "Nope. I liked all of it. It's good to say our fears out loud."

"I guess." He rubbed his hands over her hips. "Do you want to sleep over?"

She let him change the subject. She let him grind her body against his and take the intimacy she was so willing to give him. She nipped at his lower lip. "All night?"

"All night," he repeated. "I want to reach for you in the middle of the night and find out you're slick for me."

She shivered. "I didn't bring my toothbrush. Or my pills."

"I have a stockpile of toothbrushes. What time do you have to take the pill?"

"Eight."

His mouth brushed against her neck, his tongue strong and sure. "I'll get you up. Or we could go and pack you a bag now. Or I could come to your place. Or you could tell me to shut—"

"Shut up," she whispered, tightening her fingers in his hair as he kissed his way onto her chest. He tugged down the neckline of her tee, finding the curve of her bra. More shivers as he grazed the line where bare skin met see-through gauze, then roughly covered her whole breast with his hand. Her nipple beaded hard against his palm.

His movements were jerkier than usual, a little bit desperate and a lot demanding. Like he couldn't get enough of her as clothes dropped off. He sucked her breasts into his mouth, as much flesh as possible until she ached between her legs, until she needed him to fuck her senseless.

Then he carried her into his room, spread her out on

his king-sized bed, and loomed large over her. He watched her touch herself, his gaze hooded and hot, as he grabbed protection, then he was pressing into her.

No more foreplay. Her first orgasm of the evening would be on his cock, and it was barrelling toward her like a freight train already. Owen's hands clamped down on her wrists, his thighs pressing her legs apart, and she gave herself over to him and the wild, rolling sensations.

He was such a good man, and he fucked like a beast possessed. It was a wicked combination that did dangerous things to her heart.

She dug her heels into the tight flex of his ass, finding the right angle—there, oh, yes—for him to send her flying. He hunched over her, letting go of one wrist so he could find her breast again, tweak that nipple as she arched beneath him.

When she lost control, so did he. He powered into her, his orgasm ripping out of him with a shudder and growly groan, and then he collapsed on top of her.

"God," he whispered, his mouth hot next to her ear. "Fuck. Ah, fuck, Kerry, I—"

Oh, holy crap, did she know the feeling. She smiled and nodded as her eyes drifted shut.

CHAPTER TWENTY-TWO

THREE WEEKS AFTER THANKSGIVING, Becca and Hayden moved into an apartment together. The hockey team had unexpectedly come through for them after finding out Hayden was being given a rough time by some of his teammates. The coach argued that players who came to the team from out of town were placed with families—essentially, providing accommodations due to need. Local players stayed with their families, but this was an exceptional circumstance, and the coach happened to own an apartment building. It was a gift that meant Hayden could keep playing without worrying about a job, at least for the winter.

Owen helped them move, and then filled their fridge.

When he got home, his house was just as empty as it had been around Thanksgiving, but he felt differently about it now. It was empty in a forever kind of way, in a *build that home gym* kind of way, and he didn't know if he liked it.

So when he picked Kerry up for dinner a few nights later, and saw a sign that the parking lot would be closed for two weeks for re-paving, he had a Very Good Idea. "You should stay with me while the lot's being re-done," he suggested over dessert.

"I can park on Main Street and go up through the clinic," Kerry said. "It's fine."

"Sure." Owen gave her his most temptingly wicked grin. "It's *fine*. But is it *fun*?"

"Ahh," she said, catching on. Her eyes twinkled. "Are you lonely?"

"A little. The house is kind of quiet." He hastened to add, "And I'd love to have you in my bed, all night. I should have led with that."

"I can come and go, but it would be nice to not have to jostle for parking on the street."

"You can come and stay, too. Up to you." But if he could trick her into staying the whole two weeks with good food and great sex, he wouldn't be above such deviousness.

The next night she showed up with a duffle bag, which he helped her unpack into two drawers he'd cleaned out for her. "You can use the closet in the spare room, too. Or this closet. I can move my shit."

She hopped up onto his bed, kneeling on it so they were eye-to-eye, and cupped his face in her hands. "I don't need closet space. It's all good. Thank you."

"I want you to be comfortable here," he said, feeling a bit unsettled. "So you might stay over more often even after you don't have to."

She laughed and pulled him down on top of her.

The days slid by in quiet delight. Cooking with another grown-up, who shared his tastes, was totally different than cooking for a picky teenager, even one who ate a ton of vegetables and had turned into a great chef herself.

But Kerry was open to anything, and they lingered at the table, slowly talking as they ate. They discussed everything from their shared politics to very different taste in art, future hypothetical travel and curious food trends— and often, they talked shop. She'd always expressed an interest in emergency response on the interagency working group, but spending most evenings together, for hours, allowed them to dig deeper into spirited explorations of how emergency response ran into primary medical care.

And she griped good-naturedly about some of the EMTs she had run into over her career as a midwife. It wasn't that uncommon for paramedics to respond to spontaneous deliveries or assist in a birth if a second midwife couldn't get to a home birth in time. "You know who absolutely gets it? Matt Foster," she said. "If I see him come through a door, I know my client's going to be in good hands."

"He's one of my best," Owen said, proudly. "We used to be partners, before I took the supervisor role."

"I see your influence on him." She stroked her fingers down his forearm. "I'd like to see you in the field more."

"Me, too." Owen blinked. He hadn't meant to say that.

Kerry cocked her head to the side. "Are you tiring of being a supervisor?"

"I dunno." He tugged her into his side and rested his chin lightly on her hair. "Maybe."

That question kept coming back to him over the next week. There were parts of his job that he loved. He liked the sense of responsibility he had for the station as a whole. He loved making dinner for the volunteer firefighters on training nights, and ensuring that his paramedics had the schedules and training support they wanted. He liked knowing everyone was doing okay, and intervening quietly if they weren't.

But he missed being in an ambulance every day.

When he came home from firefighter training the following week, and found Kerry curled up on his couch, wearing nothing more than a pair of booty shorts and a tiny tank top, there was a little whisper in the back of his mind that he could have more time with her, more time for himself, if he went back to being a regular EMT.

She was watching a European murder mystery with subtitles, so after he changed out of his uniform, he slid onto the couch behind her, curving himself around her body.

He'd forgotten how good it felt to hold a warm body against his. Not for sex, not for release, but for the warmth itself. For the soft, squishy goodness of a lover at rest. Having Kerry in his arms felt like how he saw Becca latch on to her favourite stuffed animals at bedtime for so many years.

He laughed at the image, a rumble from deep inside him, and Kerry turned enough to look at him. "What?"

"It's silly."

She paused her show. "Try me."

"I was…" He trailed off. How to properly capture it? "I like holding you like this."

"Mmm."

"And it reminds me how kids cling to their teddy bears."

She didn't make a second appreciative noise.

He groaned. "I told you it's silly."

"I'm your teddy bear?" Her belly shook then, under his hand. "That's…really sweet." She turned around in the tight space on the edge of his couch. "But then you need to be my teddy bear, too. It's only fair, right?"

Absolutely fair. And sweet? Hell, yeah. Dangerously, precariously on-the-edge-of-no-return kind of sweet. That didn't stop him from nodding, though. Damn straight he was her teddy bear.

———

KERRY LOVED every minute of her two weeks at Owen's house. She loved the way he always kissed her as soon as he saw her, like he wanted to consume her.

She let him every time.

There was an unspoken agreement between them now. This wasn't forever. They didn't talk about it like that. It was too fatalistic, somehow. And it missed the point. They'd both worked so hard to be honest about what they wanted, how much they liked each other, to pretend this wasn't a full-blown affair with feelings and all.

Their feelings were very real. While she was caught up in this whirlwind love with Owen—and that's what it was, for better or worse—she wasn't going to diminish it by focusing on the fact it would need to come to an end one day. It was the most perfect thing in the world, if only for right now.

And it was so nice to share a bed, not needing to do the schedule comparison—in a two-pager relationship, one of them was invariably having to get up and sneak out in the middle of the night. Or crawl back into it just before dawn.

On one of those nights, when she thought she had to work, but then the labour was transferred to an OB for a c-section that went well, and mom and baby were tucked into a postnatal room at the hospital just after dinner, she texted Owen from the hospital in Walkerton.

Kerry: I'm coming back early! Do you want me to pick up dinner?
Owen: Yay! I can make something. But can you pick up condoms on the way? We're running low.

She did a happy little skip.

Kerry: On it.

She stopped at the drugstore on her way out of town. They were probably close to talking about being fluid-bonded, but with Owen's history, Kerry didn't want to rely on pills alone for birth control. As she walked back to the cash register, the greeting cards caught her eye. Was there one that properly conveyed *Thanks for the Good Sex, and all the Super Real Feelings*?

When she walked in the door at Owen's house, it smelled suspiciously like he'd also made something for dessert. "What is that delightful smell?" she called out.

He strode out of the kitchen looking like a king.

"I made oatmeal cookies," he murmured as he drew her close.

"Healthy dinner."

"There's a veggie tray in the fridge."

"Balance is important." She giggled as he helped her take off her coat, then dragged her to the kitchen.

It wasn't just a veggie tray. He'd made a beautiful cheese board, complete with little hand made paper flags that named all of the cheese.

"Artisanal store-bought cheddar," she read out loud. "Artisanal farmer's market fresh goat. Artisanal Brie…"

He cracked her up and pleased her so very much in equal measure. This was the dinner she didn't know she'd wanted, but now couldn't wait to gobble up. In between the cheeses were veggies, crackers, and grapes. He poured her a glass of wine, which also had a made-up label on it to match the cheese. *Artisanal White.* They picked at the cutting board until they were stuffed, with just enough room for cookies, then they cleaned up together.

Dessert was had standing next to the kitchen counter. Owen fed her a cookie, catching the crumbs that tumbled off her lower lip.

Then he kissed her, kept kissing her, until the cookies were forgotten. She peeled off her shirt and he chased her to the shower.

She loved Owen's bathroom. A big tub, extra deep and extra wide, with a convenient ledge at one end. He cranked up the steam, then knelt, sweeping a soapy washcloth down her leg. She sighed and leaned back against the tiles as he lifted her foot into his hand, carefully scrubbing every inch before switching to the other leg.

"You're spoiling me."

"I like taking care of the people in my life."

"I've noticed." She ignored the way her heart pitter-pattered at being included in that select group.

"Can I take care of you tonight, Kerry?"

How could she say no to that? Heat swirled through her, nothing to do with the steamy shower, as she slowly slid her legs apart.

Owen's gaze flashed dark, hungry. His shoulders pressed against her thighs and he braced his hands on her hips, curving around so his fingers cradled her bottom.

He moved his face against her, not quite kissing her. The barest of breaths, a tease, and then firmer touches. His nose against the dip between her leg and her sex, then his lips against the curls covering her pussy.

She breathed his name, and her body bloomed for him. Wet, slick, ready.

When his tongue finally slid into her inner folds, where he'd so carefully touched her before with his fingers, she nearly came undone. Jumping, she trembled as he caught her and pressed her hips firmly back against the tiles. She was his now, because he'd promised to take care of her, and he wasn't going to stop until she came for him.

He murmured for her to let go, to feel good. "You're so hot," he whispered up at her, and the compliment fed her soul. He would fuck her next, and she would love that, too.

Because she loved Owen. Because their connection was so much more than anything she'd had before, and that was both scary and wonderful.

A hot tear threatened behind her eyelid as a tsunami of sensation rolled over her. And then joyous laughter followed as he sat her down on the ledge, as he got out of the tub and found them towels.

On his bed, she pushed him onto his back. He sheathed up, then pulled her onto his cock. She rode him slowly, then faster. His hands squeezed her hips, then her breasts, her shoulders, before tangling in her hair and pulling her in close. Their foreheads pressed together. Their breaths synched up, slowing, as if their pulses aligned. And then, suddenly, as everything got hotter and needier, tighter, he shuddered, and her breath caught in her chest. *There.* He surged into her, tensing, every muscle in his body turning to granite beneath her. His thumb fell to her clit, and she followed him, that firm pressure the final stimulus she needed to get there with him.

The aftershocks rippled through her as she caught her breath, still on top of him. It was so good, she thought. So damn good.

Until she went to climb off him.

"Shit." Panic raced over her as a slick mess slid between her legs. "Owen, the condom broke."

"Oh!" He scrambled up and grabbed a towel hanging on a hook on the back of his door. "Here."

Fingers shaking, she took it and shoved it between her legs. Words failed her as her brain raced to find the right way to reassure him that the second layer of protection probably wasn't necessary. But she felt sick that it was the condoms she had bought that broke. Usually they used ones he had, and were they better? Had she not bought the right brand? Weren't all condoms equally good, as long as the size was right?

"Hey," Owen said, getting in front of her face. "Are you okay?"

She blinked at him. "Are you?"

"Sure." He shrugged. "It happens. It's been a while since I've had to have this conversation, but if you want me to get tested, I will. I don't think you have anything to worry about, though."

"I'm not worried about you," she whispered. She was shaking. Great. Why was she shaking? She took a deep breath, then another. "I'm on the pill. You know that, right? I take it religiously. It's in my purse so I can take it in the morning. You don't have anything to worry about."

Owen squeezed her hands. "It's okay. I'm not worried about that."

She looked up at him. "I thought you might...you know, because of..."

He shrugged. "I'm shooting blanks now. I got a vasectomy a decade ago, when I knew I wouldn't want any more kids. I thought it might help with the dating thing, because I never wanted that kind of surprise again. Turned out I had other trust issues that made it all more complicated."

A vasectomy.

Oh.

He searched her face. "Are you okay?"

"Yeah." She would be.

Why didn't she know that he'd been snipped? *Years ago*. This whole time, everything they had shared with each other, why didn't she know *that*?

"Kerry..." He sighed and curled up next to her. They were both still naked.

She pulled the sheet up over her body. "It's okay," she whispered. "I just thought you'd be upset."

"I'm not." He kissed her temple and ran his fingers through her hair. "We just hadn't had that talk, that's all."

"Right."

But her heart didn't feel the same as it had just minutes before. It was bruised, and she wanted to cry.

She didn't. She rolled into Owen's warmth and let him hold her. She breathed in the scent of his skin and told herself it would be easier to think about in the morning.

CHAPTER TWENTY-THREE

THE NEXT DAY, Kerry moved back to her apartment.

Her heart didn't feel any less bruised, but that wasn't why she moved back, she told herself. It was time. The parking lot was open again.

Owen said she could leave stuff in his drawers for sleepovers, but she packed everything up. Deep down, she knew she wasn't coming back, and she was sick over it. This wasn't fair—she'd known Owen didn't want any more kids. He'd told her those days were behind him. She'd known, deep down, that he would never be the guy to have her own babies with.

And yet she felt blindsided.

She was beating herself up for that, too. How could she be so foolish? And how could she be so harsh on him?

He clearly thought the vasectomy was no big deal, because he'd never mentioned it to her. Not once. She'd remember that, oh boy. And *that* was the problem. He was too sure. Too cool. And that was entirely his right. His body, his choice, and probably none of her business— up to a point. She'd feel the same way in his shoes. But she wasn't in his shoes. And *her* shoes really wanted babies.

Her heart had been in denial, and now she knew what she already knew. Owen really, really never wanted babies.

What was she doing falling in love with him? Playing house? Would he want to keep fucking her if she had a baby on her own, with sperm donation? No.

Their relationship had to end. It would end, at some point in the not too distant future, so it needed to end now.

How could she tell him? What could she say? *You're a wonderful man. You are a wonderful father. I would love to make babies with someone like you—with you, in fact, but you don't want that. You really, really don't want that. You made a permanent decision to make sure that never happened to you again, and I had no idea.*

Maybe we weren't as important to each other as I thought we were.

With each turn through her ever darkening thoughts, she whirled from angry to sad to fine, *Definitely Fine*, to lost, and then back to angry.

She didn't want to be angry at Owen. That wasn't fair.

But it wasn't fair to her heart to stay with someone who could never be a part of her future the way she wanted them to be.

Hands shaking, she texted Jenna.

Kerry: SOS. Are you free tonight?
Jenna: What do you need?
Kerry: Booze? Ice cream? Tissues?
Jenna: Oh no. I'm on it.

Jenna showed up twenty minutes later with two pints

of Ben & Jerrys and a bottle of Crown Royal. "I'm yours for the night. Let's get drunk and watch the Ghostbusters remake. Kate McKinnon makes everything better."

Kerry burst into tears.

From her purse, Jenna yanked a box of tissues. "Maybe I should have started with these. What happened?"

In halting, sniff-interrupted half-sentences, Kerry gave her the Coles Notes version. Jenna listened, and when Kerry finally finished, she poured them each a drink, and grabbed a couple of spoons.

"What are you going to do?"

"I'm going to break up with him. I have to. It's the only option."

"Are you sure?"

Kerry wanted the answer to be different, but she was certain. "If anything, this cements it as the inevitable end to our relationship. He didn't tell me he couldn't have kids. We didn't have the communication we should have, maybe because we both knew, deep down, that if we did, we wouldn't be together. But I know now, more than ever, that I definitely do want kids, so… this is it."

"I'm sorry."

"Me too. He's a great guy."

"There are other fish in the pond."

"Yep." Kerry shoved a big spoonful of Cherry Garcia in her mouth. She wasn't interested in going fishing any time soon, though.

———

SHE DID it the next day. She thought about doing it by text, but he deserved better than that, so she drove past his house to make sure he was home and alone, and then called him from her car a block away.

"Hello?"

"It's me."

"Hello, you. I miss you. Want to come over?"

Oh God. "I can't."

"Damn."

"Owen—"

"I was thinking—"

"Owen, stop."

"What's wrong?"

"I need you to listen to me." Her voice was shaking. "Please. Just listen to me."

"You've got my attention, sweetheart."

No pet names. Not now. "I need to take some time to myself. It's not you, it's me, and I've thought about it. I promise I've thought about it, and I'm sorry. But I can't come over, or hang out, or have you to my place. I need space, and I need you to respect that."

"Kerry." His voice cracked as he said her name and she couldn't handle that.

She whispered that she had to go, and she hung up the call. It wasn't her finest hour. It was sad and desperate and weak, and she couldn't do any better than that. *I'm so sorry, Owen.*

She sat sobbing in her car until her fingertips got cold, then she started the engine again. When she drove past his place, his car was gone. Steeling herself, she headed for the highway, and drove north, with no destination in mind. She just needed to not be in Pine Harbour.

It was dark by the time she got back to her apartment. She let herself in and flopped on the couch.

His knock came an hour later. She recognized his footsteps on the stairs, the heavy weight of them. He knocked twice, then waited. And then he knocked again. Would people notice if he stood out there for too long?

Go away.

At the third knock, she got up and walked to the door.

"I know you're there," he said. "Come on, Kerry."

She opened the door, and he filled the frame, his head hanging a bit. In his hand was one of her sweatshirts. "You left this at my place."

She stared at the hoodie in his hands. It was an excuse, because he needed one. Because she'd broken his heart and he needed more of an answer as to why, but he couldn't just straight up ask her for it.

And so he'd brought her something.

Hell, he could have hung on to it. That's what she would have done. Selfishly kept the thing that smelled like him.

She held out her hand. "Thanks."

He didn't let go of the hoodie. "Can we talk?"

"There's nothing to talk about," she said dully. "Please don't make this harder than it has to be."

"I don't understand." There was that crack in his voice again.

"I'm sorry." Tears were flowing freely now. Fork. And it was cold outside.

"I'm not mad at you, Kerry. Please let me come in, just so I can understand. Is that okay?"

Sobbing, she stepped back, and he moved into the apartment, gently closing the door behind him.

"Is this because I had a vasectomy?"

She shook her head no, then nodded it yes. "It's complicated. I don't—I'm not mad at you, either. I just…"

Everything she knew she needed to say to him clogged

in her throat. He handed her a tissue, and she dried her eyes. But she couldn't look up at him. She stared at his boots instead. *You're a wonderful man. You are a wonderful father. I would love to make babies with someone like you*—with *you, in fact, but you don't want that. You really, really don't want that. You made a permanent decision to make sure that never happened to you again, and I had no idea.*

And then the worst thought of all. *Maybe we weren't as important to each other as I thought we were.*

"This is all on me. You were clear about the bounds, and I knew what I was getting into." She sounded robotic, but that was better than weepy. "At some point, we would have to go our separate ways. That's all. It's better for it to happen now."

"It doesn't feel better." He leaned back against the wall, bending his knee, and more of him came into her line of sight. She could almost see his face, and oh God, she didn't want to have to look at him. But she couldn't *not*, either, so she raised her head.

What a mistake that was.

The tortured, twisted look of sadness he gave her was almost enough to make her drop to her knees and beg his forgiveness. She would get over wanting babies.

Except she wouldn't. She could put it off for a while, but not forever, and then she would resent him.

He searched her face and finally nodded, like he saw all of that. He might not like it, but he saw her. "I'm sorry."

"You have nothing to be sorry about," she whispered. She needed him to get out of there before the tears came back. "You're a wonderful—"

He caught her around the waist, holding on tight, and for another split second, she thought she might give in. Oh, how she wanted him to stay. To let him hold her for as long as he wanted, no strings attached. But she wanted more from Owen than he would ever be able to give her, through no fault of his own.

"Love makes us stupid," she said, hugging him tight. "But that's okay. I'm grateful for everything we've had."

His body shook, then he took her face in his hands and kissed her hard on the mouth. He kissed her with his whole body, and deep down she knew.

It would be their last kiss.

It had to be.

———

OWEN CALLED in sick for the first time in a decade. That was a mistake, because someone—probably Dani—immediately texted Becca to make sure he was taking care of himself, and she forwarded the message, warning him she was about to show up on his doorstep.

"Dad?" she called as she stepped into the living room.

He raised his hand from his prone position on the couch. In it was his phone. "I replied to you and told you I was fine."

"I ignored you and came over anyway. What's wrong?" She appeared above him, Charlie asleep in a baby wrap on her chest.

"Nothing."

"Is it the flu? Don't breathe on me."

"You came over here, and no, it's not the flu." He frowned. "Do I look like I'm having respiratory problems?"

"You look like you're having attitude problems," she replied crisply. "So I'm here to help with that."

"Go away."

"That's nice."

"I say it with love." Sighing, he swung his feet around so he could sit up. Sit, slump. It was all the same.

"What's going on?"

He had to swallow hard around the lump in his throat to admit the truth. "I hurt Kerry. We broke up."

"What did you do?"

He shook his head. No way was he detailing that to his daughter, no matter how grown up she suddenly was. She stood there for a minute, then disappeared into the kitchen. Slowly, he followed. "What are you doing?"

She was rummaging through the pantry cupboard. "You've moved things."

"What are you looking for?"

"You need some oatmeal."

His chest pulled tight. "Oh, it's, uh…" He gestured to the bottom shelf. "Baking stuff."

He couldn't tell her not to make him oatmeal, that it reminded him of making Kerry cookies, of feeding them to her.

Of making love, and then it all going sideways.

So he let his daughter make him a bowl of porridge. He ate it, fair comeuppance after eighteen years of forcing her to do the same. She sat across from him until Charlie woke up, then they went for a walk.

Becca didn't ask him again for details. She didn't complain when he delivered her to the apartment where she lived, and told her he was going to keep walking on his own.

But the next morning she showed up at the house again. She made him oatmeal again. And deep inside him, something tore loose.

CHAPTER TWENTY-FOUR

BY THE END of the week, he was sick of himself. Sick of lying on the couch and being miserable. So he had a shower, shaved his damn face, and went to work. They weren't expecting him. Dani was on her fourth shift as fill-in supervisor, and the white board had never looked better.

"Hey boss," she called out from his office. "Are you here to fill in for Quinn?"

"She sick?" He shoved his hand into his hair. "I didn't know. I just came in."

"Minor injury while at the hospital. She cut her hand. The docs patched her up, and Matt's dropped her at home, and is on his way back alone. All the paperwork's been completed, don't worry. You want to spell me off, then?" Dani was already tying her long dark hair into a bun.

He stopped her. "Could I..." He hooked his thumb toward the ambulance bay. "Do you mind?"

"Be my guest." She grinned. "I'm fixing the holiday schedule."

"Nothing wrong with it the way it was," he grouched.

"I know. But now it's even better."

She was probably right.

He was sitting on a bench at the back of the garage when Matt returned. "You've got me for the rest of the shift, bud."

"Partners ride again," the other man said. "You want to drive?"

"You know it." He hadn't brought himself any coffee, so they loaded up and headed to Mac's, and it was as they exited the diner, takeaway in hand, that their first call came in. A home birth support in Lion's Head.

What were the fucking chances. He braced himself for impact and flipped on the lights.

Matt reported to dispatch that they were on their way, then glanced sideways. "So much for a quiet shift, boss."

He didn't know the half of it. Either Owen was about to come face to face with the woman he loved, or her best friend and colleague, who almost certainly knew he'd broken Kerry's heart.

The road was clear, and they made it across the peninsula in excellent time. But when they pulled up in front of the address, a low rise apartment building, they didn't even need to get out of the ambulance. Well, Owen didn't at least.

Kerry was waiting with a heavily pregnant young woman, not much older than Becca, at the curb.

He killed the lights as Matt hopped out. By the time he got the back doors open and their stretcher out, she was already giving Matt the rundown.

"Jenna's at another birth, and Alyssa here is in active labour but we've got some time." Kerry said as Owen approached, barely sparing him a split-second glance. "So we're going for the transport. I'll follow you guys. No rush." She handed Matt her card, like Owen didn't have her number memorized. "If I lose you, can you text me when you get her to the hospital? Sometimes the patient handoff gets sketchy." She squeezed the young woman's hand. "But these guys are great. You're in the best of hands. I'll see you soon."

Owen ignored the way his heart hammered in his chest and let the job take over. Matt would ride in the back with the patient. They got her belted onto the stretcher, then raised it up and into the back. Matt climbed up, Owen closed the doors behind him—and then, for a brief moment, he was alone with Kerry.

She gave him a cool nod and turned, heading to her car.

Pain seared through his veins, and nineteen years of professionalism got his legs moving in the right direction instead of sprinting after her.

"All right, Alyssa," he called back. "You keep an eye on Matt back there and let me know if he starts to get a little woozy from the drive, okay?"

She laughed, then gasped as a contraction started. "Sorry," Owen heard her say. "They hurt."

That wasn't anything to be sorry for, and Matt told her as much. He kept her distracted the whole way, telling her about some of the other births he'd attended, and then the arrival of his own baby earlier in the year.

In the couple of years since they'd been partners, Matt had only improved as a paramedic. He was great with her.

Which meant Owen only had to concentrate on two things: driving, and not getting too far ahead of Kerry. He listened to her, and didn't bother to put the siren on, just the lights, but people still got out of the way for him and then slid right back onto the road in front of her, having no idea she was following the ambulance.

When that happened, he cut the gas a bit, making sure she could still see him.

By the time they arrived at the hospital, Matt and Alyssa were best friends, and Kerry managed to find them at the ambulance entrance before they even went inside. It was the best possible transfer given the circumstances. Owen and Matt got Alyssa upstairs to L&D, by-passing Emerg completely, and Kerry got her registered, resuming primary care.

So they were free to go. And they should, because she had a job to do.

But Matt was doing their paperwork and checking in with dispatch, and Owen could see the L&D nurse was getting Alyssa situated. Technically, Kerry was free for a second.

He crossed the hall to where she was standing at the nursing station. "Good following there. On the road."

She nodded without looking up. "Good driving."

"I'm glad we can work together."

That got her attention, but not in a good way. Her gaze snapped up, her brown eyes cool and hard. "Why wouldn't we be able to?"

Regret foamed at the back of his mouth. "No reason. You would never make a choice for a patient based on your own comfort."

"Not only that, I'm perfectly comfortable working with you." She frowned. "Wouldn't you say the same thing about me?"

Of course he would. But he found himself tongue-tied all over again, like their months of being close had never happened. His heart might as well have been ripped from his chest in that moment, not that Kerry would notice. His mouth moved uselessly, silently, as she pushed herself to the full extent of her five-foot-nothing frame.

"Well, I guess I'll be the professional for both of us. I will be happy to see you on any future calls I have to make, Owen Kincaid. You're a great paramedic." And with that, she stepped around him, and disappeared into Alyssa's room.

Never before had a compliment stung quite so sharply.

I love you, and miss you. Useless words. Empty words.

Matt ambled up the hallway. "Everything okay?"

No. And it might never be again. "Let's get out of here."

———

HIS HOUSE WAS SO empty that when he dropped his bag on the floor the sound echoed off the walls. Nothing had changed since that morning, when he'd gotten the foolish idea he was ready to pretend he was a whole man again.

It was tempting to flop out on the couch again. Eventually, though, someone would find him there, surrounded by empty Jim Beam bottles and pizza boxes, and force him to take a shower. Eat some oatmeal. He needed to short-circuit that pattern. He could cook himself some oatmeal, but frankly, he'd had enough, and it just reminded him of baking his girlfriend cookies.

He'd never even called her his girlfriend. Once, he'd called her his woman. They'd barely had any time together in the end. Almost an entire year of wanting her, and he'd fucked it up just as she was falling in love with him.

Owen: Can we have a team meeting?

Becca: You, me, and … Mom?
Owen: I was thinking more you, me, and Charlie.
Do you feel like company from your old man?
Becca: Always.

He threw on his coat and headed out the door.

———

KERRY DIDN'T GO HOME that night. She crashed on a cot at the hospital rather than risk driving tired on the newly icy roads in the dark. Winter was coming in more ways than one. So she stuck around to do the twenty-four hour wellness check on Alyssa and her new baby boy mid-afternoon.

The young mom had an easy delivery, but had developed some signs of pre-eclampsia afterwards, and was now in the care of an OB. She would stay in the hospital for at least two more days. "I'll see you at home once you're discharged, and you have my pager number if you need anything."

"Thanks, Kerry." Alyssa gave her a tired smile. "Now go home."

But the thing was, she didn't want to.

Her apartment was lonely and full of memories of Owen. She avoided looking at the wall inside her front door now, the spot that used to give her warm, fuzzy secret feelings when she looked at it. *Right here.*

Would she take it all back, knowing this was how it would end?

But she had known. And she did it anyway, so there were no take backs. She threw herself into her bed, her heart aching for the man who'd shared it all too briefly, and fell asleep again.

When she woke up, it was dark, and there was a text message on her phone.

Bailey: I'm going to the Hedgehog tonight, if you want to come with.

Word was spreading that she had a broken heart. On the one hand, she wanted to grieve and heal in private. On the other, every surface in her apartment still seemed imprinted with Owen's big frame.

Kerry: I'll meet you there.

She showered and then dressed with a confidence she didn't feel. Skinny jeans, black boots, a sexy top that should have made her feel good, but only made her miss Owen. She swapped it out for a black turtleneck instead, went a little extra gothic on the eye makeup, and headed out the door.

When she arrived at the pub, she half-expected it to be decorated for the holidays the way it had been the first time she'd visited almost a year ago. But after she got settled at the bar and asked Lore about it, the bartender explained that because so many army reservists came in, the owner was careful to wait until after Remembrance Day to haul out the Christmas decorations.

Kerry blamed her thoughtlessness on her disrupted sleep, and Lore waved it off. "Some of us can wear a poppy *and* hang up some holly and ivy, you know? But it's just a few more days, and then I'll be a proper elf complete with Christmas drinks, too."

A glance at the chalkboard told Kerry that the cocktail of the week was a gin and tonic. She'd pass. "Can I have a cup of mint tea?"

"Not drinking tonight?"

"I'm just here to catch up with Bailey, because I missed the last couple of practices."

As she said that, their teammate came in the door, her smile extra wide. Warning-wide. "Don't panic," Bailey said quickly and under her breath as she skidded to a stop in front of them. "But—"

Kerry's gaze slid to the front door again as Owen stomped inside. He sucked all the air out of the room.

"It's fine," she said around the lump in her throat. It wasn't, of course, but from the stricken expression on his face, it was even less fine for him than for her.

She'd bitten off his head the day before. Of course he didn't want to see her.

He stood there longer than she liked, and she wondered if he was going to turn around and head home. No fun for Owen, that was always a risk. But then he stomped past, heading to the back, and Lore poured him a stout.

Well, fork. She pointed to the glass. "I can take it back to him. And cancel my tea—I'll take the same."

Lore hesitated, clearly torn between the unwritten bartender code of ethics and wanting to be a good friend. Kerry couldn't be glib here. She lowered her voice. "I hurt him. Let me try and fix it. Better that I deal with the awkwardness tonight than it become an ongoing problem."

"Don't make a scene," Lore said as she grabbed a second glass.

Kerry blinked in surprise. "I won't."

"Good."

She hadn't opened herself up to her new friends as much as she thought she had if Lore thought whatever might happen would have any aspects of making a scene. That wasn't Kerry's style, and it wasn't Owen's, either. She chewed on her bottom lip for a second. "Lore…"

"Yeah?"

"I really care about him. You know that, right?"

Her friend paused, then nodded. "Sure, I guess."

Ouch. "Where does the *I guess* part come from?"

"You're a love 'em and leave 'em kind of woman. Party hard, go home alone."

She had been. Before coming to Pine Harbour. Now her chest had a hole in it the size of a big, surly man. "That was the old me," she whispered. "Before Owen."

Lore pushed the two drinks across the bar. "Go make sure he knows that."

Damn. Kerry hadn't meant to give Lore the impression she was trying to win Owen back. That wasn't her goal here—but they could be friends again.

She found him in the back corner, carefully laying out a set of darts on a tall table against the wall.

Taking a deep breath, she marched over and slid the beers onto the table next to his hand. She didn't miss the white knuckles. "Twice in two days." She said it extra lightly. "What are the odds?"

"Pretty fucking good," he growled. "It's a small peninsula."

"Good point."

"What do you want?"

"I came over to talk to you."

"I'm not in the mood for talking. I was, but now I'm not, so…"

"Do you want me to go?"

He froze. Then he exhaled sharply and jerked his head. No.

"You're right," she said softly. "You *did* want to talk, and I didn't. I'm sorry I couldn't before. But you're also right that it's a small peninsula, so we're going to have to learn to share it. And we have friends in common who worry that we're going to make a scene, so…"

That got her the barest hint of a smile. "A scene?"

"Maybe a screaming match."

The corner of his mouth twitched.

"I won't stay long. I just wanted to bring you your beer and promise that I'm not going to break a pool cue over my knee when you least expect it."

He laughed. It was short and cold, and it didn't completely reach his eyes, but she'd made him laugh.

"But in all seriousness, I wanted to apologize for yesterday. I could have read between the lines of what you were saying and I chose not to because…" She trailed off. He knew why.

Owen shook his head. "You don't have anything to apologize for. You're allowed to call me on my shit."

"Nah, it was thoughtless."

"You're never thoughtless," he said quietly.

Oh boy. She needed to leave before she fell into his voice and splashed around in the loveliness of it. So she reached for her glass and stepped away, but he said her name. "Kerry." Her heart slammed against her rib cage and she stopped in her tracks. He took the world's longest breath, held it, then shook his head. "Thanks."

"What were you going to say?"

He scrunched up his face. "Probably the wrong thing.

What I really meant was thank you, and I should leave it at that for now."

"Okay." She forced herself to smile, and to mean it. She did, but it was complicated. "I'll see you soon."

"Hope so."

She turned around decisively then. It wasn't any easier to walk away from him today than it had been yesterday, but with each step, she got a little bolder, because they would do this again. And again, and again.

Eventually, it would be enough, and she would be over him. She'd never loved anyone quite like this before. After loving Owen, she doubted that she'd ever actually been in love before.

It would take a while to grow out of love, too.

But she would, because loving him meant she had to accept him for all that he was—including that he had long been done having children.

But she didn't have to accept that for herself. She could love Owen and leave him in her past. She would much rather have a fondness for what they'd shared than a bitterness around what they could never have together.

It wasn't meant to be.

More than that, it wouldn't be what she would choose. There was a sweet—maybe bittersweet, sure—joy in knowing she'd closed that chapter. She hadn't clung on too long. And she was moving forward more clear than ever about what her future would look like.

CHAPTER TWENTY-FIVE

OWEN WAS STANDING at attention in the middle of the Remembrance Day parade—right in front of the cenotaph —when he heard Charlie cry.

His grandson's holler pierced the minute of silence marking the eleventh hour of the eleventh day of the eleventh month, and Owen couldn't react. He couldn't pivot his head to find Becca, almost certainly trying to shush him, and he couldn't laugh, but on the inside, he was grinning.

That was his boy. He'd recognize the cry anywhere, just the same way he'd always known Becca's cry, too. Adam's indignant voice and the unique way only Josh could slam a door.

On the other side of the cenotaph he saw a retired fire chief, who had once worked with his dad, and who had hired Owen on as a firefighter back in the day. It had been a number of years since Owen had made a point of seeking him out and saying hello. There was only so much of *"Your dad would be proud of you, son,"* that one could hear when it didn't always feel true.

Today, though, he wanted to introduce Becca and Charlie.

Once they had marched back to the armouries and were released from parade, he made a bee-line for his daughter. "There's someone I want you and Charlie to meet. Someone your grandpa once worked with."

She followed him through the sea of different uniforms until they found the firefighters, and behind them, the retired ranks.

"Sir," Owen said, finding the man who had once been a colleague of his dad's. "I'm Michael Kincaid's son, I don't know if you remember—"

The chief's face split into a broad smile. "Owen, good to see you." He did a double-take. "Don't tell me this is your daughter."

"Becca," she said, holding out her hand. "Nice to see you again."

"And this is Charlie," Owen said. "My grandson."

"Well, I'll be…" The chief leaned in and Charlie made a face. "I can see Michael in him, that's for sure. It was nice to see you. I think I heard through the grapevine that your brother Adam is joining our ranks."

"Yup."

"Your dad would have some misgivings about that, I think, but it's a good thing. It's in your blood."

Owen took a deep breath. "I think so. I admit to having my own misgivings."

"That's understandable. I always knew we wouldn't have you for long. It wasn't for you, but good to get out of your system."

Owen didn't know what to say to that. That was unnervingly accurate. "You're not wrong, sir."

The chief laughed, then they said their goodbyes.

As they made their way back to the front entrance, Owen brought up hearing Charlie in the moment of silence.

"I'm sorry," Becca moaned. "He was so quiet, and then I think he saw you? I don't know if he can recognize you that far away, but..."

Owen took his grandson, who was waving his hands for attention. "I think he can. You know me anywhere, don't you big guy?"

Charlie smacked him in the face with a tiny wet hand. Owen laughed. Was there anything better than the sweet wobbliness of infants?

Nothing. Except maybe watching a toddler take her first steps, or figure out how to dive off the edge of a pool. The soaring triumph of a kid who walked themselves home from school alone for the first time. The gentle grace and understanding a child had when they realized their parent was struggling.

"You okay, Dad?"

Owen blinked at Becca. "Yeah. I'm great."

"Do you have to get back to work?"

He looked around for Will, who was nowhere to be seen. His brother had been right behind him on parade. "I need to find your uncle."

"Which one?"

Fuck it. He didn't know. "All of them, probably."

Owen was pretty sure he'd chicken out if he waited for each brother to get back to him one by one, so he sent a group text instead.

Owen: Anyone free to listen to their older brother talk about his feelings?

Seth was the first to reply.

**Seth: You jerk, you had to have a crisis while I'm
running supplies? I can be home next week. You
better still have feelings when I get there.**
Owen: Pretty sure this is a chronic condition now.
Seth: Excellent.
**Will: Didn't I just see you twenty minutes ago?
What happened after I left the armouries?**
Owen: You left already?
Will: I have to prep for a staff meeting tomorrow.
Owen: …
Will: You don't listen to me anyway.
**Owen: That's not true. But I'll wait and see if Adam
and Josh are free—and then I'm coming to you,
because I need your help specifically.**

Neither Adam nor Josh replied immediately, so Owen
decided to head home. By the time he pulled into his
driveway, they'd both chimed in.

**Adam: I was at the armouries but missed you. Let
me know where to meet up.**
**Josh: My place. I just put a basketball hoop in
behind the garage.**

Basketball? It was consistently below freezing every
day now. Slightly off-season. Owen went inside and
changed out of his army uniform, and re-dressed for
shooting hoops in the winter.

Then he went digging in the crawl space for another
box he hadn't looked at in years. Once he had what he
needed, he drove to the garage.

In the time Josh had been back, he'd made huge progress on the building. The boarded-up front window was now replaced with a brand new pane of glass. It had a newly whitewashed façade, and *Kincaid's Garage* was outlined in paint on the wall. Owen liked that even more than the *Pine Harbour Garage* his brother had been considering.

And the garage doors were now apple red.

The whole thing looked retro, and hipster, and very much a success before it had even opened.

He walked around the side, following the sound of rubber slapping against concrete, then a backboard. *Bounce, bounce, bounce, thwack.* Behind the garage was a parking lot—although right now, it was a big, echoey, private basketball court.

"The net is an integral part of the renovations, eh?" Owen called out.

Josh caught the ball and spun it on his finger as he glanced over his shoulder. "Gotta burn off some steam as the paint dries. I didn't know that you'd want to call around for tea."

Owen snorted. "This won't be nearly that polite."

"What's going on?"

He glanced around.

Josh swung his arm wide. "There's nobody here."

Fuck. Owen's courage had fallen out of the truck somewhere on the hill down to the harbour. "I'm not sure where to start."

The fond smile on his brother's face helped. So did the way he slung the ball under his arm and gestured to an old bench against the wall—and the cooler underneath it. "Want a beer?"

"Hell yes."

It took Owen half a beer and a good amount of sorting through his thoughts before he could begin. At first, the story came out in fits and starts, but once he got going, it poured out.

"The last thing she said to me when we broke up was, *love makes us stupid*. And I just stood there. I heard her admit that she loved me, that she'd been with me *because she loved me*, even though we were all wrong for each other, and I turned on my heel and walked out on her."

"Shit."

"The thing is—the worst part? My first reaction, as the stunned stupid ox that I am, was who said anything about love?" He shook his head. "That kept reverberating in my head, even as I knew that of course I loved her, too. We never said it to each other. I think deep down I knew, but when she said it I was still shocked. I should have stayed and fought for her. Tried to work through the problems. I don't deserve her. But I miss her, and I love her, and I never got a chance to say that."

His brother's mouth dropped open. "Wow."

"That's all you've got?"

"It's just...so much."

He was miserable. "I know. And she's made it crystal clear she's moved on. And she's been really kind, actually." Owen's chest hurt. "So I can't ignore that, but the thing is...."

Footsteps from the side of the building interrupted him, and Josh looked almost relieved. When Adam appeared, Josh pointed. "Get Adam's thoughts, because I'm the last guy to give good advice when it comes to mending relationships."

Owen frowned. "Why is that, exactly?"

"Not the subject of our conversation today." Josh filled

Adam in, and hearing the bullet points of his breakup with Kerry repeated back was just the bruising one-two punch Owen deserved.

The youngest Kincaid frowned. "We're missing something. Kerry was head over heels for you a month ago. What happened?" The back of Owen's neck got hot as Adam looked back and forth between him and Josh. "What else did you do?"

"Kerry wants kids," Owen admitted, his voice cracking. "We broke up because she found out I got fixed."

"Ah, man, no." Josh groaned.

"You didn't tell her up front?" Adam asked.

Owen scrubbed a hand over his face. "No. It didn't occur to me."

"You knew she wanted kids, and…just dodged that conversation for the entire duration of your relationship?"

"It wasn't that long of a relationship." Owen's voice cracked as he said it. "We were still in the having fun stage, and yes, I know how fucking stupid that sounds in retrospect. We talked around it, though. She was Becca's midwife, for God's sake. She knows my life."

"Well, I don't know what we're doing here," Adam said. His brows were two dark thunderclouds above his glaring eyes. "I think you misled her and she's right to be done with you. You should have been upfront with her about being done with kids."

"That's the thing," Owen said, his throat dry. "I don't think I am."

"You don't think? With a question mark on it?"

How could his mouth be bone dry and his hands slick with sweat at the same time? "No question mark."

"This cannot be a thing you do to get a girl back."

"I know that. It's not."

Adam looked skeptical. One day, he would realize everything he'd prioritized in life was ass-backwards, and it might be a woman who unlocked that epiphany for him —but if it stuck, it would be a product of his own mind.

At least, that's how this was playing out for Owen.

He wasn't changing his mind *for* Kerry, but he might be changing it because of her. Because of how she looked at Charlie, how she looked with Charlie in her arms absolutely. Maybe that was the moment his subconscious had started a drumbeat of its own. *Raise more kids. Raise them with this woman. Fill her arms with children, as many as she can hold.* He hadn't been listening. A decade ago, and probably even years before that, he'd made a decision to protect himself, because his life had been hard and he'd been all alone.

There was nothing harder than middle-of-the-night parenting. At every age, it was the hardest, and loneliest. But on either side of those struggles were moments of absolute joy, and Owen wanted that again.

If Kerry didn't want him anymore, he would accept that. But she didn't have all the facts. "I need to talk to her about this, but I wanted to say it out loud first. And also figure out how to have that conversation with her in a way that doesn't make any false promises."

"Don't be halfway," Adam said. "If you go to her with something like that, you gotta be all in. Are you?"

Owen nodded. "All the way. I love her."

"Then what can we do to help?"

He had a half-baked idea, and he needed it to be fully baked as soon as possible. "We need Will—or at least the keys to his school."

CHAPTER TWENTY-SIX

OWEN FELT like a stalker as he cruised by the community centre the next evening, but he wanted to make sure Kerry wasn't at home. Sure enough, he spotted her car. Adam's intel that she had indoor soccer practice was accurate.

Which meant the coast was clear for him to drop off the first part of his surprise at her apartment.

He looped back to the main drag, pulled into the lot behind her building, and quickly climbed the stairs. She didn't have a mailbox, but he'd come prepared with a roll of tape. He carefully fixed the envelope to her door.

That was as far as good luck got him, because as he descended the stairs, headlights lit up the parking lot. He recognized the car. Damn it. She was home early from practice.

He might as well face the music. He leaned against the railing and watched as she got out, her white parka bright in the darkness. She climbed the stairs slowly, her gaze locked on his face the whole time, and stopped in front of him.

He shoved his hands in his pockets. "Hi."

"What are you…?"

"I was trying to be stealthy and leave you a note while you were at practice."

Her eyebrows curved high. "Keeping track of my schedule?"

"Trying to stay out of your way," he clarified. "I really want to get this right."

"What is *this*, exactly?"

"There are things I want to say. If you want to hear them. I have a seven-step plan to carefully communicate those things."

"Seven steps?" Her voice tightened. "Owen…"

"Read the note. Think about it, please. If you're open to listening to me, let me know."

There was a long pause as she looked toward the stairs. Owen rocked back and forth on his heels. She had to be freezing.

"Go inside," he said in a rush. "It's cold tonight. Think about it, okay?"

She lifted her head again, her chin jutting and her eyes bright. "This is a bad idea."

"It might be, but I've done a lot of thinking, and realized some things. Big things."

"Don't make me promises," she whispered. "That's not what I'm looking for."

He shook his head. "That's not why I'm here." She shivered, and he took a step closer. "Please. Go inside."

She craned her neck, but didn't move.

He took a step toward the parking lot, then another. "Go on, read it," he said. "I'm gonna go stand by my truck. I'll stay there in case you want to throw something heavy at me."

Her lips twitched.

It had always been the humour between them. If he could make her laugh, it might just get him enough of an opening to show her why she could trust him.

He turned to face his truck, and from behind him, he heard her climb the stairs. He waited until the footsteps ended, then he turned again. He couldn't see her on the balcony, but he heard her door swing open and saw the interior light flip on.

She didn't shut the door.

He pictured her reading the note, which he'd memorized.

Kerry,

I didn't know what I wanted when I met you. I knew, but couldn't say, how I felt when I lost you. And losing you made me realize what I value most in the world. Now I want a chance to tell you what I couldn't before.

Please let me explain.

Owen

In the space of time it took him to hear it again in his head, her door stayed open, warmth and light spilling out into the darkness. He braced himself for a slam, or a silent close and an end to that warm light, but neither came.

Finally her head appeared at the balcony's edge. She didn't say anything. She also didn't throw anything, which was an excellent sign.

He rolled the dice.

"I love you." It felt good to say out loud. Scary. He'd

thought about putting it in the note, but he wanted her to first hear it in his own voice. He knew it might not be enough. Because she already knew he loved her. She'd seen it. In hindsight, he could see it, too. He'd shown it to her before he even realized it himself. But it hadn't been enough. He lifted his voice again. He didn't care who heard him. "I hurt you. I didn't mean to, but I did, and I'm sorry."

"That's what I said to Lore," she said, her voice drifting down to him. "I told her that I hurt you and I needed to make it better."

He couldn't do this from a distance. Taking the stairs two at a time, he stopped just short of her landing. "You didn't."

"Owen…"

He shook his head. "Please don't. I was living deep in denial, and that wasn't fair to either of us. But you did *not* hurt me. I should have said it all a lot sooner, but to be honest, some of it I didn't really understand until very recently."

"How recently?" Her voice shook, and he couldn't get a read on her face in the shadows.

"Yesterday."

She laughed weakly. "That's recent."

He rolled the dice again. "Can we go inside? Just for a minute?" It was selfish. He wanted to see her face again.

Her exhale was long, audible, and shaky. But then she nodded. Heart pounding, he followed her into her apartment. Every moment was amplified. The click of her door closing behind him, the way her hands shook as she took off her parka and boots. The pause when she straightened up, squared her shoulders, then gave him a look that was equal parts terror and bravery. "Do you want tea?"

He wanted anything she would give him. "Sure. Or a glass of water? Water would be fine. I'm fine, actually."

She hesitated, then went to the kitchen. He heard the water run and closed his eyes. *Get a grip.*

When she came back to the door, she was holding two glasses. "You might as well take your stuff off."

He hurried out of his winter gear and followed her to the other end of the apartment, where her sparely decorated living room set-up was. She perched on the padded ottoman, clearly leaving the couch for him.

Owen sank into it and gathered his thoughts. "When you said, love makes us do stupid things, that hit me hard." He paused, because this was so important. "I want you to love me because I'm right for you, not despite the fact that I'm wrong for you. I have a lot still to say, but I want you to know that I'm not asking for a compromise.

"I was twenty-one when my dad died. My mom needed me. I had Becca, and Rachel and I were still working out co-parenting, but suddenly there were four younger brothers to take care of, too. My mom never recovered from losing Dad. Six months later, she was gone, too. It was a stroke, they said, but I've always thought that she really died of *his* heart attack. I don't know if that makes sense.

"And suddenly I had a toddler, two teenagers who saw themselves as my equals—and fuck, I was barely out of being a teenager myself. A complete fuck-up on so many levels, barely working part-time as a relief paramedic, supporting everyone with the job that killed my father. Somewhere in there, I came to resent my brothers." That was hard to say out loud. "I got the vasectomy when Adam was in his last year of high school. I don't think about it. And I don't mean that to be glib, I mean, I buried that shit. I don't *look* at it. Becca's teen years were hard, too. It's all hard, and for a long time, that was all I could see."

Kerry's eyes were wet. Her cheeks were, too. Silent tears. He'd gone off the rails a bit there. He hadn't planned on telling her all of that, not up front. But he wanted her to know everything, even the darkest parts he hadn't properly admitted to himself yet.

"I regret it." That was even harder to say. "I regret not trying harder with Rachel, I regret not being happier when she moved on. I regret not following her example and finding love again on my own sooner. I regret the bitterness, and the anger at my brothers. I regret not being happier when Becca told me she was pregnant. The only thing I don't regret in all of this is waiting for you. You are perfect, and I went and fucked that up, too.

"When you told me you knew you wanted to have children, and you knew I wasn't the guy for that, I should have had an epiphany in that moment. I am deeply sorry that I didn't. I'm sorry it took me weeks to sort out my feelings."

Owen knew he should pause and check in with Kerry, but he'd opened the flood gates and he couldn't stop.

"I know better than most that no one should have a baby for the wrong reasons. But I also know that sometimes life throws a wrench in the best laid plans and it's the greatest gift ever. Do I regret becoming a dad at eighteen? Sure, on some level, and I never dealt with that feeling of being conflicted. Do I regret *Becca*? Never. She's made me a better person more times than I can count. And then she had Charlie, and that humbled me all over again, right when I was ready to be selfish."

"It's not selfish, though," Kerry whispered. "What you want, that life…that's perfectly normal. I don't want to get in the way of you having your independence."

"God damn it, please do. I've had a taste of that, and it turns out, I don't like being lonely. More to the point, I've had a taste of loving you, laughing with you, being with you, and it's the best thing in the world.

"I spent a long time being afraid. Having a big family is stressful. A young family is stressful. But you know what else I've learned? Being alone is stressful. It's not the make up of the family that's the problem. I don't want to be driven by fear anymore."

"Oh…"

He swayed toward her, wanting so much to draw her into his arms. But he kept going, because this was the most important part. "Making more of a family with you would be a gift, not a burden."

"I—" She stopped. And then she burst into tears.

"No, no, no," he murmured.

Her fists clenched tight in her lap, her knuckles turning white. Her nostrils flared as she struggled to control herself.

"It's okay." Helpless, he moved off the couch and knelt in front of her. "Let it out."

"I'm scared, too," she finally admitted. "I had this narrative in my head. We would be a fling, we would have an end point, because we wanted different things in life. And that was safe. Even though it hurt."

"Give me a chance to show you what I should have shown you the first time. That I'm the guy you can trust to hold your hand when you get scared."

"I don't know how." Her voice hitched.

"We'll figure it out together. I didn't know what I wanted in life until you walked into it. So I've got some baggage I'm carrying around, these rules I made for myself, but they don't make me happy. You make me happy. I'm willing to do the hard work to figure out the rest of it." He held out his hand. "Give me a chance."

Time stood still.

Then she slowly slid her fingers over his and gave his hand a tentative squeeze.

"That's what I'm talking about," he whispered. "It's okay to be scared."

She nodded.

"I love you," he repeated. It felt damn good to say.

She nodded again, and he smiled. Her lips worked their way into a delicate smile. "I love you, too."

The world's most beautiful four words.

She slid into his lap and he embraced her as tight as he could. He held her until her breathing softened, slowed, and then he kissed her.

It was like taking a first big gulp of air after being under water. Two weeks without oxygen, and now his soul was full again. Her lips tangled with his, her tongue darting out to welcome his. He deepened the kiss, hungry for more of her sweet, warm, sunshine-y taste. She gobbled him up in the same way, her hands finding his face. Holding on.

It took them a while to get their fill of each other.

As she gazed at him, her eyes glowed almost golden with unshed feelings. "It was so hard to be apart from you, and I couldn't make sense of it. I thought I could just grieve and move on, but I couldn't. I was in denial, too."

"Maybe we were both afraid of getting this close to someone, for different reasons."

"But you aren't now?"

"No."

She screwed up her face. "I still am."

"That's okay. I'm never going to break your heart again."

"You didn't. I did that to myself because I couldn't bring myself to say out loud that I wanted to make babies with you. I told myself that wasn't on the table, and still dove headlong into wanting what I couldn't have."

"You can have it." He took her chin between his thumb and forefinger and held her still when she tried to duck her face into his neck. "Kerry, if you want kids, I want to have kids with you. I can be alone when I'm dead. I'll get the vasectomy reversed. They do that. And if that doesn't work, we'll find the best quality donor sperm your uterus could ever imagine."

"Owen!"

"Only the best for you."

"You're the best for me," she whispered. "I love you."

He let her fall onto him then, to hug him tight until there was no space between their bodies. He kissed the top of her head. "I have to tell you about yesterday."

"What happened?" The question was muffled against his skin, but he got the gist.

"I introduced Charlie to an old friend of my dad's. It had been years since he'd seen Becca, too. And then Charlie gave me a slimy high-five to the face..." He smiled. "And I just started thinking about all the wonderful parts of raising a little person. And then a not-so-little person. My brothers...they're such good guys now. And I couldn't be prouder of Becca. I did okay. But I'll do better next time."

"You did great the first time." She took a deep breath. "And you will the next time?"

He laughed gently, deeply, at the disbelief and wonder she poured into that question. There was no question about it, though.

He brushed his fingertips over the flutter at the base of her throat. "Let me take that question mark away. Let me make love to you."

She trembled.

"Does that scare you?" He kissed the delicate skin he had just caressed.

"You're so much better at this than I am." She licked her lips. "Lore said she thought of me as the love 'em and leave 'em type."

Owen shook his head gently. "You're not."

"I don't want to be. Not with you."

He caught her hand and brought it to his chest so she could feel his heartbeat. "Feel that?"

She nodded.

"I'm sure."

With a breathy inhale, she leaned in and kissed him. "What do you want?"

"Make love to me."

Her eyes sparked. "Take that question mark away..."

"Yeah. You get the idea."

"It's a good one." She licked her lips and hooked her fingertips into his waistband. "This is real."

"It's love."

"Yes."

"So make love to me. You've already done it once."

"Owen," she whispered.

He'd figured this out, somewhere in the middle of their conversation. Hell, she'd made love to him many times over. But that last time, when the condom broke…he'd been indifferent, and she'd been so desperate to protect his feelings and make him feel safe, to reassure him that the way she'd clung to him wouldn't have any forever consequences.

And then so hurt when he'd shrugged it off, because he knew it wouldn't.

Making love wasn't always about making babies. But for Kerry, maybe there was a bit of that tangled up in it, a future potential, and he'd crushed it by being a callous goon.

He wouldn't be callous again. "That last time together, I think it felt like making love for you. And I seemed like I wasn't there. Not in the same way. But I am. I want to be laid bare for you, in every way."

She slid off his lap and stood on shaky legs beside him. He leaned in and pressed his head to her spandex-clad thigh.

"Come with me," she said softly. She tangled her fingers in his hair and tugged.

His heart jolted and he scrambled to his feet. He had more than a foot on her in height, but standing there together in her living room, with the shattered fragments of their fears all around them, he felt as small and vulnerable as she looked.

Small, vulnerable, and still brave. He kissed her again, holding her face the way she had held his. She pressed into him and that sunshine-y flood of oxygen filled him once more.

Not so small. Still vulnerable.

Together they stumbled to her room. They didn't bother to turn on the lights. In the dark, they stripped each other down to nothing.

Kerry took his cock, hard and throbbing, in her hand, and stroked him slowly in the tight space between their bodies. "Do we need—"

"Nothing. Unless you—"

"No…"

She whimpered as he rolled her onto her back. He stroked her breasts, her hips, worshipping the shape of her, before sliding his fingers against her slick pussy. God, she was soaked for him already, and that made him rut against her hip like a monster.

"Yes," she breathed.

Her monster, who loved her so much.

She hitched her leg around his hip and tried to flip him back. "Owen, I need you."

He needed her, too. With a roar, he fit them together and thrust home, sliding into her body where a moment before there had been nothing but desire.

She fit him perfectly, hot and wet, and when he bottomed out, he thought he might never want to leave. "So good," he growled.

And she laughed.

Fuck, that made him hard. She laughed and her breasts bounced against his chest. "So good," she repeated in the sweetest, huskiest voice. "I've missed you."

"I love you."

She repeated that, too. They said it back and forth as they found a rhythm. Breath against skin, hands around flesh. Pushing and pulling to get closer, feel more.

Arousal climbed. It spiralled and bloomed in a kind of technicolour Owen had never imagined. He never wanted to leave her body and he never wanted this to end, but at the same time she was getting closer beneath him, he could feel it. And he wanted to come with her, to chase her orgasm with his own.

He wanted to fill her up and then hold her after.

She arched her back, her breath gasping nonsensical words that sounded like music, and deep inside, he felt his response let loose. Darkness closed in around his vision as he pumped his hips one more time and felt the rough first spurt jolt out of him.

CHAPTER TWENTY-SEVEN

"WHERE DID that fall into the seven steps?" Kerry heard the wild, crazy laughter in her voice. It made her smile, and she didn't even need to look over at Owen to know he probably had a matching expression on his face.

He coughed. "We skipped a couple."

"I'll be right back." She rolled off the bed and went to the washroom, and when she got back, Owen had pushed himself up in the bed and turned on the light.

She stopped in the doorway.

His gaze raked over her naked body, making her skin tingle. Slowly, she climbed on top of him and settled on his chest. They were both a bit damp.

"Should we take a shower?"

"We should get dressed and go to my house."

She raised her head and gave him an *are you out of your mind?* look. "Why?"

"Step three."

"You've already got the girl."

"Trust me, I think this is worth it." She went to move, and he clamped his big hands down her on her butt.

"Not yet, though. I like having you draped on me like this."

She wriggled against him and fell quiet, listening to his heartbeat.

When she lifted her head again, he was looking at her. His gaze was relentless. Once upon a time, she'd read it as harsh and piercing. Now it washed over her as gentle and tender. Wonderful.

"You're looking at me."

"I like to do that."

She shivered. "I know." Reaching out, she traced the hard line of his jaw. "You always have."

His eyes darkened, but he didn't look away. "I couldn't help it. And then I didn't want to, because I thought looking at you might be all I'd ever get."

Her chest hurt at the idea of not having this love, because of one or both of them being too closed off or stubborn. "I could never have resisted you. Since the beginning, this was what I wanted. You have always been irresistible to me."

"Same." He caught her hand and kissed her open palm. "Do you have any lingering doubts?"

She thought about it. "No. Questions, maybe, but not doubt."

"Questions about what?"

"Kids."

He spread his arms. "I'm an open book. Dig."

"Everything you said makes sense. But are you sure you want to start all over?"

He didn't answer right away. His gaze dropped away from hers, then came back. "What I have realized is that I was blessed to grow up with a large family, to be able to raise a daughter and support my brothers as they moved into adulthood. That was a joy, truly, as much as I fixated on the negative aspects. But I never chose it. Next time… this time, I want to choose it."

"Babies," she whispered.

He nodded. "Babies, and maybe we could be foster parents down the road. There are kids who need adults in their lives to make a safe space. Queer kids, kids who have escaped abuse—"

She climbed up him higher, kissing his face all over. "Yes."

"Maybe one thing at a time." He dusted his fingers over her cheek, then brushed his hand back into her hair. "I want some time with just you, too."

It took them another hour to get dressed. He'd offered to go and get the mysterious step three, whatever it was, but he had the bigger bed—and the bigger shower. "I like your place." Then she corrected herself. "I *love* your place. It reminds me of you, and it makes me happy to spend time there."

"Maybe one day soon we can talk about making it your place, too." He zipped up her parka. "What would you think about that?"

"One step at a time," she said, her cheeks heating up. She thought it sounded lovely.

———

STEP THREE, it turned out, was a present. A gift bag of smallish proportions and decent weight, that inside had two boxes, one significantly heavier than the other.

Each of them had a card that matched the one Owen had left on her door.

"I had this whole plan worked out," he admitted. "You

would read the note, and then reach out to me, and I would leave this on your doorstep next."

A delightfully romantic idea, although Kerry thought the way it had gone was better. She wouldn't have wanted to wait another day to hear all that Owen had shared.

She picked up the lighter, smaller box, but her fingers were shaking.

"Help," she whispered, and she realized her voice was shaking, too.

He leaned in and kissed her, softly, then covered her hands with his. "Here."

Inside was a cassette tape box. Clear plastic, with paper covered in black marker writing. **Owen's Mix Tape for Kerry**, it read in big letters in the middle. Song titles were written in smaller print around the title.

She picked it up, and it actually felt like there was something inside it.

It was an actual tape.

"What did you do?" Now her voice sounded full of wonder, and that was accurate.

She looked up at Owen, and he flexed one shoulder. A little shrug. "I made you this."

"How?"

"I'll tell you after." He reached for his bag and pulled out an honest-to-God first generation Walkman. "I want you to listen to it first."

He helped her put the tape in the deck, then he sat in the corner of the couch and pulled her into the crook of his arm. She held the headphones to her ear, angling them a bit so he could hear too, and she pushed the Play button in with a ka-chunk.

At first there was nothing but a crackle. Then she heard Owen's voice from a bit of a distance. "This tape is a little bit of a love letter, and a lot of an explanation. It's the story of falling in love with you, and that started from the very first moment I laid eyes on you. This one's for you, Kerry Humphrey."

It was a country song she recognized that was a few years old, but it had been in heavy rotation all summer on the local station. She looked at the handwritten playlist notes. **Brett Eldredge, "Wanna Be That Song"**. Owen held her as she listened to every word, and tears gathered in the corners of her eyes.

When the song faded out, Owen's voiceover returned. "Did you know a cassette tape only holds thirty minutes of recorded material? I had forgotten that. So we're going to have to zoom way back, to when I was taping songs off the radio the first time around. To when I found out my girl-friend was pregnant, and we decided we wanted a baby long before we were really ready. I feel like that's been my entire life to this point, Kerry. Never quite ready for what life puts in front of me. I wasn't ready for you, either. But I am now. So here's an inside look into that eighteen-year-old boy's heart."

That did it. The tears slid down her face as his voice cracked in her ear, as his arms wrapped tighter around her body. She listened to "November Rain" by Guns and Roses and "My Favorite Mistake" by Sheryl Crow and tried to picture Owen—this mature, capable man—in Becca and Hayden's shoes. She couldn't quite picture it, but he would tell her more, over time.

When his voice came back on the recording, it was to introduce two country songs he listened to a lot when he was away from Becca.

She turned in his arms, and he relaxed his grip, but

gestured for her to keep listening. Biting her lip, she nodded and sank onto her heels, kneeling beside him.

This was him. He was showing her his life through songs, and it wasn't just angsty feelings. It was slices of fun, snuck in where he could. It was three lives in one. The father, the single guy, and the responsible firefighter and paramedic determined to have a respectable career. She'd seen all three of those men, and she'd seen them war against each other, too.

The final song was a Dire Straits song that had been his father's favourite.

When the tape clicked to an end, Owen slid the headphones off and their hands stayed tangled around the Walkman. Neither of them spoke.

She looked at the box. There was no side B.

Owen followed her gaze. "I thought we could make that playlist together."

CHAPTER TWENTY-EIGHT

ON CHRISTMAS EVE, Becca and Charlie went to Hayden's family get-together, so Owen and Kerry went to the Green Hedgehog with his brothers. They played darts, drank Lore's dangerously good Egg Nog, and when they were dropped off at home, they had happy, laughing sex under the mistletoe.

Then they put on matching Christmas PJs, just in case Becca showed up at dawn. The last thing Owen did before bed was slide one more present for Kerry under the tree.

In the morning, it was Kerry who got up first. He felt her slide out of bed, and told himself he would get up, too, but he drifted off again.

The next thing he knew she was back with two foaming lattes—because she'd bought him an espresso machine, too. An early Christmas present, and smart planning ahead. She'd decided to give up her lease at the end of January, which would mean she was precariously far from the lattes in the clinic.

"What time is it?" he mumbled. Owen usually didn't

have any problem getting out of bed, but that egg nog had hit him like a ton of bricks.

"Just after eight."

"I'm up." He shoved himself out of bed. "Do you know where my phone is?"

Kerry found it on the bedside table and handed it to him. "Are you okay?"

He stopped and grinned. "Great. Just... you know. First Christmas in a while that's a different routine, and I didn't see Becca and Charlie yesterday, and they'll be over soon, so..." He tapped his screen. "Nothing yet. I'll text her."

She slid the latte into his hands. "Here. Drink this."

He took a big sip, then pulled her against him. "Last night was a lot of fun, but this old man isn't cut out for early mornings after a party."

"You're not old." Kerry wiggled her eyebrows at him. "Come on, I've got a surprise for you."

He followed her into the living room.

She had been busy this morning.

"Wow. A year ago, I thought my days of huge present piles under the tree were numbered." Owen shook his head in disbelief. "Where did all of these come from?"

"I may have gotten carried away..." Kerry bounced up and down. "I had to get stuff for Charlie, and Becca, and Hayden. Your brothers have presents there, too."

"Hayden doesn't need anything," Owen muttered, but he didn't mean it. He had a couple of gifts in the pile for Charlie's dad, too.

His phone lit up as he was still taking in the stack of presents.

Becca: We're on our way over!
Owen: See you soon!

He showed it to Kerry. "Your enthusiasm for Christmas is contagious. Note the double exclamation mark."

"I love it." She picked up a flat rectangle wrapped in shiny red paper. "I want you to open this one before they get here."

Owen nabbed his special present for her, too. "Let's trade."

"You first." She beamed at him.

He ripped off the paper. Inside was a leather notebook, embossed with his name on it. Inside there were Post-it notes on the first few pages, all in Kerry's neat handwriting. Things he had said he wanted to do.

Buy a four-wheeler
Unplug for a whole weekend
Smoke a joint
Spend the weekend naked with Kerry, laughing

He liked her modification to the last one the best. "This is amazing."

He clasped it to his chest and embraced her around it, holding the book between them as he kissed her.

"I'm still a big fan of your plan to do all the things you couldn't before," she said. "I think it's time to start writing down your wish list so we can start crossing things off."

He couldn't agree more. "Do you have a pen? Let's start now."

She grabbed one from the side table and handed it over.

"You open yours while I do this." Owen carefully removed the sticky notes on the first page and put them on the next one.

As she discarded the gold and silver paper around the

ring box, he dropped to one knee, then turned the notebook around so she could see what he had written at the top of page one: **Owen Kincaid's Great Husband Plan**.

"I have a new plan." He grinned up at her as she bit her lip and bounced in place. "No more bachelor dreams for me. You're it." He reached out with one hand and opened the ring box in her hand. "You make me happy every single day. I want to wake up next to you, and tell you that I am in love with you, forever and ever. Will you marry me?"

Her head bobbed three times in quick succession. "Yes."

He jumped to his feet. "Yes?"

She nodded as he picked her up and swung her around. That was how Becca, Hayden and Charlie found them, spinning in a circle in the living room.

Becca closed the door behind them. "What's going on?"

"She said yes," Owen shouted.

Charlie started to cry.

"Oh, no no no," Kerry gasped, tossing the ring box to Owen as she reached for the little guy. "Come here. It's okay."

She got him out of his winter bunting bag, then handed him to Owen, who had arms big enough to hold them both. He wrapped Kerry in one arm and cradled Charlie in the other, and beamed at his daughter over both of their heads.

Becca clapped her hands together, then looked at Hayden.

It wouldn't be long before that kid did some ring shopping of his own. Owen didn't know how he felt about that, exactly, but it was nothing like how he'd worried a year earlier. It would sort itself out, that was for sure. And he'd be happy for the little moments in between, like how Hayden gazed back at Becca, and then stepped forward to take Charlie, who had chosen the most inopportune time to need a diaper change.

"He knows the number one job of a dad, at least," Owen said quietly to Becca as she gave him a hug.

"Stop." She poked him in the belly.

"Probably never," he chuckled in her ear. "Merry Christmas."

"Merry Christmas, Dad." She turned to Kerry. "Does this mean we get to start planning a wedding? I can get you a good deal at the country club…"

EPILOGUE

August

THEIR WEDDING WAS NOT at the country club. They put off the planning too long, not because they didn't want to get married, but because none of the options Becca suggested to them felt right—and then all the dates filled up.

Owen and Kerry didn't mind in the least. Over the spring, they had collected all the pieces they needed to make a wedding happen. But while Adam was away at school, and Hayden was playing hockey every weekend, there was no time when everyone would be available to celebrate together.

So they waited. And then the perfect opportunity presented itself—Nashville star-turned-Pine Harbour local Liana Hansen announced she was pregnant, and instead of touring, she would headline a weekend of concerts right in Pine Harbour. It would be called County Country, and she hoped to make it an annual event.

The whole town got involved. Permits were issued to

turn Main Street into a walking mall. Farmers' fields were turned into camping venues, and Owen was tapped to coordinate the safety committee.

He volun-told Matt Foster to handle it instead. And then he went home and asked Kerry how she felt about maybe not having a wedding reception, but having their first dance in the middle of a street party instead.

She loved it.

They exchanged vows in the same church Owen's parents got married in, then led a parade of friends and family to Mac's for burgers before dancing the night away on Main Street. Everyone who mattered made it. Kerry's parents drove up, and were very polite to each other. Adam arrived shortly before the ceremony, but he stayed until the next day.

The accelerated program was no joke, he reported, but he was in the final days of it. "I'll be back in a couple of weeks for good. Graduation's around the corner."

The next morning, they had everyone over for brunch in their backyard before they took off on their honeymoon—an entire week completely unplugged. They left their pagers and cell phones on the kitchen counter and drove to the city for two nights. They slept on thousand-thread-count sheets, ate at five-star restaurants, and had wild monkey sex against the dark windows, overlooking the glittering metropolis below.

Then they got extra-large lattes for the road, piled into Owen's truck, and headed north again, to a camp site they had to hike out to. They didn't pass a single soul on the way, and as soon as their tent was set up, Owen stripped down to nothing.

"Come on," he said, peeling her out of her clothes.

"We're going skinny dipping. It's not just my wish list we're checking off on this trip."

She scrambled out of her clothes and chased after him, splashing into the cold lake water. He caught her in his arms and pulled her close to warm her up.

She wiped damp tendrils of hair off his forehead. "You didn't forget."

"I keep many lists in that book you gave me. Things my wife wants to do."

"Nice."

He licked at the corner of her mouth. "Things I want to do to my wife."

"Even nicer."

"And my favourite list of all…"

She arched an eyebrow.

He grinned. "Baby names. Here's hoping we'll need to consult it in a few months."

————

LABOUR DAY WEEKEND meant tourists galore in Pine Harbour. Ever since County Country, their town had been overrun with people looking for famous singers on the weekend. The lack of lattes usually discouraged them from sticking around too long. But Owen couldn't hunker down at home and avoid the traffic, because his wife wanted to go to the farmer's market.

They had a hot date night planned. Cheese board, veggie tray, and an over-the-top vampire slayer TV show. They needed supplies.

While Kerry slept in on Saturday morning, he hopped in the shower, then made them both fancy coffees. By the time he got back to the bedroom, he realized he had missed eight text messages from his brothers on their group chat. He clicked the screen open.

> **Seth: What's the plan for Adam's graduation ceremony? I can fly south and could collect folks on the way, shorten the trip? Let's coordinate.**
> **Adam: Countdown is ON.**
> **Josh: We can't wait. I'm coming down early to party.**
> **Will: Seth, can you pick me up? Unlike Josh, I have a full-time job with responsibilities.**
> **Josh: Hey, I'm an entrepreneur with a million followers on TikTok.**
> **Will: As I was saying...**
> **Adam: Owen, what's your plan?**
> **Seth: Newlyweds don't answer text messages this early on a weekend. We should all be so lucky.**

Time to put a stop to that speculation.

> **Owen: My wife is still sleeping, thank you very much. I was making her coffee. I think we'll drive down, though. Wouldn't miss it.**
> **Adam: Cool. Hey, do you remember Captain Petersen? We're going to meet up for drinks.**
> **Owen: I'm not sure if I know Petersen.**
> **Adam: You've met her. Tall blonde. She was my boss on tour, worked in Meaford for a while.**
> **Will: Rings a bell.**
> **Adam: She's given up the army life and is a baker now.**
> **Josh: Is she hot?**
> **Adam: Shut up.**

Seth: Shut up.
Will: I was going to say, but they beat me to it.
**Owen: I'm going to go wake up my wife now. We
have a farmer's market to get to.**
Josh: Words I never thought I'd hear you say.

Owen put his phone away and shook his head, smiling.
They were still young and had years ahead of them before
they settled down. But once they did, they would learn
just how rewarding a trip to the farmer's market could be.

———

If you want to keep in touch with Zoe, please sign up for
her VIP reader email list at www.smarturl.it/
ZoeYorkNewsletter! She shares new release information,
amazing sales, and behind the scenes writing news!

ACKNOWLEDGEMENTS

I started writing this book in October 2017, and then my life went sideways, as lives sometimes do. I wrote two other Pine Harbour books before I felt ready to pick this project up again, and I'm grateful to my editor, Kristi Yanta, for helping me stumble through all three novels. Completing them has been therapeutic, and for the first time in a long time, I'm not carrying around parts of untold stories.

It is a joy to say that. And I'm sure it won't last for long! I can't wait to dig into writing Adam's book next.

As I was out of my element with Hayden, Kerry Rubel graciously answered a lot of questions about junior hockey. Most of that discussion didn't end up on the page, as research so often falls to the wayside when there are grown-up characters more interested in the bed that is right there! But it was important for me to know what Becca and Hayden would be dealing with from the hockey side of things, and if I messed any of that up for story-telling purposes, that's on me.

Thanks as well to Sadie and Jessica, who read this in chunks, and my family, who were really very good about being ignored at long stretches as we came down to the end.

Finally, thank you to every single reader who discovered Pine Harbour in the first series and pre-ordered this book, sight-unseen, because they couldn't wait to go back. I'm so glad to have your trust.

~ Zoe

Marriage is for suckers—Adam and Isla agreed on that when they got hitched.

Adam Kincaid has a lot to prove: as a brand-new firefighter, as the youngest of five brothers in a small town where everyone is curious about your business, and as an unexpected newlywed.

Isla Petersen knows exactly what she's getting into: a marriage of convenience with a younger man, a soldier she once commanded when she was an army captain. And she knows what she's getting in return: a bakery all her own

This is a standalone story of two friends who don't believe in love, but do believe in each other. Welcome back to Pine Harbour!

ABOUT THE AUTHOR

Thirteen-time USA Today bestselling romance author Zoe York lives in London, Ontario with her young family. She's currently chugging Americanos, wiping sticky fingers, and dreaming of heroes in and out of uniform.

www.zoeyork.com

facebook.com/zoeyorkwrites
twitter.com/zoeyorkwrites
instagram.com/zoeyorkwrites
youtube.com/zoeyorkwrites
pinterest.com/zoeyorkwrites

www.ingramcontent.com/pod-product-compliance
Lightning Source LLC
Chambersburg PA
CBHW011031190726
48290CB00011B/2787